WITHOUT SIN

A Novel

Praise for Without Sin

"*Without Sin* exemplifies the tragic outcome of the United States' increasingly dysfunctional immigration policy. McCabe renders personal the horror that thousands of young undocumented women experience daily. Weaving social commentary into a compelling and entertaining story is a task few writers can accomplish. McCabe does so admirably here. Readers and advocates of social justice should not miss the opportunity to engage with the written work of such an outstanding, new talent."

—Marisa Ugarte
Executive Director of the Bilateral Safety Corridor Coalition

"Arguably, the 2000 mile US-Mexico Border is the most socially, economically, and politically tumultuous space in the world. *Without Sin* successfully weaves harsh reality with moving prose and takes readers to the line that divides the two countries to tell a human story that may and likely does occur."

—Mark Salinas
Chicano & Ethnic Studies Professor and Hayward City Councilman

"McCabe has written a novel that offers a poetic dance between brutality and beauty—consistently honoring the sanctity of humanity. Our youth need works such as this to guide them into grappling with questions of morality. I am hopeful that the dialogues that emerge—within themselves and perhaps more importantly with others—will mark our future generations in ways that we will be able to witness through an increase in the value of honor and respect for all living things."

—Silvia Villanueva
Assistant Professor, Pasadena City College

"This book is 'a good read,' but McCabe offers us more than a page turner. *Without Sin* gives readers detailed renderings of what is most absent from our society's current dialogue about immigration policies: the faces and the personal stories of those who suffer most as a result of these policies."

—Kris Sloan
Assistant Professor, St. Edwards University

"*Without Sin* by David McCabe, which placed in the *William Faulkner—William Wisdom Creative Writing Competition*, is a must read for all who would understand the complexities, as well as horrors, of the lives of undocumented immigrants in the United States, as well as those still trying to get here in search of a better life. Those who would send them all packing, especially, should read this novel and then examine their hard-hearted souls."

—Rosemary James
Co-Founder, Pirate's Alley Faulkner Society

WITHOUT SIN

A Novel

David S. McCabe

SUNSTONE
PRESS

SANTA FE

Sunstone books may be purchased for educational, business, or sales promotional use.
For information please write: Special Markets Department, Sunstone Press,
P.O. Box 2321, Santa Fe, New Mexico 87504-2321.

Book and Cover design › Vicki Ahl
Body typeface › ITC Benguiat
Printed on acid-free paper
♾

Library of Congress Cataloging-In-Publication Data

McCabe, David S., 1970-
  Without sin : a novel / by David S. McCabe.
    p. cm.
  ISBN 978-0-86534-878-3 (softcover : alk. paper)
  1. Murder--Fiction. 2. Mexico--Fiction. I. Title.
  PS3613.C323W58 2012
  813'.6--dc23
                                    2012007833

WWW.SUNSTONEPRESS.COM
. SUNSTONE PRESS / POST OFFICE BOX 2321 / SANTA FE, NM 87504-2321 /USA
(505) 988-4418 / ORDERS ONLY (800) 243-5644 / FAX (505) 988-1025

For Lisa always

Thalia, Liz, Maria, Juan, Humberto, and Karia
your strength and perseverance
inspire me daily

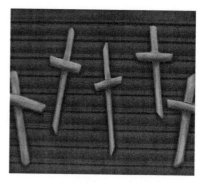

In Memoriam:
Bryan Hargreaves (1972–2006)

When love for family is stronger than fear,
when the desperation sets in
A man will cross any line that is drawn,
and who's to say it's a sin?
—Slaid Cleaves, Borderline

Do not forget to show hospitality to strangers,
for by so doing some people have shown hospitality
to angels without knowing it.
—Hebrews 13:2

PART I

1

The way I figure it, there are two kinds of people in this world. One is the kind that takes stock in their dreams. They will read books about dreams and their meanings. They'll keep a note pad next to their bed and as soon as they wake up, they'll try and write down as much as they can remember about what they dreamt before it vanishes from their memory. These kinds of people might even go as far to pay someone to interpret their dreams and try to find some significance in them. The other kind of people don't think much about dreams at all.

Before I was sent to Iraq during the first days of the Second Gulf War, I guess I was more of the second kind of person. I didn't so much as give my dreams a second thought. Truth be told, I could hardly remember even having any dreams when I woke up. After I came back, it was a different story altogether. I would fight sleep because I knew what was waiting for me when I closed my eyes and faced the darkness. I feared my dreams. Not because there was some boogeyman waiting for me, but because each time I closed my eyes, I found myself back there. Each dream was a terrible repeat of the human cruelty that I bore witness to and even had a hand in; and I was helpless, but to watch it play out over and over again in the brutally honest cinema of my memory. I had one stretch that was so bad that I didn't sleep more than one hour in four days—so I finally broke down and went to the V.A. Hospital in Mission Valley and spoke to a doctor.

One of the reoccurring dreams that haunted me on so many nights found me outside the port city of Umm Qasr, where me and my team worked with the 15th Marine Expeditionary Unit to clear out the insurgents that were reported to have been holed up there. Only in my dream, I was alone and on horseback and I was dressed up like one of them old time cowboys from the American West. It was dusk and the wash of fiery colors contrasted starkly against the bleak countryside. When I looked around, I saw destruction stretch out before me as far as my eye was good. Charred craters dotted the landscape and black smoke rose up from the burnt out edifices like thin, twisted pillars winding up toward the heavens. There was not a single building that remained standing; markets, homes, even the mosque had been razed. The narrow streets were littered with the dead. They lay bloated beneath the fading sun amidst large circular pools of blood that had spilled from their torn flesh before soaking into the dust and drying into cracked, black stains upon the earth. As I rode through, I could hear nothing but the sound of my horse's hooves striking the ground and the soft, ominous chorus of groans that would emanate from the bloated bodies as the buildup of gases would force their way from the bellies and through the mouths of the dead, softly vibrating their stiffening larynxes on the way out.

I turned and looked back over my shoulder in the direction of the city's entrance and I felt an ice cold shudder of fear bolt through me. I could see in the distance a horse and rider thundering toward me. The horse was large and muscular and as black as the night and sparks of blue and red would explode from its hooves when they struck the ground. I could not see the rider's face. He was dressed like an Arabian knight, veiled from head to toe in black, holding high above his head a large curved sword rushing wildly onward like some dark oracle of destruction. I put my spurs into my horse's side and sped down the road past the smoldering ruins of human devastation and headed toward the setting sun with the pursuing dark horse and rider closing in fast behind me. I could feel my horse strain against the bridle and hear the leather saddle creak and groan beneath me as my horse galloped frantically away from our shadowy pursuer. In the distance, I could see a type of fortress rising up against the horizon. It was a U.S. military encampment. Two lookout towers rose above the entrance manned with turret guns. I yelled for them to open the gates. I could feel the hot breath of the black horse on my back and could hear the swordsman's blade slice through the air. And then, just before either reaching the gate or meeting my demise at the horseman's dark hand, I woke up.

The V.A. doctor told me that I was suffering from Post Traumatic Stress Syndrome. She said it was common among veterans and prescribed me some medication to help me sleep and some Venlafaxine to help with the depression. I didn't recall feeling all that depressed, but she was the doctor.

She suggested counseling too and at first I was open to it until I filled the prescription and read the paperwork that accompanied the pills when I got home. It seemed to me that the medication she was prescribing caused more problems than they cured. Some of the side effects included blurred vision, loss of libido and constipation. None of those sounded all that appealing to me, however one of the warnings listed on the label concerned me more than the others. It said "If you experience thoughts of suicide or self harm while taking this medication contact your physician immediately."

All I wanted was a good night's sleep. I had no interest speeding up my date with eternal rest... so I flushed the pills down the toilet. I didn't go see a counselor as the doctor suggested and I didn't see that doctor again either. Instead, I put away a couple of beers and I put pen to paper and write down my thoughts in this journal before I lay my head down every night. I read once that writing is therapeutic... this novelist explained how he had spent a good many years as a "shopping cart soldier" left homeless and adrift in Los Angeles' Pershing Square after returning from Vietnam. He was a broken man, haunted by flashbacks, wracked with guilt and contemplating suicide until he attended a veteran's writing workshop. He discovered that putting his nightmares into words helped him face his demons. He said he was an empty shell and writing made him feel like he had a soul. I don't know about that. I can't say that I fully subscribe to the writing as catharsis school of thought, but if you ask me, it sure beats the hell out of constipation or erectile dysfunction.

For the most part, I sleep better nowadays, but I still take no comfort from my dreams.

Monday, September 15, 2008
G.H.

The desert, with its immense emptiness, has a way of making you consider your own mortality. This has always been so. Even before there were cities, roads, or fences scaring the landscape, men would huddle together and look beyond their flickering campfires into the darkness and comfort themselves with tales of ancient gods and their struggles to bring order out of the abyss.

He stepped out of the cold yellow glow illuminated by the porch light and cast his eyes for a moment at the immense starlit sky above. He didn't know much about gods. The older he got, the more he realized that he didn't know much about God for that matter. But deep down, he had always believed that the desert must be one of the old gods. Hot, brown, and just about as angry and unforgiving as they come. The thing he found to be most ironic was that he had tried his entire life to escape the desert. But then again, how does one hide from the gaze of God?

When he was 18, he signed on with the Navy. Things had begun to sour between him and his father and he reasoned that being on a boat at sea would take him just about as far away from the sand, rock and other discomforts of home as a person could get. Then suspicions arose regarding Iraq's role in September 11th and whether Saddam Hussein might be stockpiling weapons of mass destruction and he was back. He found himself in a different part of the world, but subject once again to the same god.

When he came back to the world, he tried to stay away; he figured that if he was going to wake up with sand in his hair, it was going to be because he was soaking up the sun on some tropical beach. How he had fallen into work with the United States Border Patrol in Southern California, he wasn't sure. Perhaps he was bored. Perhaps desperate times call for desperate actions. He had completed six years with the Navy, he was unemployed, he was fluent in Spanish and gasoline was over three dollars a gallon. Whatever the reason, he couldn't be certain, but he now found himself wearing the uniform of the United States Border Patrol, stationed just a few miles outside of Tecate, Mexico near the desert border town of Potrero.

His father used to tell him that with time, we all end up being who we're supposed to be. He thinks about that now and again but is often troubled by the thought that the man he is now is nowhere close to the man he hopes to become.

Potrero is a cotton mouthed, dreary-eyed hangover of a town that lies curled up like a sidewinder rattlesnake, south east of San Diego off old Highway 94. Potrero is a unique town in Southern California: it has no manicured lawns, no franchised restaurants, and no coffee shops or gas stations to welcome travelers with their sterile but familiar signs. What it has is the Mexican frontier on one side of what some locals refer to as the "taco curtain." A fourteen-foot high iron fence erected to keep the Mexicans, Guatemalans, Salvadorians and who knows what else out. To the north is National Forest land, all protected, and still wild, open desert. The actual terrain is populated by a disagreeable form of ground cover, which includes a variety of sage and wild rosemary to tough manzanita, yucca and a variety of unidentified plants with burrs and thorns. The dense undercover makes light of the fact that this is a desert, while at the same time, reminding you beyond doubt that you are in a godforsaken place.

Nobody lives out here, except for the 287 recluses who call Potrero home. The inhabitants are a mix of farmers, ranchers, artists and outcasts who live in seclusion and some for good reasons. Still, he enjoys the silence. On a quiet night, and most nights are quiet, when a big, full moon rises up over the mountains, the coyotes sing out in numbers too great to count that a person can, for a moment, forget he is part of humanity. The worries and responsibilities that attach themselves to the modern world rise up and fade into the ether along with the calls of the coyotes.

Potrero has a general store that sits directly across from the Fire Station. Martin and his wife, Ester, have run what has served as the general store for 25 years, providing the locals with groceries, gossip, feed and tack. Every morning, they open at 4:30 and have a fresh pot of coffee waiting for any early customers who happen to stop by. Garrett is there every morning, and Martin always greets him with a black, fresh steaming pot.

The wooden screen door creaked as he pushed it open and stepped into the lighted shop.

"Morning Garrett!" Martin grinned holding the black handled coffee pot in his wrinkled hand.

"Morning Martin. What happened to Ester? It's four forty-five a.m., the day's half over. Is she sleeping in?" He sat the Stanley Thermos coffee mug on the counter top.

"No, nothing quite like that. She's in San Diego with our daughter trying to catch up with all the grand-mothering she has to do." He poured the inky essence from the pot. Steam rolled off the black surface and dissipated in the air.

"Well, ain't that just about the sweetest thing! What about you Martin? Don't you have any grand-fathering to catch up on?" Garrett screwed on the lid to the thermos sealing in the aroma and the heat.

"Oh, Ester does enough grand-parenting for both of us. Besides, if I spent my time spoiling my grandkids, who'd make your morning coffee?" He chuckled as he placed the pot back on the hotplate.

"Don't go thinking that I can't manage without you Martin," Garrett shot back.

"Well, you'll get your chance to prove it. Ester and me are going to take a little vacation next month. We're renting one of them motor homes and taking our grandson with us to Baja for a few days. I just hope you don't go through caffeine withdrawals while I'm gone," Martin replied.

"Don't go worrying about me. Besides, I've been looking for a reason to try some of them specialty coffees. I guess I'll have my chance to upgrade while you and Ester are gone." Garrett's eyes twinkled as he took a slow sip from the insulated mug.

"Oh shit! You ain't going frappa-mocha half-crap, de-caf, whatever the hell they drink at Starbucks on me now are you?" Martin chided.

"Nope. I'm fixing on trying that Kopi Luwak coffee that is all the rage." Garrett grinned.

Martin's brow wrinkled. "I don't follow you. Copy Lou what?"

"Kopi Luwak. You ain't tried it?" Garrett laughed.

"If it don't come already ground in a sealed can, I can't say that I have." Martin leaned in against the counter, his blue shirtsleeve pulled up just above the faded eagle tattoo on his forearm.

"Well, let me bring you up to speed here old timer. I'll get you into the twenty-first century of fine caffeinated beverages yet!" Garrett leaned against the counter and took another sip from his mug.

"Oh Christ! Garrett, why do I get the feeling that I should be putting on my hip waders?" Martin asked.

"I'm serious! This is top grade stuff. If you start selling this Kopi Luwak coffee, you'll put this little market of yours on the map."

"All right then, lay it on me." Martin unscrewed the metal lid to the half empty sugar jar and topped it off.

"Well, it turns out this coffee ain't something you're gonna find grown by any local boys on account of a little critter called the luwak."

"The what?"

"The luwak. It's like this little cat or monkey or something that lives in the rainforest of the Philippines. I saw them when I was stationed over there."

"And it makes coffee?" Martin raised a thick gray eyebrow.

Garrett laughed. "Not exactly—but it helps. You see, the luwak was considered a pest by the folks around there for years because it climbs the coffee trees and eats the coffee cherries. Apparently it enjoys the sweet fleshy part of the fruit, but it's unable to digest the beans, so they pass right on through."

"So then, what you are telling me is that this monkey shits coffee beans?" A broad grin began to spread across Martin's furrowed face.

"Yeah, apparently, the digestive fluids in the animal's stomach add something special to the coffee's flavor through fermentation." Garrett took another sip and sat his mug on the counter top.

"I'll bet it does! But I don't suspect that folks around here would be too hot on monkey ass flavored coffee."

"Don't be too sure now Martin. Folks in the city pay as much as five dollars a cup for this brand of java."

Martin leaned across the counter and stared into Garrett's chestnut colored eyes. "I knew it! You are so full of shit Harrison that your eyes are all brown! But I'll give it you—you had me going there for a minute."

"I am telling you the gospel, Martin. This stuff is for real and it is good to the last dropping." Garrett grinned.

Outside, the gravel covered driveway crackled and crunched under the broad all terrain tires of a white Wrangler Jeep followed by two sharp blasts from the horn. The blinding glow from the xenon gas headlights turned the dark, pre-dawn sky into day.

Martin held his hand above his eyes as he looked toward the glowing screen door. "Your ride is here Garrett. Goddamn. I hope you all are a little more discreet when you're sneaking up on them wetbacks trying to steal across the border. No wonder the goddamn state is being invaded by illegals, they see you guys coming a mile away!"

"That . . . or maybe they've heard about your fine coffee." Garrett winked.

"Get the hell out of here. My tax dollars don't go to pay you to drink coffee and bullshit with me."

"All right then, I know when I've worn out my welcome. I'll see you same time tomorrow?" Garrett grinned.

"I'll be here."

"All right." Garrett laid a dollar bill on the counter and stepped out into the morning coolness. The wooden screen door slammed shut behind him and rattled several times against the frame.

"Coffee shitting monkeys," Martin mumbled to himself as he placed the dollar bill in the cash drawer.

Taylor Brophy was behind the wheel. Brophy wasn't much older than Garrett, but he had been with the Border Patrol for six years and had taken it upon himself to mentor Garrett and help him adjust to the demands of the job. From the very beginning, Garrett was impressed with the ease in which Brophy dealt with the human tragedy they often encountered along the border, while keeping a sense of humor about it all. Garrett didn't think that he had many of them, but he felt comfortable counting Brophy as one of his friends.

Garrett climbed into the cab of the government issued Wrangler. He leaned over, pulled the nylon strap across his chest and snapped the seat belt into the latch. Big and Rich's "Save a Horse, Ride a Cowboy" was blaring from the speakers.

"Christ, Brophy. You don't do anything quiet do you?" Garrett reached over and turned the volume down.

"Whatcha do that for Harrison? That's a good song." Brophy put the Jeep in reverse and backed out onto route 94.

"I'm not arguing that it ain't. I just prefer to ease into my day as opposed to being shot into it like a cannon. Besides, you can't possibly think that that crap qualifies as real country music?"

"I'm just trying to get you into the mood brother! 'Cause today is your day and this Friday, we're gonna celebrate!" Brophy slapped his hands on the steering wheel like he was issuing a drum roll.

"What are we celebrating exactly?"

"Don't be a dumb ass! Today you complete your probationary period with the patrol. Unless you screw up, that means you get bumped up from your lousy ass GS-5 level to GS-7. You'll actually start earning some real folding money instead of the pocket change you've been living off of these last six months." Brophy grinned.

"Oh, that." Garrett smiled. "Well, you know I never got into this line of work for the money. It's all about the prestige and the respect that comes with the uniform for me."

"Oh yeah, the chicks do dig a man in uniform." Brophy laughed.

"So, how do you reckon we should celebrate my sudden windfall into wealth?" Garrett inquired.

"Don't cheapen this milestone." Brophy took a serious tone. "It's more than a celebration. You have been here half a year, at day's end, you will be earning a man's wage. It is time for your initiation. It is time for you to become a man, my son." Brophy cast a knowing look at Garrett and patted him on his shoulder in a fatherly fashion.

"Just mind the road dad," Garrett replied sarcastically jutting his chin toward the windshield.

"Don't worry about me. You see, when you reach GS-7 status on the government pay scale, you can multi-task."

"Cow!" Garret shouted as he pointed ahead.

"Shit!" Brophy jerked the steering wheel to the left and swerved, narrowly missing a nearly solid black Holstein standing halfway in the lane.

"Dammit Brophy! Watch the road!" Garrett yelled clutching the dashboard.

"Did you piss your britches Nancy boy?" Brophy laughed.

"Just keep an eye on the road and watch for the little distractions that might meander into your lane, like a twelve hundred pound cow! I want to live to see that GS-7 pay, you reckless bastard."

"All right, calm down there Susan. You're okay and the cow's okay, and I am going to make sure that you live at least long enough to regret celebrating your promotion." Brophy smiled.

Brophy steered the Jeep off of Highway 94 and pulled into the gravel driveway of the Otay Lakes Border Patrol checkpoint.

2

*I*t's tough to actually peg the number of illegal immigrants now living here in the United States. Estimates by the Census Bureau, the Pew Hispanic Center and others who try to account for such things, put the number somewhere between eleven and twelve million. These folks also figure that the U.S. Border Patrol apprehends only about ten to thirty percent of illegal border crossers, meaning that a whole lot more of them manage to get through than what get sent back.

Smuggling people across the border has turned out to be big business. There are coyotes and guides that are paid good money to move people to the North. But there are some of those wanting to cross that don't hire help and they just go it alone . . . by the hundreds. A couple of months back, I was patrolling a stretch of border along the badlands. The night was pitch black and graveyard quiet when all of a sudden, as if on cue, a hundred or hundred and fifty men and women just charged out of the darkness and hit the wall. It was just me, Brophy and seven miles of fence that night. I hit the lights and Brophy called it in and then we set to chasing them down. Brophy yelling, "Alto! Alto! Goddamnit!" But not one of them stopped, they just scattered like jackrabbits and disappeared like ghosts into the inky blackness. Between the two of us, we caught four before the ghetto hawk flew in with the spotlight. Even with air support, we didn't catch any more of them. They blitzed us, and as far as we could tell, nearly all of them got through.

I've been with the patrol for nearly six months and I've seen people do some desperate things out here, but the thing that troubled me most (and I mean the type of troubling that makes it hard to close your eyes and sleep at night) was what we came across about four months ago. By now, most folks have either read about it in the papers or saw it on television, but that just ain't no substitute for witnessing the real thing.

We were patrolling our section of the canyon off of Highway 94 when we came across this semi-truck hauling a refrigerated trailer parked off to the side of the road. Weren't nobody there and there wasn't anything around for miles . . . not a gas station, house . . . nothing. So Brophy and I went to check it out. It was an independent rig. One of them owner operator outfits that seem to be increasingly rare in these days of three-dollar diesel. The Rig was a cobalt blue Peterbilt with a sticker placed on both the driver and passenger side windows that read in bold block letters: "No Passengers." We found the door was unlocked so we climbed up into the cab. The passenger seat had been removed in the event that the driver should ever contemplate violating the edict of the window stickers. Brophy found the registration and logbook in the glove compartment, but there weren't no sign of the driver.

It was a scorcher that day too. Must've been 110 degrees in the shade, if there were any shade. So we were a little concerned about what happened to whoever was driving the rig. We was just getting ready to radio it in and give it over to the Highway Patrol when I heard something that sounded like crying come from inside the trailer. I took my flashlight and tapped on the door and then the crying got louder and other voices joined in filling the air with the unmistakable moans of people in misery.

The door on the trailer was secured with a large brass padlock. So, I took out a pair of bolt cutters from a toolbox we found inside the cab and cut the lock off. Brophy helped me pull the doors open and a wall of heat and human stench belched out of that trailer and nearly dropped us both to our knees. Inside, we found seventy immigrants packed in like cargo. None of them had any water or food. They were just sitting inside that trailer, parked off of the roadside out in the middle of the desert. When we got inside, we saw that insulation had been pulled off of the walls and scattered all around and you could see scratch marks on the walls and the doors where several of them had attempted to literally claw their way out of the trailer. You knew which ones had tried because their fingertips were all raw and bloody. Many of them had passed out from heat exhaustion and weren't responsive. Four had enough fight left in them to help Brophy and me move the rest out into the fresh air. Nineteen gave in to dehydration and the suffocating heat and there weren't a thing we could do for them. Three of the dead were children—the youngest was only five years old.

Turned out, the driver of the cab was offered a lump sum payment of three thousand dollars if he would pick up a group of migrants outside of Tecate and drive them to some undisclosed location near San Diego. The driver got nervous on account of some heavy police activity that was taking place in the area at the time. This bastard already had two strikes on his record and didn't want to risk a third, so he abandoned his truck along with everybody inside. Didn't let them out. Didn't even bother to turn on the refrigeration unit. He just left them inside for God, fate and luck to sort out.

The law eventually caught up with him and filed 19 counts of first-degree murder charges against him, along with false imprisonment and 70 counts of conspiracy and harboring and transporting immigrants. His trial is coming up soon.

I have only been wearing this uniform for six months, so I guess I don't know anything different that what I have seen, but I listen to some of the old-timers when they get to talking about how it used to be and how it is now. They say that the situation along the border is only getting worse. When some of the younger officers hear them go on like this, they tell them that they're all full of shit and the fact that they think things are getting worse is proof that they are just getting' old. I wasn't sure what to believe when I first signed on, but I do know that the desert can be a cruel place; I have bore witness to this fact on more than one occasion and in more than one desert. Now, all I can say is that the longer I wear this badge, the more certain I am that those old-timers got it right.

Friday, September 19, 2008

G.H.

If you drive north along the two lanes of Highway 94 for about 13 miles, just before you reach the fork where the 94 and Otay Lakes Road split, you will find the Otay Lakes Border Patrol Checkpoint nestled between the scrub pine and manzanita. There are three modular buildings, a moveable kiosk and several three-foot tall bright orange safety cones that make up the checkpoint. Behind the buildings is a large gravel lot where the agents park their vehicles while manning the station. Typically, there are no fewer than ten agents staffing the checkpoint at any given time. The Otay Lakes Checkpoint has been in full operation on a continuous 24-hour basis since September 11th, 2002. It opened precisely one year after the Twin Towers fell, and was funded in part by a grant issued by the Department of Homeland Security in an effort to improve the safety of the United States borders and prevent further attacks from Islamo-Fascist terrorists.

John Parker was the senior supervising agent at Otay Lakes and has been serving at this station since it opened. Taylor Brophy joined the ranks several months later after earning his Paramedics license at Palomar College. While neither of them have had any encounters with terrorists, both have enjoyed the occasional exploits of preventing vehicles loaded with migrant workers from entering the country, and confiscating the occasional stash of weed from vacationing college students returning from their adventures in Tecate, Mexico.

Garrett checked in with his shift supervisor and took his position at the kiosk. John Parker had not arrived yet, but figured he would know about it when he did. Parker never missed a chance to celebrate. He was only curious as to what his initiation into his new salary rank would entail. He was on rotation, and for the next two weeks, it was his responsibility to be observant. He would keep a keen eye out for drivers exhibiting suspicious behavior or carrying questionable cargo. Of those travelers that raised no suspicion, he simply waved them on through.

For those that provoked his curiosity; he had a series of questions to ask. In some cases, he would search their vehicles. Seldom were his searches rewarded. That was why he hated this part of the job. The coyotes, the drug smugglers, the feared terrorists, had become too sophisticated. They knew the terrain; they knew where the checkpoints were and how to avoid them. Garrett knew from experience that if he were going to be successful at catching anyone illegally crossing the border in an area this vast, it would be from a plane. He would have to fly.

A total of 300 agents are assigned to patrol approximately 33 miles of international border between the United States and Mexico along the eastern San Diego corridor. This checkpoint was a rather quiet assignment. Otay Lakes is a substation of the larger Campo Station situated some twenty miles southeast of Potrero. The human smugglers, known as Coyotes, responsible for spiriting their cargo of flesh and bone, hope and fear, knew of both checkpoints and easily avoided them. Instead, they would use a network of underground tunnels to silently move their cargo across the border and beneath the wire. Once on U.S. soil, they would travel for miles along desert trails too treacherous for most four wheel drive vehicles, and slowly, relentlessly, make their way to a better way of life. On many occasions, tragedy would strike a band of immigrants. They would get lost in the vast backcountry, suffer injury or abandonment at the hands of their smugglers. Left without adequate food or water, they would sometimes quickly, sometimes slowly, perish and their flesh-encased bones would wither and whiten, becoming just another form of excrement upon the landscape.

The old way of patrolling the border no longer worked. One could not sit and watch and wait, staring at the fence, waiting for the moment of desperation to arrive, and move in to herd off the multitude of souls stampeding across the imaginary demarcation that separated the two worlds. This geographic region is arguably the harshest, most rugged, and isolated terrain in all of Southern California. It is largely undeveloped high desert land with roads that are barely recognizable as roads at all. The region consists of rocky peaks interconnected by steep-walled canyons. Elevation ranges are extreme and treacherous, ranging from a few hundred feet above sea level, to as high as 4,500 feet at the mountain peaks. With the exception of a few grassy valleys, the entire area is densely covered with thick brush, native vegetation and rocky out-croppings. In order to truly secure the borderlands, new strategies and innovative technologies were required of the agents. In 1994, the Border Patrol launched a high tech crackdown that was dubbed "Operation Gatekeeper." During the last decade, over a hundred million dollars have been invested by Washington in this endeavor.

The Border Patrol began utilizing military drones that would fly along the California/Mexico border, taking live video of the terrain below. If any human movement were identified, the coordinates would be transmitted to agents on the ground so that they could quickly head off any illegal entry into the States. The agents also utilized more traditional modes of prevention too, such as mountain bikes, all-terrain vehicles and horse mounted patrols. Garrett Harrison was familiar with all of these modes of border protection, but his preference was patrolling by air even though he had participated in air patrol operations only once. He had the opportunity to patrol the southeastern border regions aboard an old Army issue 1968 OH-6A Cayuse helicopter. It was an antique for certain, but an excellent light reconnaissance helicopter.

From the air, one can see the many trails leading from the southern border through the ravines and canyons. They pass and weave across each other as they lead northward toward some promise of work, or of a better life; however for many who are lost, the paths lead them toward the unknown abyss.

From the air, you can see how the northbound trails dip in and out of the washes that run through the arroyos. Migrants hide in these washes, taking shelter from the sun under the thick, low chaparral where their predecessors had built sturdy lean-tos from cut wood and brush. They become little communities, abandoned and populated for short durations throughout the day and night by thousands of people migrating through miles of desolate wilderness. They move slowly and silently, like an invisible human caravan, crossing the desert sands like Moses and the Israelites in search of their Promised Land.

For some agents, catching migrants is routine, and the incidents blend and cross one another like the trails of the landscape. For Garrett, one afternoon stood out in his mind above the rest. It was more than the thrill of assisting in the air patrol—it was the people themselves, and it was their stories that fixated him.

It was two months ago, after locating a band of migrants by air, he radioed their location to the ground patrols and he and the pilot landed to assist the agents on the ground. There were nine in all. Seven of those apprehended in the group were young men. There was a young couple with one small child among them. Garrett and the agents sat by the side of the dusty road and waited for a transport bus to take them to the Campo Station for processing. Garrett was the only agent in the group who was fluent in Spanish; to pass the time he began to speak to them in a manner that moved beyond the regimented formalities of inquiring their names, age and town of origin. He spoke to the couple. They were both not much younger than Garrett and had their five-year-old son with them. The boy was dressed in dirty jeans and a blue and gold Chargers jersey that looked two sizes too big. He slept deeply, curled up in his father's lap, exhausted from a night of walking.

As they talked, the parents smiled warmly at Garrett. They spoke openly to him about their son and their lives, what they hoped to do now that they were being sent back to Mexico and whether they would again chance a crossing into el Norte. Garrett asked them about their son's name. They told him that his name was Cristian and that he had been named after his paternal grandfather who lived in Jalisco. The young woman asked if Garrett had a wife or children of his own. He explained that once, he had had a fiancé, but things did not work out so well. She asked if it made him sad that he had no one at home waiting for him. He told her that sometimes it did. The woman asked what his former fiancé was like and laughed when he told her that he thought her hair was brown.

They asked him how it was he knew Spanish so well. He told them he learned from his mother.

"¿Ella es de México?" she asked in surprise.

Garrett explained that she was not from Mexico, she was Cuban.

He joked that she used to yell at him in Spanish when he would get into trouble.

"¡Mi mama también!" shouted one of the young men from the group. The whole band burst out into laughter while the other two agents and the pilot looked on with disinterest. When the white and green bus arrived, Garrett bid farewell to the migrants. He took his two fingers and gently touched the little boy, who was now wide-awake, on his forehead. This was a gesture Garrett learned from his mother, who had learned it from her own mother in Cuba. When you come across something so precious as an innocent child, you touch them there and pray for God to watch over them and protect them from *el ojo malvado*, the evil eye.

Garrett did not believe in breaking protocol. In his line of work, becoming too familiar was a liability. But he did respect the old ways. He did believe that such a simple gesture, even to strangers, that tells them their children are valued, is worth taking a moment to exercise. He never saw any of them again after they boarded the bus. Garrett often wondered what became of them. He wondered what future, immediate or distant, he had set in motion for that family on that day. Did they return to their old lives in Mexico? Did they make another attempt to travel to the North? Were they even alive? What, he wondered, might have happened if they had not spotted them from the air?

He stared at the two lanes of Highway 94 stretching out before him. There were no cars, just sage, dirt, blacktop and blue sky. He watched the metallic waves of heat dancing off the road before him, bending light and the world itself as each oscillating current broke free from the horizon and vanished into the air.

"God. I want to fly," Garrett whispered to himself.

Garrett's radio began to crack in a cacophonous medley of voice and static at the same instant he saw the smoke rising from the southeast. It started out white and wispy, and very quickly turned black as coal. Black smoke is usually an indicator that something man-made is on fire. Tires, oil from an engine, a structure . . . something.

"This is eagle eye calling the eagle's nest. We have a confirmed 11-71 Northwest of Sycamore Canyon. Repeat, we have a confirmed 11-71 to the Northwest of Sycamore Canyon. The fire is burning hot and the smoke is black and thick. I can't make out the origin," the voice called out.

"Eagle eye, this is the eagle's nest. Do you see any movement in the vicinity of the fire?"

"That is a negative. There is no movement. The smoke is black and as thick as molasses. Can't make out anything. Hold on eagle's nest, I am going to give it another pass."

Garrett listened intently. He could hear the helicopter's blades slicing the air in the distance. He could see the plume of smoke rising against the blue sky.

The radio came alive once again.

"Eagles nest, this is eagle eye. We have a definite 11-8. I repeat, there are people down. I can confirm three. Requesting assistance. Over."

"Eagle eye, this is the eagle's nest. Do you see any other activity at the site?"

"That is a negative eagle's nest. All is quiet. Over."

"Eagle eye, we have notified Agent Brophy. He is getting the med packs ready. Return to the nest and escort him to the scene."

"Copy that eagle's nest. I'm coming home."

Garrett had been listening to the radio dialogue so intently that he did not notice Brophy standing at the kiosk window until he rapped the glass sharply with his blue carabineer key ring.

"Hey, Harrison. Get your ass out of the kiosk. I might need you to speak Mexican if we find anyone alive down there."

"What makes you think they don't speak English?" Garrett asked.

"Well first of all, that pass is a thoroughfare for illegals. Second, it's too hot for a white man out there, and third . . . just get your ass out here. The ghetto hawk is gonna be touching down any minute!"

In ten minutes, the OH-6A had landed, and Brophy and Garrett boarded and were in the air.

When they arrived on the scene, the fire had nearly died out. There were inconsequential wisps of gray smoke rising from the blackened earth. In the center of the burn zone was a man. He waved to them, and then he struggled to rise to his knees only to collapse onto the blackened Beyond him were two more figures lying motionless, like discarded things on the ground.

The pilot made another pass in order to make certain that it was safe to land. He brought the chopper down a hundred yards from the burn site. Brophy grabbed his med pack and leapt from the chopper as soon as it touched ground and took off running across the embers with Garrett following close behind.

As they drew closer to the first two figures, it became apparent that they were young women, probably not more than twenty years old. They were lying on their backs with their eyes cast wide open and clouded over by the dust that had collected over them. Their lips were leathered and curled back as if to protest some offense and their blouses had been torn off of them and the shreds of bloodied cloth were cast aside.

Both women had been cut open from below their navel up to their sternum and their entrails had been pulled out and strewn across the ground. Their intestines had been crushed flat as though someone had tried to squeeze something out of them. Concentric pools of dried blood blackened by the sun encircled the two bodies and joined together like some grotesque Venn diagram.

"Aw fuck!" Garrett covered his nose in an attempt to blunt the smell of blood, decaying flesh and fecal matter. He turned his head and scanned the surrounding country. Just beyond the dead women were broad tire tracks pushing north across the rock strewn terrain.

"Goddamn. There's nothing we can do for these two except call the coroner." Brophy jutted his chin toward the third figure lying still on the ground. "Let's see if this guy has any fight left in him."

When they reached the man, he was barely conscious. By the time they carried him out of the burn zone the smoke had mostly dissipated.

As Brophy began administering first aid to the fallen man, the pilot approached Garrett and commented to him on how odd it was that the fire burned so black. Upon close inspection, it was nothing more than a grass fire. But both the pilot and Garrett had come to the same initial conclusion that it was probably some sort of vehicle burning. The pilot said that he would not have bothered to investigate it if he had thought it was only a small grass fire. He would have left it to the California Department of Forestry to sort out. But that's exactly what it had been, a grass fire and now it had burned completely out and there wasn't even any smoke. Except for the small patch of blackened earth, there was little evidence at all to testify that only moments before, a fire had raged there.

Garrett turned his back to the disemboweled corpses and shook his head. "I've heard of things like this happening in Brazil or Columbia. I've even seen it back in Iraq . . . but here?"

The pilot squinted in the glare of the sun and scanned the ravine. "This damned place went to Hell a long time ago and it's all just getting worse. I've seen some bad stuff around here. Probably the worst happened a couple of years back. We came across three men left in the ravine. Them sons a bitches had crossed somebody and had their eyes plucked from their sockets and their tongues cut out for their troubles. The worst part was that they was alive when we found them but they couldn't tell us a damn thing. All three of the poor bastards was corpses before we could get them to the county hospital. I tell you, it's like something out of a Mad Max movie out here. You'd think you was in Iraq or Afghanistan. But you ain't. You're here, in America. This goddamn drug war has moved right into our own backyard and the cartel is getting more and more brutal and twice as bold. If you get in their way, it don't matter who you are, you end up like this. I'm telling you son, Hannibal is at the fucking gate here."

"The Mexican Cartel did this?" Garrett asked not looking up from the emaciated figures lying on the ground.

"Well, not the Cartel exactly. The Zetas." The pilot pulled out a red and white package of cigarettes and patted the bottom of the box against his palm.

"The what?"

"Los Zetas."

"Never heard of them," Garrett replied.

"I ain't surprised. The DEA has kept pretty quiet about them. Otherwise, it might give the impression that we're losing the war on drugs." The pilot lit a cigarette and took a deep drag from it.

"So what are they . . . a gang? Drug smugglers?"

"Not quite. The Zetas are elite soldiers recruited from the Mexican Army by the cartels to keep order, collect information and when necessary, make their problems disappear."

"So they're hired thugs," Garrett replied.

"They're a little more sophisticated than that. These boys are the equivalent of a Special Forces unit. Mean, smart and mobile. It works out pretty well for them. They are paid more money by the cartels than they would ever see in their military career. Affords them the good life. They can buy homes, cars, clothes and jewelry for their girlfriends. Let's just call it the Mexican GI Bill." The pilot laughed.

"Which cartel?" Garrett asked.

"What?"

"Which cartel do they work for? The highest bidder?"

"These boys are bought and paid for by Felix Cárdenas."

"Cárdenas? Wasn't he captured awhile back? I remember hearing about him getting arrested before I was shipped out to Iraq. Ain't he in prison?" Garrett asked.

"Yeah." The pilot flicked the ashes from the end of his cigarette and spit on the ground. "It was a regular Mexican standoff between Cárdenas and damn near the whole Mexican Army. Both sides were loaded for bear with machine guns, grenades and rocket-launchers, the whole deal. The Federales finally got the bastard though. But if you talk to any of the boys from the DEA, they'll tell you that a prison cell is just a minor inconvenience for Cárdenas. He still calls the shots and the Zetas make sure everyone walks the line. Those who don't, end up just like them." The pilot nodded toward the two bodies and shook his head.

"It's a damn shame about those girls. They ain't nothing more than babies. My daughter just started college and they're probably close to her age." The pilot removed his mirrored sunglasses and wiped the beads of sweat that had collected among the wrinkles on his forehead.

"Nothing more than babies."

The pilot seemed to lose himself in thought for a moment, blinked hard, returned his sunglasses to their proper place, took a long drag from his cigarette and smiled at Garrett.

"Smoke 'em if you got 'em." He exhaled. "We're not going anywhere for awhile. This place is going to be crawling with sheriff's deputies and DEA agents before long, we have ourselves a bona fide murder scene."

The pilot patted Garrett on his back and laughed. "I hope that you don't have any plans for tonight." He walked back to the helicopter and began shouting something into the radio and Garrett pulled some bottled water from his pack, broke the seal and approached Brophy. The man turned his gaze to Garett with a look composed of both fear and relief; as though Garret might be some dark prophet, coming forth from the shadows to absolve him of past sins, before casting him headlong into the abyss. A full body shiver enveloped him, and then he lifted his hand and gestured to Garrett as though to call him forward.

"Agua, por Dios. Agua fría, por favor," the man whispered hoarsely. Garrett held the bottle of water to the man's inelastic, cracked lips. He began gulping voraciously and immediately began to vomit the water back up.

"Lentamente. Beba lentamente," Garrett whispered as he propped the man's head up while Brophy took his pulse. The man had no papers on him. Like many lost in the desert, his identity was a mystery. Garrett could not be certain if he was Mexican or Guatemalan or of some other origin. All he knew is that he was a man somewhere between 25 and 35 years old and he was clinging to life. His hair was damp and matted with sweat, dirt and clotted blood. He was exhausted and weak, but after a few swallows of water, he began to slowly and deliberately tell his story.

"Garrett, I believe this old boy's ready to talk. Can you make heads or tails of what he is saying?" Brophy asked.

"¿Cómo se llama?" Garret asked.

"Blas. Mi nombre es Blas," the man replied in a dry murmur. His clothes were stiff and black from dried blood and crusted, charcoal colored chips cracked and flaked off of his shirt as he attempted to sit up.

He told Garrett that he was a coyote and that he was helping his girlfriend and her sister make their way across the badlands. He explained that his girlfriend worked as a *mula* for a very wicked man, who smuggled drugs and people across the border. *Mulas* would carry drugs and other contraband inside their body in an effort to escape detection from corrupt coyotes, *banditos* or police that they may encounter on their way. On her last trip into the United States, he did not pay her. He said that she took too long to cross and it cost him money. So she decided that this time, she would cross, only she would not meet the contact. She would instead keep the drugs and she would sell them and keep the money and try to start a new life in the North.

"Le dije que, era una idea muy mala." He began coughing violently.

"Es bueno. Tómelo lentamente," Garrett whispered to the man. After a moment, the coughing subsided and he continued to tell how his girlfriend's sister wanted to join her, and the two decided that they would work as *mulas* and cross the border together. He insisted that it was a very bad idea and that it would be too dangerous for them to go alone. After considerable debate, he decided that he would help them cross. He explained that between the two girls, they had swallowed 100 packets of cocaine wrapped in tinfoil and encased in small balloons. He told him how on a moonless night with their bellies full and hard packed with their cargo, they traveled across the desert to the North.

But somehow, he heard about the plan. Somehow, he knew that they would betray him, and he made sure that they were punished for their disloyalty. The man continued to tell how three days earlier, they had arrived in this place to find that he was waiting for them with several of his men. The men had guns and they grabbed the girls and then proceeded to beat him. Then, without saying a word, he cut open their stomachs with a hook.

"Quién?" Garrett asked.

"Él," Blas replied.

He continued to explain how terribly the girls screamed as they were disemboweled. He thought he was in Hell. He had tried to fight and free himself from the men. He had managed to take out his knife and cut himself free from one of the men that held him—but then another man took out his pistol, and then everything went black. He told how he awoke in the evening to a great searing pain in his head. He found his girlfriend and her sister lying on the ground only a few meters from him. The man had cut out their stomachs and removed the cocaine packets from them, and then cast their intestines aside like excrement on the desert floor. He explained how for three days and three nights he had protected their bodies from the ravens during the day and from the coyotes at night. He had thrown stones, and made noises—but they were becoming more and more bold, while he was growing weaker and weaker.

Brophy had removed the IV packs from his bag and continued to prep the man for transport. Sure enough, above his left eye, beneath a thick crusty layer of blood and dirt, was a hole. A bullet had entered his skull and remained lodged somewhere in his brain. The man had survived three frigid nights and three blistering days in the California desert. He had survived an execution attempt, with a bullet in his head. He had survived three days without food or water. He explained that he was certain that he was going to die in the middle of nowhere and that he was afraid that the bodies of his girlfriend and her sister were going to be eaten by coyotes and would never receive a proper burial. So he prayed to the Holy Mother for deliverance from this place and in one last desperate hope, he started a fire with his pocket lighter, and that fire burned quickly and belched out a pillar of smoke just as black as the night into the clear blue sky.

The pilot had finished shouting orders on the helicopter's radio and had returned from walking the perimeter of the burn zone. He approached Brophy, Garrett and the injured man and scratched his head in puzzlement.

"It just don't make much sense to me," he said. "I just finished walking that black patch over yonder, and I could not find a single man-made thing that would explain all that tar black smoke we saw. Nothing but burned grass. It's like the desert simply offered them up."

"Well." Brophy smiled at the pilot as he worked the IV into the man's arm. "It seems to me that he is one lucky son of a bitch. But we'd better get him loaded into the chopper and get him some real medical attention before he just up and quits on us."

The blades from another helicopter could be heard slicing the air in the distance. The pilot shaded his eyes with his hand and squinted in the direction of the sound.

"San Diego County Sheriff. Good, let them have this one. I don't envy the paperwork those guys are going to have to file. Hell, I don't envy the paperwork we're going to have to file when we get back. Damn, I was looking forward to having dinner at home tonight," the pilot protested.

Garrett disregarded the pilot's complaint and tapped Brophy on the shoulder. "He seems to be coming around. Do you think he'll be all right?"

"Hard to say," Brophy replied. "To tell you the truth, I'm a little worried he might up and die right here, and right now. I've seen it before. Folks can be put through the paces, and literally will themselves to live through just about any horrible thing and then, right as help arrives, they relax. They feel safe and let down their guard for one second only to die in the next."

As Brophy explained this, Garrett thought it strange coming from him. When it came to the practice of emergency medicine, Brophy had a cool head. He was a practical, calculating practitioner who held to a modern view of science leaving little room for a metaphysical concept like "the will to live." He would write in the report that the bullet killed him, or the loss of blood, or perhaps heat exhaustion and dehydration. But the notion that the man had a choice to either live or die but he felt tired, and decided to lie down one last time seemed beyond the realm of acceptable possibilities that Brophy would offer up, and the fact that he would suggest it surprised Garrett.

The chopper lifted off the ground. Garrett could see the sheriff's deputies ambling about below measuring, photographing and cataloging the crime scene. They had wanted to get a statement from Blas, but Brophy explained that if they didn't get off the ground and to a hospital, the only statements Blas would be making would be a request for his last rites. Brophy continued to monitor his pulse and breathing the best he could while Garrett held the IV.

"He's fading!" Brophy shouted over the rotors.

This man didn't want to lie down. Garrett could see it in his face. He faced extreme odds in the desert, and he didn't lie down. When the ravens danced mockingly around the corpses and the coyotes came at night trying to feed on the remains of the two girls, he didn't lie down. Through the three days and nights of solitude and extreme temperatures that only the desert can fashion, he never let himself rest. But now, as Garrett held the IV, blood began to fill his left eye, and eternal sleep was creeping over him. His breathing slowed, and his voice became more hushed. Garrett needed a name. The Sheriff's Deputies would want a name; the DEA would want a name. He leaned in close to the man.

"¿Quién hizo esto?" Garrett shouted into Blas' ear, and then pressed his ear to Blas' lips so he could hear his reply.

"Cacique... el Cacique." he murmured in a hoarse, throaty whisper and spoke not another word again.

3

About two years ago, the President signed into law the Secure Fence Act, a law that pretty much calls for the fencing of over 800 miles of desert between the U.S. and our neighbor to the South. In absence of an actual physical border, we're compelled to make our own. I guess we figure that we got to protect that real estate purchase we made in the name of some virgin over one hundred and fifty years ago.

I hear people talk a lot about the Mexican-American border these days; and the more I hear them talk about it, the more convinced I am that most of them have no idea what it's really like. They'll talk about it like it was this tangible thing, like the Rockies or the Grand Canyon or something . . . but it ain't nothing like that, what it is, is this arbitrary line cut through the middle of the desert that divides economic prosperity from depression. Separating the haves from the have-nots.

In nature, there ain't no bright lines of demarcation that neatly divide one space against the other either. Yeah, if you go out into the wild you can find wide rivers that separate one shore from another— or mountain ranges that spill out onto the landscape, jutting upwards into the sky presenting formidable barriers for travelers to pass. But these are natural boundaries. They ain't political ones. Nature don't acknowledge race or politics. Natural demarcations like the Grand Canyon and the Rockies are gonna still be here long after we have faded into history. But the fact is, in absence of natural boundaries such as these, folks tend to make their own. Whether they're stringing barbed wire or drawing imaginary lines of longitude and latitude, they tend to want to carve up whatever corner of the world they find themselves in and call it their own. It's a primordial instinct imprinted on us and it is just as strong as the drive that sets us longing to see whatever might lay beyond the horizon. For as long as there have been people wanting to migrate someplace, there have been other people wanting to stop them.

Unlike natural boundaries, the man-made ones are quick to move. They'll change in shape and size and often they are renamed to fit the image of the namer.

I remember reading about the Mexican-American War when I was a kid in school and how the American troops chased Santa Anna and his boys deep into Mexico and pretty much forced him to sign away over half of Mexico's territory to the United States in a treaty named after the Virgin of Guadalupe. The U.S. Government wanted to be fair about things, so they paid the Mexican government a lump sum payment of fifteen million dollars in exchange for the territory. The new border was marked by the Rio Grande in Texas and if you crossed over into New Mexico, Arizona and California, the markers were seldom anything more than a pile of rocks. This lack of clearly defined demarcations led to more disputes, which resulted in the U.S. "purchasing" more land from Mexico in another treaty some five years later. I guess it was ironic that the first treaty was named after the Virgin, because she is believed to be the manifestation of the Virgin Mary in Mexico. Hell, two revolutions were carried out with her likeness painted on the flags. In hindsight, neither of the rebellions worked out exactly as planned, but if you take the time to ask, you'll find that most Mexicans believe that she blesses and protects her people even still. If you ask me . . . that's faith!

Nowadays, it's considered patriotic to defend the borderlands between the United States and Mexico, although nobody says much about defending the border between the United States and Canada. When you bring this up in polite conversation, it tends to get folks on both sides pretty riled up. You got people on one side saying that a million illegals cross the border each year from Mexico into the U.S. and they have got to be stopped. Others argue that Mexico is just working on reclaiming her old territory . . . one migrant worker at a time. I laugh at that . . . but I guess I can understand how one might fall into either line of thinking.

Politicians don't miss a chance to join in on the debate either.

There are some who go on about us being a nation of laws and that we can't abide people disregarding that fact and taking the easy way in. One of them even shot a campaign ad of him riding on the back of an elephant across the Rio Grande to make a point of how easy it was to get into the country illegally. The last time I checked, risking life and limb to cross miles of open desert under conditions of extreme heat with outlaws on both sides of the border looking to take you for whatever you got doesn't qualify as the easy way into anywhere—and as for the politician—I don't figure his crossing into the U.S. on the back of an elephant broke any laws . . . no matter how ignorant it seemed, but who knows, maybe them folks with the People for the Ethical Treatment of Animals might want to have a word with him.

I guess if you pay close enough attention to the way that people talk these days, you might find it easy to accept the notion that you can't really consider yourself an American unless you believe that better fences make better neighbors. On the other hand, I guess you can't really consider yourself a Mexican unless you believe in the Virgin of Guadalupe.

Friday, September 26, 2008
G.H.

Garrett rented a space behind Martin and Ester's General store where he parked his 1976 Airstream trailer. Martin and Ester had a detached garage that provided the perfect location for Garrett to work on restoring the 1947 Indian Chief he had inherited from his father. He and his father had begun the restoration project before Garrett enlisted in the Navy, and was not able to finish it before the cancer took him. It had been a slow process, but Garrett took satisfaction in seeing the motorcycle come along. It was nearly complete and he couldn't wait to take it for its first ride down the 94. He was cleaning rust from the carburetor when he heard Brophy and Parker pull into the drive.

They had to postpone Garrett's initiation last Friday due to the vast amounts of paperwork that had to be filed detailing the discovery and recovery of the shooting victim and the two disemboweled women in Sycamore Canyon. Garrett struggled to reconcile the dichotomous nature of his work. On one hand, the people he encountered were living, breathing people, with histories, hopes and fears just like him; but on the other, they were breaking the law. Many of them were guilty for more than just trying to cross without visas. What happened to Blas and the two women was proof of that. Garrett realized that if he allowed himself to get caught up in the details, if he allowed his work to become personal, it would bury him.

Garrett wiped his hands on a blue rag as the men got out of their truck.

"There he is Parker!" Brophy shouted. "The man stands before us a bona fide GS-7 son of bitch! You know what that means?"

"Sure I do! First round of drinks are on him!" Parker grinned.

"Now get your ass in the truck. We have an initiation to get underway." Brophy motioned to the black Chevy Silverado parked in front.

"I know that may qualify as sweet talk where you come from, but your red neck foreplay won't work on me you horny bastards!" Garrett grinned. "Let me get cleaned up first."

As you approach the crossing to Tecate, Mexico from Highway 188 and top the hill, one is taken by surprise by the sudden emergence of humanity upon the scenery. After traveling several miles on a secluded two-lane road without seeing as much as a solitary structure, the horizon is transformed by the thriving city to the south. The desert landscape is suddenly and vibrantly divided by a series of city streets and buildings all of which are illuminated by both artificial lights and the tireless energy of a living city. A weary traveler unfamiliar with the region might at first question if what they see before them is real, or a mirage manufactured by an isolated and barren wasteland.

They pulled into a dirt lot surrounded by a sagging chain link fence. Brophy spoke to the woman sitting at a tiny desk at the kiosk near the entrance. She explained that for seven dollars, he could park the truck for 24 hours. He paid her and inquired if she could exchange U.S. dollars for pesos. She indicated that she would. He motioned to Garrett and Parker and each of the men handed her several hundred-dollar bills from their wallets and waited as she counted out the pesos in exchange.

The three men walked toward the entrance to the crossing, and passed by a bullet riddled sign that read:

PERMIT REQUIRED TO EXPORT FIREARMS – 22 U.S.C. 2778.

"Hot Damn! I love Mexico," Parker sang out, patting Brophy and Harrison on their backs with his enormous hands.

"So, the big initiation is taking me to Tecate to get piss drunk? I could've done that from the comfort of my own trailer." Garrett glanced up at Parker and squeezed the back of Brophy's neck.

"Oh, we never said nothing about getting drunk partner. Well, maybe you will if you want—that's on you. I told you that it is time for you to become a man! The best place to do that is at Casa de Diana's." Brophy winked at Parker.

"You got that right Brophy," Parker cheered. "Now we'd better hurry up before all those young little darlins' are used up."

"You're taking me to a brothel?" Garrett's brow raised in surprise.

"What's the matter Navy boy?" Parker replied. "You didn't get so used to being cabin bound with all them sailors that you forgot how comforting a nice piece of feminine ass is, have you? And no, we ain't taking you to no brothel. Casa de Diana's is a respectable whorehouse."

"Don't go listening to Parker here neither," Brophy responded. "He'll have you convinced that the young ones are the way to go."

"Oh Christ! Not this shit again," Parker groaned.

"I'm telling you brother. My old dad was right, the older the violin, the sweeter the music." Brophy's smile widened.

"There's something definitely wrong with you Brophy, this unhealthy infatuation with the geriatric testifies to it," Parker remarked shaking his head.

"All I am saying brother, is that a slim waist and a tight ass is a poor substitute for experience," Brophy replied. "Some of them abuelas are as wild as alley cats I tell you. Don't let appearances deceive you. A little snow on the roof don't necessarily mean there ain't a roaring fire in the furnace!"

"Jesus, Brophy!" Parker gulped. "You're gonna make me lose my lunch here."

"You just say that 'cause you're ignorant on the subject and don't know what you're missing." Brophy grinned. "Some of these women got enough years and mileage on them that if a man pays attention, he can learn some things."

"I think you better stop all this talk about your lust for the grannies or you are going to scare Garrett here away," Parker said.

"I don't know about that. Garrett might appreciate the kind of loving an experienced woman can bring to a man." Brophy laughed.

"Hey Garrett, your abuela's still alive, ain't she?" Brophy asked in mock sincerity.

"Shut the hell up you sick bastard!" Garrett shoved him off of the sidewalk into the street.

Without missing a step, Brophy skipped out of the road back onto the sidewalk facing Parker and Garrett as he walked backwards.

"Does she knit afghans? Cause I love afghans! Better'n silk sheets I tell you. It's kind of sexy how your toes poke through the little holes too!" Brophy laughed.

"The man's certifiable, ain't he?" Garrett asked Parker.

"You ain't telling me anything new." Parker grinned. "I've been working with this deviant for the last four years."

Dusk was falling upon the town of Tecate as the three men continued down street. The sky blended and melted into deep hues of orange, red and purple when they approached the corner of Lazaro Cárdenas and Calle Libertad. Adjacent to the street was Miguel Hidalgo Park, named in honor of the Creole priest who called for Mexico's independence from Spain in 1810. The street lamps in the park began to flicker on as ranchero music played by four gray haired men floated across the plaza. Several children clutching melting ice cream cones ran about playing in front of the fountain as their mothers gossiped while keeping a watchful eye on them. It seemed to Garrett Harrison that Tecate stood apart from other larger border towns. It evoked a sense of dignity, and held a sense of self that was absent from places like Tijuana. There were no children running up to the tourists trying to sell them gum. Taxi drivers were not climbing over each other trying to convince you to allow them to meet your transportation needs. There were no crosses adorning the border fence bearing the names and giving silent witness of the men and women who lost their lives attempting to cross into el Norte. Tecate held its own unique sense of place in the world.

Across from the park sat the Hotel Tecate. It was an old building constructed in the 1930s following a traditional mission style design with a rust colored terracotta tile roof. A flickering blue neon vacancy sign hung in the window winking in the darkness like a woman too old to flirt. Adjoining the hotel was Casa de Diana. The exterior walls were coated with a thick white plaster. The windows facing the street were stained glass designs depicting the goddess Diana embarking on a variety of adventures. Decorative wrought iron adorned and protected each windowpane. The steps leading to the entrance were capped with yellow brick. Two large doors sat at the top of the steps leading into the foyer. Each door was artistically crafted from railroad ties and hand pressed steel. Wrought iron adorned the center of each door making a variety of geometric shapes. Hanging above the entrance was a round steel plate measuring about four feet in diameter with the initials C D cut into the center.

"All right boys, here's the place!" Parker began herding the two men toward the steps.

"Don't forget Garrett. First round is on you!" Brophy reminded.

"On me? I thought this was my initiation. You're gonna make me pay for my own initiation you cheap bastards?" Garrett shot back in disbelief.

"It's tradition," Parker replied. "Besides, we'll cover whatever little honey you pick out. It's more'n fair, so quit your bitchin' an let's get on inside."

They pushed the large doors open and stepped into the foyer. An older man wearing a white suit directed them toward a second set of doors, which opened into the cantina. It was a narrow rectangular shaped room with high ceilings. A long polished mahogany bar with brass railings ran the entire length of the room. Behind the bar stood the barkeep, who worked under the watchful eye of an oil painting of the goddess Diana. The painting depicted the goddess standing bare-breasted in a golden field drawing back on her bow preparing to slay a boar. The room was nearly empty of patrons but for three men surrounded by six whores sitting at the far end of the bar playing a game of dice. Occasionally the group would explode into bouts of laughter when a member of their party either won or lost a round.

Toward the back of the cantina, the whores sat on crushed velvet sofas waiting for their next client. They all looked up with interest as the three Americans crossed the floor and approached the bar. Each took a barstool and placed their boot heels on the brass railing.

"Well, what are you fella's having, mezcal?" asked Garrett.

"Oh no! No! No! None of that cheap Mexican hillbilly liquor," Brophy protested. "That stuff tastes like warm piss anyway. I'm having me some Don Julio Real."

"Hot damn! The man may be pervert, but he has expensive tastes. I'll have one too!" Parker exclaimed.

The barman reached behind the counter and filled three shot glasses from a bottle of Don Julio Real Tequila.

Brophy held up his shot glass and winked at the barkeep. "Leave the bottle amigo. Gentleman." He nodded at his companions. "I would like to make a toast."

"Ladies and gentlemen, you had better lock up your grandmothers and hide your guns—Taylor Brophy is about to get himself juiced!" Parker shouted as he pounded the counter with the palms of his huge hands.

"To Garrett Harrison. The best goddamn rookie border agent to come out of the U.S. Navy! Welcome to the brotherhood my brother!" Brophy winked at Garrett.

"Cheers!" Parker chimed in.

The three men clinked their glasses, tossed the tequila shot glasses back, and then sat them on the table. Parker nodded to the barkeep and he returned to the bottle and refilled their glasses.

Garrett scanned the perimeter of the room, sizing up its inhabitants. In much the same way a photographer uses filters and soft light to reduce the imperfections of his subject, the pale yellow bar light diffused through the suspended cigarillo smoke creating an odd halo effect around the occupants, thus making each seem more attractive than the honest light of day might otherwise reveal.

"You got yourself a little sweetie picked out yet Garrett?" Brophy asked.

"We just got here you horny bastard. Don't rush the man," Parker barked.

"What about that one over there?" Brophy jutted his chin toward a rotund woman wearing a purple tube top and jeans that were straining to hold in her curves.

"I don't know Brophy, why don't you go on and get her?" Garrett replied.

"Are you kidding me? That one's a baby. Hardly even green broke yet. That one is more my style." He pointed out a gray haired woman wearing a long red silk robe who was barking orders to the whores sitting on the sofas.

"I don't know Brophy. I think she's the Dueña," Parker whispered. "She might not be open for business."

"Now look here Parker. She is the most seasoned woman in here, hands down and you know I have got my needs. When a man gets a taste in his mouth for an older woman, there just ain't no substitute for it," Brophy asserted.

"All right then, you better go get her." Parker grinned.

"All right. I will . . . and you boys are just gonna have to get along without me." Brophy tilted his shot glass back, emptied it and sat it on the counter, and walked over to introduce himself to the Dueña.

"You know—he ain't right in the head," Garrett offered up.

"I know it." Parker sipped at his tequila all the while eyeing the girls at the end of the cantina.

"Harrison. You speak Mexican pretty damn fluent, don't you?" Parker asked.

"I speak Spanish fluently, yes," Garrett replied.

"Mexican, Spanish, same difference." Parker shrugged. "I got a problem that you might be able to help me with."

"And what exactly might that problem be?" Garrett asked.

"Well, it's pretty damn embarrassing. So much so, that I almost quit coming here," Parker explained.

"If it is a performance problem, they got pills for that, you know?" Garrett grinned.

"It ain't that asshole," Parker growled.

"Well then, you tell me. What's the problem?"

"Well, I don't speak Mexican . . . and these girls ain't exactly English scholars . . . and when I am with them . . . well, it's sometimes hard to communicate certain things," Parker whispered sheepishly.

"What kind of things?" Garrett asked.

"A lot of things. For starters, when I'm ready to . . . you know . . ." Parker began to stammer.

"I know . . . what?" Garrett grinned.

"Oh goddamnit to Hell. You're going to make me spell it out, ain't you?" Parker groaned.

"The only way I can help you is if I know what you're talking about." Garrett took a sip from his glass.

"Okay. Here it is." Parker took a hard swallow from his shot glass and sat it back down on the bar and leaned in close and whispered to Garrett, "When I am ready to . . . cum, I don't know how to tell the girls that in Spanish."

Tequila sprayed from Garrett's lips as he burst into laughter.

"Christ, Harrison! Pull yourself together and act like an adult!" Parker growled lowly.

"You want to know how to tell a woman that your are cuming in Spanish?"

"Well, yeah. It ain't exactly something that comes up in your high school Spanish class. I tried doing a direct translation from an English to Spanish dictionary once . . . and well, that was pretty useless."

"Why? What did you tell her? " Garrett asked grinning.

"Well, I translated I am coming into Spanish. I was hammering away, and when I felt the spirit move me, I tried to warn her by telling her: estoy viniendo."

Garrett laughed.

"It ain't funny!"

"Oh, yes it is! What did she say? What happened next?"

"Well, she just got all confused. She stopped and looked at me with all of this concern and asked me where I was going."

"You can't tell me that ain't funny Parker! Goddamn!"

"Well, there is more."

"Oh shit! I bet there is." Garrett grinned.

"Well, you know, sometimes, I like to go a little crazy and do it doggie style," Parker whispered.

"All right."

"Well, how do you even ask that of a girl in Spanish?"

"Don't tell me. You used your dictionary again didn't you?"

"Well, yeah, I did. I wanted to say, let's do it doggie style. So once, I asked this girl here: Hagámoslo estilo del perrito."

Garrett burst out laughing. "You jackass! You basically told her that you wanted to fuck her like a dog."

"Yeah, well, I figured that it must have a different meaning in Spanish than it does in English, because she got madder at me than an old wet hen! She got so offended, she got up, threw my pesos at me and left."

"Well, it only goes to show you, Spanish is a romantic language. Some of these crude English phrases don't always translate." Garrett grinned.

"Well, I need your help, or I am going to be forced into a sex life where my only option is the missionary position and I cum without warning."

"Can I ask you something?" Garrett asked grinning.

"Go ahead." Parker drained the tequila in his shot glass.

"Why haven't you just taken the time to learn Spanish? I mean, they offer classes, there's even a pay upgrade if you're proficient. It'd help you in the job and sure as hell couldn't hurt your odds with the brown eyed señoritas." Garrett laughed.

"No, thanks. I was hired before they pushed that bullshit bilingual requirement. I don't need to habla to deport anyone. As far as working with the brown eyed señoritas goes . . . I don't need to be proficient in Spanish. I got pesos and I got you. You gonna help a brother or not?" Parker asked.

"All right. I'll help you Parker." Garrett spoke slowly and deliberately, "The first thing you gotta do is remember that you can't literally translate an English phrase word for word because, as you've already discovered, they don't always hold the same meaning."

"I figured that much genius!" Parker replied.

"I'm just saying is all. Now second, well, you had better get a pen and write this down, because I know that you are going to get liquored up here and forget." Garrett laughed.

"Hold on a minute . . . " Parker searched his pockets. "Damn, I don't have a pen."

He turned to the barkeep. "Do you have a pluma por favor?"

The barkeep nodded, he reached into his coat pocket and handed parker a pen.

Garrett handed him a napkin from the bar.

"Okay, when you feel the spirit move you, as you said, and you want to warn the girl that you are ready to shoot . . . all you have to say is: prefiero caballeros."

"Pre . . . fee . . . air oh ca bay air oh's," Parker spelled out.

"Okay, thanks a lot buddy. This is really going to help me out! What about doggie style? How do I say that?" Parker asked.

"Well, that is a little more complex. Let me see here . . . " Garrett tapped his chin pensively. "Ah yes! You would want to say: ¿Puedo coger su culo?"

"Okay, wait a second . . . Puh way doh co gair sue coo low, got it! Man! This is going to make such a difference! Thanks old buddy!"

"Don't mention it." Harrison smiled. "Always willing to help one of my gringo buddies learn how to speak proper Mexican. Want another round?"

"Sure, I'll take one more shot . . . for courage."

"Courage? Parker, I don't know if anyone has told you this before

. . ." Garrett leaned in close as if to bestow some secret wisdom onto his friend without anyone hearing. "This woman . . ." he jutted his chin toward the prostitute in the riding boots "all of 'em. . . . They're a sure thing. You don't need any extra courage. You've got pesos, remember?"

The barkeep poured them each a fresh glass.

Parker grinned. "You're probably right, but since you are buying. I won't turn it down. Especially when Don Julio Real goes for about four hundred dollars a bottle back home!"

"Four hundred bucks! Damn Parker, I ain't seen my raise yet. You two bastards are gonna put me into hock before I get my paycheck!"

Parker lifted his shot glass and grinned. "Consider yourself initiated!" He drained the glass and set it back on the counter top.

"Well I'll be damned! Would you look at that!" Parker exclaimed. "Looks to me that Brophy has sweet-talked that ol' Dueña after-all!"

The two men watched in amazement as Brophy, escorted by the gray haired woman in the red silk robe, left the cantina.

"Well, we had better get busy then," Parker commanded. "Do you have one picked out for yourself Harrison? "

"No, not yet. You?"

"I'm thinking about that one with the blue jeans and them knee-high riding boots. Yee-Fuckin-Haw!"

"Yeah, she looks like a winner." Garrett sipped at his tequila.

"Well, I don't want to leave you here all sad and alone. You want me to help you pick one out then?" Parker offered. He reached into his hip pocket and pulled out a round tin of Copenhagen and tapped the can three times before he pinched a wad of dip and worked it into his lower lip.

"That ought to really impress the ladies." Garrett raised his eyebrow.

"Been chewin' since I was fifteen years old and I ain't never had a problem yet with tape worms or long relationships." Parker grinned. "You sure you don't want me to help you pick one out?"

"No. You go on. I'll be all right." Garrett laughed.

"You sure?"

"Yeah. Go on."

"Well, I appreciate your help. Next round is on me. Barkeep!" Parker reached over the counter and tucked a wad of pesos in the bartender's shirt. "After my amigo finishes that one, and picks out a little *señorita*, you set both of them up with a drink of their choice. *¿Comprende?*"

The barkeep nodded his head.

"Damn, I am throwing down with the *habla* already. Look at me Harrison, ain't I a Spanish speaking son of a bitch?" Parker grinned.

"You are at that!" Garrett smiled, and thanked the bartender. "Go on now, get after them girls and avoid the rush!"

"You know I will!" Parker turned and headed toward the woman in the black knee-high boots.

Garrett Harrison was sipping at his tequila when he saw her enter the cantina with him. She wore a red dress that fit tight and smooth, complimenting every line and curve on her body. Her ebony hair shone almost cobalt in the bar light and flowed off her shoulders, hanging low down the middle of her back. The man spoke with the two whores sitting on a red love-seat. They stood up immediately, and vacated their post. The man motioned to the girl, and she sat down where the two whores once resided. He was tall and lean with wisps of gray contrasting sharply against his jet-black hair. He was dressed in a dark black suit, with a yellow silk shirt. His hands were adorned with an assortment of gold rings.

The barkeep moved from behind the counter carrying a brown envelope. One of the whores followed him carrying a glass and a bottle of liquor. A broad smile spread across the man's face. He embraced the barkeep and took the envelope and placed it in his coat pocket. The whore offered to pour him a drink, to which he politely declined. The girl sat quietly on the couch looking at the floor. She gently brushed her bangs from her eyes with her fingertips. The barkeep and the man finished their conversation, and the man left the cantina.

When the bartender returned to the counter, Garrett asked him if the girl worked here.

He indicated that she did, she was new to Casa de Diana. Garrett asked him who the man was.

"¿Qué hombre?" asked the barkeep.

"El hombre en la ropa negra," Garrett replied.

"No se. Él no es nadie," he replied nervously, and moved to the other end of the bar and began polishing glasses.

The men in the corner erupted into laughter once again and began a friendly argument over who was going to buy the next round of drinks.

He rose from the bar and crossed the cantina and approached the girl sitting on the red sofa. As he drew closer, he could tell that she was young; perhaps only sixteen or seventeen years old. She lifted her eyes to meet his. They were a light golden color and shimmered in the pale light. She smiled at him, and for a moment, he lost the ability to speak. She lowered her face slightly.

"Um. Good evening. May I sit down with you?" he managed to splutter out.

"Mis disculpas, hablo solamente español," she replied.

"Está bien. Sé hablar español." He smiled.

She shifted on the sofa slightly, offering up enough room for him to sit. He sat down beside her on the red sofa and smiled nervously. The woman from the bar approached them and asked if they would like something to drink. The girl indicated that she would like tequila and Garrett indicated that he would have one also.

"¿Cómo te llamas?" He asked.

"Me llamo Angelina Marguerite," she said softly.

He told her that it was indeed a pretty name. He asked her if Marguerite was French. She said she was not certain if it was, she explained that she was named after her mother who had died when she was a very little girl.

He told her that he was very sorry to hear of her loss. He understood that losing a member of one's family was a difficult thing. He explained that he too was an orphan in this world. He had lost his mother when he was younger and his father had passed away only two years ago.

She made the sign of the cross and said that she hoped that his parents were rejoicing in heaven with God.

The woman from the bar returned with their drinks.

"Gracias." He smiled and attempted to pay her with the pesos from his billfold. She refused, reminding him that his friend had paid for their drinks in advance.

She sat silently for a moment running her slender finger around the edge of her glass. Then she asked him if he was married.

He was surprised at the question. He told her that he was not. She explained that many of the men that come here have wives or girlfriends at home, and it was curious to her why they would come here to pay for attention that they could get at home for free.

He admitted that it was questionable that men would do such things. He wasn't sure why, but he felt that it was important that she knew that he had no one waiting for him at home. So, he again emphasized that he was single and that he did not even have a puppy waiting at home for him let alone a girlfriend. She told him that it did not really matter if he was single or not, but that she believed him.

She asked him how old he was. He smiled and asked her how old he looked. She frowned and told him that it was bad manners to answer a question with a question. He laughed. He told her that he had turned twenty-four about seven months ago.

He asked her how old she was. She frowned again and asked him if he had ever talked to a girl before tonight.

"¡Por supuesto! Hablo con muchas señoritas," he replied.

She insisted that it could not be true, because if he had experience talking to women, he would know that asking them their age was taboo. He smiled broadly and told her that it was okay if she was sensitive and did not want to reveal her age to him. He actually preferred older women like her. She held her hand to her mouth letting out a sound that was part gasp, part laugh and playfully nudged his bare forearm with her other hand.

"¡Qué rata!" She laughed.

He felt something swell within him when he realized that he made her break into a genuine smile. His skin felt warm from where she had touched him with her hand and he liked the way her eyes danced when she laughed. For a brief moment, he forgot where he was.

Parker suddenly burst through the cantina door wearing his pants and clutching his boots in one hand and shirt in the other. A woman wrapped in a sheet wielding long leather boots chased after him shouting all sorts of profanities in Spanish. She hurled one of her long black riding boots in his direction striking him in the side of the head.

"Ow! Son of a . . . Somebody get this crazy whore off of me!" Parker shouted.

Several of the whores who sat watching the spectacle jumped up and restrained their sister, attempting to offer words of comfort. However the woman would not be consoled, she just kept shouting "¡El americano está loco! ¡El americano es puto!"

Just then, Brophy emerged from his visit with the Dueña.

"Just what in the hell is going on?" Brophy asked tucking in his shirt.

"I don't know. She's crazy is all I can figure." Parker had put on his shirt and was attempting to pull on his boots.

"Well, she is saying the same about you. What happened in there?" Garrett asked.

"All I did is tell her the things you told me to say. I said them exactly like you . . ." Suddenly a look of enlightenment and anger crossed Parker's face all at once.

"You son of a bitch! What did you make me say?" Parker shouted.

Garrett burst into laughter. "I'm not sure."

"What in the hell do you mean that you ain't sure? Either you are or you ain't." Parker's face grew red.

"Well, it's just that my Spanish is excellent, but my Mexican is a little rough. You may of told her that you prefer to be with men . . . and that you are going to fuck her in the ass—or something like that. Why? Do you think she was offended?" Garrett grinned.

Brophy burst into laughter. "You taking Spanish lessons Parker?"

"Goddamn, I should've known better than to trust a Mexican." Parker grabbed a sliced lime from the bar and threw it at Garrett who caught it in his hand.

"For the last time you ignorant hillbilly. I ain't Mexican, I'm half Cuban!" Garrett threw the lime back at Parker, striking him in the shoulder.

"Damn it all to Hell!" Brophy shouted. "A food fight? Name calling?

Junior High level practical jokes? This is the last time I take either one of you to a whorehouse again; you just can't behave in a respectable adult manner!"

When Garrett looked back at the sofa, the girl was gone. She had joined the other women in an attempt to comfort the still screaming prostitute.

Just then, the barkeep along with two other darkly dressed men approached the three and suggested that they pay their tab and get on their way. Garrett pulled his billfold from his pocket and paid the barkeep and provided him a little extra to compensate for the unanticipated excitement. The occupants looked on with interest as the three men were escorted to the door.

Somewhere in the stillness, a clock bell chimed midnight welcoming the new morning when they stumbled out of the doors of Casa de Diana and into the streets of Tecate. Brophy's laughter rang like a clap of thunder through the darkened, nearly vacant streets, echoing off of the plastered walls and fading into the night.

"Garrett Harrison, if you ain't the damnedest . . . funniest rookie I ever did see! Whoo! Hoo!" Brophy slapped Garrett on his back and his huge laugh resounded again, enveloping the three men and echoing into the night.

"Yeah, he's a regular comedian." Parker spat a thick brown stream onto the sidewalk. "Thanks to this asshole, I spent good money, and I didn't even get laid. If I were up for that, I would've tried going out on a date."

Garrett laughed. "Well Parker old buddy, you should just chalk this experience up as a little lesson in humility. It ain't easy getting by when you don't know the language of the land. Maybe this will inspire you to take a little time out of that busy schedule of yours and learn a little Spanish. I mean Christ, Parker, you work with Spanish speakers just about every damn day, and it wouldn't kill you to broaden your vocabulary a little."

Parker spun on his heels and turned to face Garrett. "Let's get one thing straight Harrison, I don't work with these people, I deport them. Besides, them border crossing sons a bitches are the ones sneaking into our country, invading America—the least they could do is learn to speak English!"

A grin spread across Garrett's face. "Parker, I have news for you . . . you're the border crossing son of a bitch tonight."

"Don't be ignorant, Harrison," Parker shouted. "It ain't the same thing and you know it. Besides, I think you owe me the forty dollars I gave that whore. You're the reason we got throwed out before I got anything."

"Girls! Girls! You need to stop this catfight before one of you says something that you can't take back," Brophy interrupted, stepping in between the two men draping his arms across their shoulders. "Now, the way I see it is you are both right. Parker, Harrison here makes a good point. We are all border crossing sons a bitches. And Harrison, Parker here is right, you are a comedian. That was some funny shit back there!" Brophy burst into another volley of laugher.

"Look Parker, I'm sorry that you lost your money." He jutted his chin in the direction of the slow moving figure ambling down the road. "I tell you what, I'll treat you to some roadside tamales. Fresh tamales always seem to make even the darkest situation look just a little better," Garrett offered.

In the distance, an ancient, sandal clad Indian woman pushed deliberately at a white cart making her way slowly down the *calle*. She looked as though she was rising from the earth as she made her way up the dark, asphalt road toward the three men. Her silver braids nearly touched the white apron that was tied securely around her ample waist. Though her shoulders were slightly stooped, she walked with the grace of one accustomed to carrying a basket upon her head.

"Ah! Ain't she something!" Garret declared.

"Christ, Harrison, not this perverted shit again! Don't tell me that Brophy's infatuation with the elderly has rubbed off on you! I am not in the mood for it," Parker groaned.

"Ease up Parker, the man has finally acquired some taste in women!" Brophy replied draping his arm around Garrett's neck. "Go on Harrison, tell us more about this little honey."

"Get your mind out of the gutter Parker! I don't mean what you're implying," Garrett replied shoving Brophy to the side. "This tamale woman is it."

"Is what?" Parker asked puzzled.

"She's the answer," Garrett replied.

Brophy raised his eyebrow. "The answer?"

"Yep."

"The answer to what?" Parker asked.

"The answer to everything," Garrett replied emphatically.

"The man has had too much tequila I think, it's gone to his head." Parker pointed his index finger at his temple and made a circular motion with it.

"Parker, Parker, Parker. You don't see it? I'm sure that Brophy sees it, don't you?" Garrett asked quizzically.

"I can't say that I do," Brophy replied puzzled.

"When you consider the tamale woman, you consider the very heart of the human condition. When you consider the tamale woman, you're considering the shared histories of humanity . . . the tragedies, the triumphs, the joy and sorrows, the things that bind us all. She is the story behind the story, don't you see?" Garrett pressed.

"I see an old woman pulling a cart." Parker blinked.

"You notice that she ain't wearing a wedding ring?" Brophy whispered to Parker.

"Yeah, so?" Parker replied.

"Well, I heard it said that the many of the tamale women are widows. They marry their men, and then something happens . . . perhaps their husbands are unfaithful . . . or abusive or they just lose interest; but the tamale women . . . they get their vengeance, along with a special ingredient to add to their tamale recipe! As for their husbands, well no one ever sees them again. At least not without a masa and cornhusk ensemble." Brophy winked at Parker.

"That's just plain sick Brophy!" Parker laughed.

The old woman came to a rest at the edge of the sidewalk, stopping before the three men. She gazed up at them and offered up a smile made soft by the lack of teeth beneath her wrinkled lips. Here was a woman whose brown eyes would soon be completely clouded over with cataracts. Garrett looked at her and wondered how it was possible that she could see well enough to guide her tiny cart down the road.

"¡Buenas!" Garrett smiled down at the woman.

"Buenas noches. ¿Gustas algunos tamales?" The woman inquired.

"¡Sí, por supuesto! Compraremos tres, por favor," Garrett replied.

"¿Rez o pollo?" She asked.

"Pollo por favor," Garrett replied.

She lifted the lid to her cart and pulled out three tamales wrapped in hot, moist cornhusks and placed them into individual plastic bags and handed them to Garrett.

"Gracias." Garrett smiled, not certain if she could see his face.

"Treinta pesos por favor."

Garrett passed the bags to Parker and Brophy and then handed the woman thirty pesos. She slid the coins between her fingers, feeling their contours, then placed them into a coffee can and closed the lid and placed it back into the cart. The old woman turned back to face Garrett and grasped his hand in hers. Her fingers were gnarled and rough from years of labor, but had a youthful radiance that warmed his hand.

"Ella es una muchacha fina, y ella está enamorada de usted," she whispered softly.

"¿Qué muchacha?" Garrett asked.

"Usted sabe. Usted sabe bien." She gently patted his hand and slid the metal lid of her tamale cart closed and returned to her journey down the dimly lit *calle*.

The three men stood beneath the street lamp and peeled back the cornhusk wrapped tamales and bit into warm masa.

"What'd she say to you?" Brophy asked biting into his tamale.

"I am not sure," Garrett replied.

"You ain't?" Parker asked in disbelief.

"Mark my words boys." Garrett smiled and patted Parker on his back. "Until you learn to appreciate the unvarnished simplicity of the tamale woman, you'll know absolutely nothing of the human condition or your place in the world."

4

*B*eing a nation at war is tough business. If you're on the home front, you figure out pretty quickly that everyone has an opinion and everyone thinks that their side of the debate's the right one to be on. It's tougher still if you're personally invested in the argument by having a loved one serve and never knowing if the next knock you hear at the door will be accompanied by bad news. If you're in that boat, political views take a back seat to the simple desire to see that empty chair at the end of the dinner table occupied once more by the one who should be sitting in it.

I served for six years and never really got too wound up in the politics of what I was doing. I had my orders and I carried them out. I never once stopped to try and rationalize anything I did, or attempted to make sense of the world that I found myself in, because if I ever tried, I would've come completely unhinged. I'm sure of that.

Some of the men and women I served with believed in the cause. Like me, they were following orders that more times than not, didn't make a lick of sense, but they carried them out all the while knowing that they were upholding the banner of liberty and bringing democracy to oppressed people. Sometimes, I envied them. They had a sense of purpose that seemed much bigger than mere survival. Many of them soldiers were just common folks earning a soldier's wage, which I can tell you first hand, ain't a whole hell of a lot. Others were with the reserves, which meant they had to leave their families and their jobs back home to make a stand a world away for a lot less than they was accustomed to earning. One day, I saw this soldier up and fall apart in the middle of the mess hall. He hit his knees and set to crying like a baby, all broken up because he couldn't make his mortgage. His family had struggled to make ends meet ever since he deployed. His wife picked up another job and bought their kids school clothes at a second hand store. But in the end, the bank repossessed their home, his wife left him and he just lost it. I don't figure he had cornered the market in that particular brand of misery either.

When I woke up this morning it was all over the radio about how four U.S. civilians were killed in a grenade attack by a group of masked insurgents outside of Fallujah. The reporter described in elaborate detail how crowds took to the streets cheering and dancing as they pulled four charred bodies from the burned out vehicles and then hung two of them from a Euphrates River bridge. The crowds then drug the other two bodies through the streets, beating them with sticks all the way.

On every broadcast, the reporters used terms like civilian or contractor to describe the slain men. Bringing forth images of red blooded, flag waving construction workers or truck drivers, who found themselves in Iraq for no other purpose than the reconstruction of a broken country. They was all a little slow to mention the fact that these boys was hired mercenaries, bought and paid for by private U.S. security firms to do the same thing U.S. soldiers do, but for nearly ten times the pay.

No one is quite sure how many private soldiers we have on the ground in Iraq and Afghanistan. Some put the number between twenty to thirty thousand. It's also a bit unclear as to how much tax dollars are being paid out to these companies. One Californian congressman conducted an investigation into the matter and claimed that one of these private military companies received a no bid contract for over $830 million dollars. Now the notion of armies for hire ain't something new. In medieval times, professional soldiers were hired by kings to fight their wars; until the tendency of these demobilized companies to loot the countryside brought about the need for organized armies made up of citizen soldiers, loyal to a national identity, paid for by taxes and accountable to a centralized government.

These mercenaries that we have deployed are better paid and better equipped than conventional soldiers and can act with total impunity. The way things sit, none of these private security contractors are bound by military regulations nor can they be prosecuted under Iraqi or U.S. law for crimes they commit. Some argue that this is a good thing. Being unencumbered by bureaucratic red tape makes these private soldiers more agile and more efficient . . . sort of the Federal Express of national security. These companies recruit heavily from the FBI, CIA and Special Forces in an effort to enlist the best and the brightest. I knew several guys who wouldn't re-enlist for another tour in Iraq with the military but were all too happy to return as soldiers for hire. If you did the math, it ain't too hard to figure out why. As private contractors, some of these guys brought in close to $450,000 a year.

In my experience, most of these rent-a-cops were arrogant and difficult to work with. I remember when I was in stationed in the Green Zone in Umm Qasr, I witnessed a Marine commander order a squad of private contractors to put their weapons on safety when entering the base post office. To which the leader winked at the officer, wiggled his trigger finger in the air and replied, "This is my safety" and walked right on past the officer as if he was nothing more than one of them greeters at Wal-Mart. Their attitude was, "We're fuckin' security and we don't have to answer to nobody."

Six months later, that same squad leader was fired after he got piss drunk at a Christmas Eve event and shot and killed the bodyguard of Iraqi Vice President Adel Abdul Mahdi. This jackass killed the personal bodyguard of the Vice President of a sovereign nation, and all he got was fired. The real kicker of the whole deal was he was seen two months later in Fallujah working for a different security firm.

I feel bad about those four men that were killed and desecrated in Fallujah. No one deserves to go out of the world like that. But I am guessing that not one of them lost sleep at night worrying about how they were gonna pay their mortgage or if their kids had clothes.

Tuesday, September 30, 2008
G.H.

She was brushing her hair when she heard his approach. Before his knuckles made contact with the door, nausea descended upon her rapidly and fiercely like some terrible clawed raptor. She drew a breath and welcomed him in.

"*Buenas Noches, mi cielo.*" he smiled warmly at her. He stood before her in the entryway, with a black leather satchel slung across his shoulder and holding a single red long stemmed rose in his hand. She knew what the rose meant; this was the gift that he brought to all of the women that worked for him on such occasions.

"*Buenas Noches* Juan Carlos." she pinned her hair back and smiled at him through the mirror. "I was just on my way to the cantina. I am not late?"

"No!" he laughed. "You are not late. In fact, I have arranged for you to have the evening off."

"Really? What is the occasion?" she asked in surprise.

"You have been working hard for me and I appreciate it. He smiled at her as he sat his satchel on the edge of her bed and pulled from it a bottle of merlot and two wine glasses. "I thought it would be nice for both of us to have a little time off. As they say, *trabajar sin descanso agota a cualquiera.*"

He sat the bottle and the glasses on her nightstand and walked up behind her, delicately tracing the contours of her face with the tightly folded petals of the rosebud.

Hating him was something that she tried desperately to avoid. Since he deserved nothing from her, she attempted to feel nothing for him at all. For the most part, she was successful, except for the fear. The fear of him remained ever present.

"I am flattered that you wish to spend your free time with me, Juan Carlos... but I am certain that there are other women who are equally as hard working and much more beautiful than I." she felt a momentary stab of guilt at the thought that she might be steering him in the direction of some other unfortunate woman, but had a morbid sense of relief at the realization that he would not change his mind. Juan Carlos was the kind of man who would run over a dog in the middle of the road before he would ever consider altering his path.

"Angelina, *mi amor*, how can you say such things? There is no woman in all of Mexico that can match your beauty, of this I am sure you are aware...and false modesty, is that not a sin?" he laughed.

"I just do not wish to be perceived by the others as receiving special treatment from you when they work just as hard, it is not just." she lowered her head.

"*Mi cielo*," he spoke softly, placing his hands on her shoulders turning her to face him. "I would never dream of doing a thing that would cause you distress, or be against your will. If you bid me to go, I will go. You have only to say the word." His mouth curved upward into a smile that contested the kindness in his words. This was not the first time he came to her, nor would it be his last. He would always enter bearing the gift of a single rose and a bottle of a fine vintage wine or champagne or tequila. The greatest offense to her was not the gifts, or even the fact that he came to her, it lay in the fact that he always presented his intentions in a manner that presumed that their meetings were consensual.

He kissed her neck and it took all of her strength not to cry. He moved up to her chin and then to her lips, occasionally expressing small cries of appreciation, like a hungry infant at its mother's breast. She closed her eyes and tried to imagine herself somewhere else, at the old church near her grandparents home, on the docks of Yelapa watching the waves break as they rolled into shore while she waited for her father to return from the sea. When these images could not fully subdue her desire to scream or to vomit, she would remind herself: *this will be over soon. It means my grandparents are safe tonight. That is all it means, that and nothing more.*

†

Chato waited silently inside the cab of the old primer gray Chevy pickup parked outside of Casa de Diana's. For Chato, silence was not just a professional courtesy, but a matter of survival.

When the men would come to him and offer him a job, sometimes, they would specify that they wanted it to appear accidental. Other times, they would want to make clear that it was to be an obvious act of retribution. If the men did not specify how the job should be carried out, he would take their silence as permission to command creative license. He would not question the morality of the task set before him nor would he make attempts to negotiate a higher wage. He would not even bother to count the money given to him; he would merely accept the envelope and nod his head in solemn agreement. If the men ever thought it strange that Chato did not speak, they never made their concerns known to him.

When he first began to talk, he could never seem to get a proper hold of his words. His tongue would always stumble and his speech would rattle from his lips in rapid, uncontrollable repetition. His father ignored his condition and would often avoid speaking to him at all. However, his mother worried about his speech and would constantly make him stop mid-sentence and repeat himself hoping that on the second or third attempt, the words would emerge stammer free.

When he was five years old and the tremors in his speech had not ceased, his mother took him into the hills to see the Curandera, a healer that many from his village would visit in search of cures and hope. The Curandera was an old woman who smelled like sage and dust. She had only one eye and used it well as she examined him with the careful precision of one about to buy a horse. She looked in his eyes and peered down his throat. Her gnarled skeletous hands felt the contours of his head and firmly squeezed the glands beneath his jaw line.

The Curandera had determined that the spirit of some trickster, a *duende,* had bewitched him binding his tongue and bestowed upon him both a gift and a curse. She explained that the tongue of the boy had been enchanted with two languages. One of course was his mother tongue of Spanish and the other was something older, and darker, a language that did not originate in the human mind or the throat. This language is one that surges up from the heart, from the blood in his veins drawing upon the memories and the customs of the ancients.

"When the boy speaks, his tongue becomes confused and does not know which language to use to express itself, so his speech becomes repetitious, like the drumming of a woodpecker," the Curandera explained.

It was determined that she should perform a *purépecha*, a purification ritual on not only the boy, but the home as well. It would be important to cure the house and remove from it all of the elements that may have served to bewitch the boy.

So, it was that the Curandera came to his grandfather's *rancho* and smeared a foul smelling grease all over his body and for three days she burned incense and prayed in a language not understood by him. On the third day, she entered his room with a branch from a sage bush in one hand and a white chicken in the other. She waved one, then the other over him chanting rhythmically all of the while. She then placed the chicken in a brown woven basket and tied the lid securely so it would not escape and then she carefully wrapped the sage branch in a white cloth and tied it with a white ribbon.

She told his mother and his father that the air throughout the entire house was thick with magic and it required all of her skill and her most powerful prayers to cleanse it. She explained that in her prayers, she thanked the *duende* for its generosity in granting the boy with an enchanted tongue, but explained that it was a gift that the family feared would hinder his growth and acceptance into the world of men. She told how she had used the incense to purify the air and to drive the magic from every corner of the house. The chicken was used to draw the magic from the boy directly and to capture it within the feathers and flesh of the animal, while she had used the sage branch to sweep the home of any remnant energy.

The Curandera explained to his mother that the chicken and the sage branches should be taken far from the home. The chicken should be killed and then burned along with the sage as an offering. The smoke would return the magic to the *duende* from which it came, releasing its hold on the boy forever. The ashes of these offerings should then be sprinkled around the four corners of the house.

She advised his mother that the boy should not speak until the dawn of the Sabbath and on that day, the family should pray and give thanks—for the *duende's* magic would have been fully driven from him. His mother explained this to him, and he did not speak until that Sunday morning as directed. His mother was a woman of faith and she believed in the healing ability of the Curandera. She told him that he would lead the family in prayer before breakfast that morning and he would do so without stumbling over a single word. With the family gathered around the table and the smell of chorizo thick in the air, Chato bowed his head and at the age of five discovered that in this world there were mountains that neither faith nor magic could move.

As Chato grew, he became increasingly more silent, speaking only to those in his family and even then, only when necessity demanded it. He grew accustomed to the ridicule and the unkindness in words uttered so easily by others, but came so difficult to him.

In the solitude and open spaces of his grandfather's *rancho*, he discovered that he had a gift that did not require a steady tongue, only a steady hand. There he could fire *pistolas* and rifles without worry of the authorities. For Chato, the world of the gun provided him a mystical realm in which he could submit himself fully. In this world, he was not bound by customs or tradition or matters of principle. Here, it did not matter that his tongue stumbled clumsily over the words he tried to express. In this place, Chato learned how the elements of space and matter connected and transformed; he mastered the laws that governed their interactions and nothing else needed be known or understood. The gun became an extension of his body. Steel and oil, powder and lead become one with his own flesh and bone. He would pull the trigger and as if by will, navigate the bullet to hit the most challenging target from any distance. To those close to Chato, his mastery of this realm seemed otherworldly and his achievements effortless and unholy. When word of his skill spread, the unkind words about his speech stopped and laughter and insults were replaced with silence and nervous glances.

Chato learned that there is a debt to be paid for every gift. He discovered that the curse that accompanies the gift of genius, whether the gift is mastery of music, math or the gun, is loneliness. The one bearing the gift is often obsessed with the perfection of it and loses himself in its pursuit. The wonders of invention and the possibilities that unfold in the young mind intoxicate the bearer of the gift and provide them with their only source of validation and sense of accomplishment. The outside world, with its messy human interactions, emotional conflicts and complex histories, is cast aside so that attention can be given to the intricate and bounded universe over which the genius alone has dominion. Such was the cross that Chato had to bear. His youth had been one of lonely silence until he met a young woman who offered him words of kindness. In time, her kindness grew into something deeper. She worked at her family's restaurant in Totatiche. They called their restaurant La Candelaria, in honor of the Virgin who was said to have tested and rewarded a benevolent *hacendado* for his kindness and generosity toward the less fortunate.

In the corner of the restaurant sits a statue of the Virgin de La Candelaria and above it, enclosed in gold picture frame, is written the miracle of the pearls for the patrons to read. Throughout all of his visits and all of the meals he ate in the presence of the Virgin, Chato never read her story. He didn't have to. For he, like all of the residents of the region, had committed the legend to memory.

The story goes that during the turmoil of the French occupation of Mexico in 1866, Don José Ignacio, the *hacendado* of El Cabezón, distributed all of his dwindling stock of corn and beans to the suffering residents of his estate and the surrounding war torn villages. One morning, an elderly woman came to his hacienda seeking corn. Although his warehouses were by then empty, Don José took pity on the old woman and encouraged her to forage for any remaining grain that might still lie in the cracks and corners of his storehouses.

Early the next day, a worker came to him complaining that the doors of the granary were bulging and he was unable to push them open. After much effort, several men managed to force open the doors, from which began to spill large, round kernels that more closely resembled pearls than corn in their luster and transparency. Everyone was stunned, as it was well known by all that Don José's storehouses were empty.

Don José believed that he had been blessed with a miracle and went to the hacienda chapel to offer thanks. When he arrived, he was humbled to find a string of real pearls hanging around the neck of the statue of the Virgin of La Candelaria. Word quickly spread throughout the region and all were convinced that the old woman who had visited Don José on the previous morning was in fact the Virgin herself, come to test and reward the *hacendado's* generosity and compassion.

The owners of the restaurant were known for their generosity as well. In the tradition of Don José, if someone came to them hungry and unable to pay for their meal, they would feed them. Their daughter was known throughout the village for her beauty and how freely she gave her smile. But it was for Chato alone that she reserved her warm kisses. One night, while walking home un-chaperoned, her father discovered this and his reputed benevolence vanished. He told her that nothing good would come of his daughter having secret rendezvous with a stammering peasant who had no other gifts to offer the world than swiftness with a gun. He forbade her from seeing him again. This devastated Chato. In spite of his pleadings and desperate proclamations of love, she would not disobey her father and she would not see him. In the long days and nights that followed, Chato realized that she was lost to him and he felt something deep within him break.

When he turned eighteen, he traveled to Guadalajara, Jalisco and reported to the military recruitment center to register for the conscription program. Mexico employs a draft system where every young man must register for service on his eighteenth birthday, after which his fate is determined by lottery. The boys present to the recruitment officers their birth certificates and then wait their turn. When the names of all potential new recruits are recorded and the young men are assembled into the auditorium, they stand at attention until their name is called. Selection for service is celebrated as a fair and evenhanded process whereby the son of a peasant or the son of a banker may be called to serve. Chato was ushered into a large auditorium with hundreds of other young men from all over the region. He could not help but notice that many of those who were waiting with him were dressed in little more than rags.

It was hot that day and the auditorium was crowded. The boy standing beside him collapsed onto the floor and had to be ushered out to receive medical attention. Chato's shirt was damp with sweat when his name was called. The solider before him was close to his own age, but stood with a sense of dignity and purpose that made Chato envious. When Chato stepped forward, the soldier reached into the canvas bag he was carrying and pulled from it a black stone. This indicated that Chato was to be excluded from military service. Had the stone been white, he would have been directed to the testing center to determine which branch of the military and what duties he was best suited for, as this was how such things were decided.

The soldier directed him toward the exit. The disappointment that welled in Chato at that moment surprised him. He had arrived at the recruitment center because that was what he was supposed to do. He was numb and had no ambition to serve in the military. In fact, in those days, Chato had little ambition for anything at all. But as he stood in line and watched the uniformed soldiers moving about he began to imagine a new life for himself. One where polished boots and a crisp uniform might command him the respect that his shattered speech could not. A life where he could finally forget the illuminating smile of the girl from La Candelaria.

He approached one of the recruitment officers and told him that he did not wish to return home, but that he wanted to serve. The officer told him that there was a process to determine these things and now since the black stone was drawn, he was under no obligation to serve and the military was under no obligation to take him. With great difficulty, Chato forced his words forward and told the officer that he did not believe that such things as the lives of men were fated and that the lottery was nothing more than a game of chance. Men make their own way and do not live their lives by default.

The officer smiled at this and agreed. He told Chato that it was the responsibility of the military to protect the sovereignty of Mexico and to serve the people in times of crisis. The military needed men with skills. He asked Chato what gifts he had that he might give to his country.

Chato told him that he could shoot. The officer laughed and told him that a monkey could pull a trigger, to which Chato stammered that he could hit anything he aimed at. The soldier asked him if he wanted to make a wager. Chato pulled from his pocket a roll of pesos and presented the wadded mass of wrinkled bills to the officer. This brought a smile to his face and he asked him why he suddenly felt compelled to waste his money with games of chance.

Chato told the soldier that this was not a game of chance and that if he were not afraid to lose a few pesos, he would prove it to him.

The soldier thought about this for a moment and agreed that he would meet after his shift to take Chato to a place where he can demonstrate his skills.

Chato waited outside of the recruitment center for the rest of the day and as the sun began to move slowly toward its rendezvous with the horizon, the soldier appeared. He told Chato to follow him and walked him through the recruitment center out into a plaza. As they walked past the barracks, several other soldiers began to follow them wishing to witness this peasant demonstrate his marksmanship.

They stopped just beyond the barracks and the soldier announced to the gathering crowd of soldiers that Chato claimed to be a marksman and he asked Chato if it was true that he could hit anything he aimed at.

"Suh . . . suh . . . sí," Chato stammered.

"Well . . . puh . . . puh . . . pick a target," the soldier mocked.

A darkness fell over Chato's eyes. He did not like being ridiculed for his speech and he believed the soldier's mockery in the world of the gun, a world where Chato believed himself to be a god, was nothing less than blasphemy.

He pointed to the golden locket that hung loosely around the neck of the soldier. Surprised, the man fingered the chain and smiled at Chato and asked him if perhaps he wanted to choose a slightly larger target, like the wall surrounding the compound. The group of soldiers burst into a volley of laughter to which Chato's eyes grew darker still. He stood silent, staring coldly at the mocking officer until the smile disappeared from his face.

"Okay then. So we know that you are not wasting our time, how much do you wish to lose on this little gamble?"

Chato reached into his pocket and once again handed the soldier his roll of pesos, which he quickly counted out.

"Two hundred pesos, this is not much. Hardly worth my time. But I will tell you what I will do. Two hundred pesos will buy you two bullets. If you can hit this locket with either one of them, you will double your money and I will draw the stones from the bag once more. If you do not hit the locket, I will keep your pesos and you will get the hell out of my sight. Claro?"

Chato nodded in agreement.

The crowd of soldiers had negotiated their wagers against one another, each bearing their own rationale for why the peasant before them might or might not hit the target, turning their attention to the officer and the boy.

The officer nodded at Chato, signaling for him to follow, and with a crowd in tow, the two walked to the center of the plaza in the crimson light of dusk like boys about to engage in a schoolyard brawl.

The officer unclasped the strap on his holster and removed his service pistol. He ejected the magazine clip and proceeded to remove all but two of the ten rounds. He told Chato that this was a Heckler and Koch 9 millimeter pistol. He asked him if he had ever seen a gun like this before. Chato shook his head no. The officer laughed and told him that he was not surprised and explained that this was the service pistol presented to him on the day that he had graduated from the military academy.

"Perhaps you think that you may have one just like this someday, eh?" The officer smiled.

Chato said nothing.

"Very well then." The officer handed Chato the pistol and reiterated, "Two hundred pesos. Two bullets. Listo?"

Chato nodded that he was ready.

The officer took several long strides away from Chato and removed the golden locket from his neck. He held the chain between his forefinger and thumb, allowing it to hang loosely at his side and smiled at Chato and the mob of curious onlookers standing behind him. He flicked his wrist, which spun the locket in a circular rotation, bound tightly in orbit by the chain and then he released his grasp, jettisoning the locket and chain high into the air like a tiny golden tailed comet.

All eyes fixed on the gleaming object spinning pale against the darkening sky as they waited for Chato to fire. Then he raised the pistol and fired off two shots. The locket jerked and spun in the air and seemed to divide against itself before falling to the ground. The sound of gunfire echoed off of the barrack walls and vanished into the various noises of the living city that dwelled beyond the compound.

The officer walked across the plaza and bent over and picked up the broken chain. He scanned the ground and found the locket laying five meters away. He knelt down and picked it up. The clasp that bound the locket to the chain had been severed by the first bullet and the heart shaped family keepsake, which had once held the portrait of the officer's mother, now bore testimony to the path of Chato's second bullet that had passed through the very center of the pendant before vanishing into the sanguine sky.

Chato quickly found his way into the Fuerzas Especiales, the special operations unit of the Mexican Navy where his gift was celebrated. When he turned nineteen, he had an anchor with the words "Fuerza, Espíritu, Sabiduría" tattooed on his right arm and by the time he was twenty, he was renowned as one of the best snipers in all of Mexico. His country had called him into service on numerous occasions, from helping to silence conflicts in Chiapas to thwarting assassination attempts against heads of state. He had become a hired gun for the government, a man to be reckoned with—a man to be feared. Other men might be content with such accomplishments and the attainment of such a place in the world. However, Chato knew that fear and respect were not the same thing and he grew increasingly restless with this knowledge. He could not forget the girl from La Candelaria and he thought about how her father might see things differently if he returned to Totatiche a decorated officer. So, he applied to the Naval Officer's Academy at Reglamento del Centro de Estudios Superiores Navales with thoughts of her weighing heavily on his heart.

When he received the letter denying his admission, he approached his commanding officer in search of an explanation. He cautioned Chato to not take this rejection too hard and reminded him that less than half of those who apply are admitted and only half of those accepted even make it to graduation.

"Besides, you are the best sniper in the Fuerzas Especiales. Here it doesn't matter if you can't talk straight, it matters only that you can shoot straight. Officers are expected to speak with pretty words. You are a sniper, not a poet. You should accept this."

That evening, Chato took a bottle of Mezcal and several pieces of sandpaper and proceeded to remove the anchor and the motto of the Fuerzas Especiales from his arm, along with much of the flesh that bore it.

Three days later, while Chato was running, four men in dark suits driving a black Mercedes approached him. The driver explained to Chato that a very important man wanted to meet him for dinner on the following night. He handed him an envelope with an address and a time. The next evening, Chato sat down to dine with Felix Cárdenas and his life changed, forever.

Immediately after taking office in 1994, Mexican President Ernesto Zedillo declared drug trafficking to be an issue of national security and called on the armed forces to increase their interdiction efforts to take on a more visible role in counternarcotics activities by establishing checkpoints along all major roads and highways, as well as increasing surveillance of the maritime approaches. The United States further pressured Mexico's Defense Ministry to issue what is known as the "Azteca Directive" which called for the modification of the Mexican Constitution and the Criminal Code, establishing the military's permanent campaign against drug trafficking and organized crime.

To support this effort, Zedillo sent the first of several thousand young soldiers to Fort Benning, Georgia to study American military tactics that they would apply at home to combat the drug cartels. Chato was familiar with these elite Mexican commandos. They were known as "Los Zetas" and many were lured to work for the very cartels they were trained to dismantle. Felix Cárdenas was especially aggressive in his recruitment tactics. The soldiers he approached either accepted his offer and became wealthy beyond their imagining, or they vanished and became one of the *desaparecidos*. When Cárdenas courted Chato, he accepted. Not out of fear, but simply because it occurred to Chato that respect would be something that he would never own and in its absence, fear and wealth seemed to be a comforting substitute.

His eventual capture by Mexican authorities and extradition to the Federal Penitentiary in Victorville, California only served to delay Cárdenas, but failed to end his control over the cartel. Chato and other members of Los Zetas made certain of that. Whenever the men approached Chato to employ his services, there was little ceremony. They would simply hand him the large manila envelope that contained all which needed to be known for the contract and leave. Generally, this included several photographs of the target, addresses, schedules and of course payment. Cárdenas always established the price and Chato never contested it. He never asked for more than was offered, nor did he question the justification for requesting his assistance. For Chato, each contract was a task just as important as the last. Whether the target was a priest, a child or a member from a competing cartel, Chato never concerned himself with the ethics of the errand before him, only the best method of executing it. This moral flexibility was something that Chato had developed in la Fuerzas Especiales and had served him well with his new employer.

In each package, Cárdenas would always include a handmade rosary, which held special significance. It served as a final gift from Cárdenas to the target and a way of communicating to Chato how the deed should be done. If the beads of the rosary were red, that indicated that he wished the job to be carried out swiftly and mercifully. In these cases, Chato would most often employ a snipers bullet through the heart from a safe distance. If the beads were white, that meant Cárdenas wished the target's demise to appear accidental, to which Chato would utilize a lethal dose of heroine. However, if the beads were black, this was Cárdenas' way of telling Chato two things. First, he wanted the target to know that it was the hand of Cárdenas alone that was responsible for their end and second; Chato was given discretion over how that job should be executed.

On this occasion, when the men delivered the envelope to Chato, he sensed that it was going to be a unique request. The package was heavier than the ones he received in the past. When he broke the seal, an ebony rosary fell onto his lap. He reached in and removed six neatly banded stacks of American currency, double what he was accustomed to receiving. He sat them aside, disregarding them in a manner that rendered them unimportant and reached in deeper and removed the file that contained the information that Chato required. When he opened the folder, he found several pictures of Juan Carlos Salizar, Cárdenas' former apprentice and current rival. The man who betrayed him. The man responsible for Cárdenas' imprisonment. The man known as "El Cacique."

An ancillary gift that accompanied Chato's mastery of the gun was his ability to foresee future events where life and death were concerned. When it came to executing a task, he could witness the entire occurrence in his mind's eye as though it were something unfolding before him. On occasion, these visions would be so vivid they would conflict sharply with the demands of reality. For in the realm that Chato ruled, the lines between the present and the future were often blurred, compelling him to test constantly the history of what has already been done against what yet remains to be done.

As he sat in the truck waiting for Juan Carlos to arrive at Casa de Diana's, he began to imagine how he would put out his flame. Cárdenas had made it clear that he wanted Juan Carlos to know that it was he who was ushering him into oblivion. Chato knew that it would be difficult to get close to him as his aspirations had forced El Cacique to become a cautious man.

He had loaded the truck bed with bales of alfalfa stacked in such a way that the center was hallowed out, creating an enclosed channel that was large enough to accommodate a grown man with a narrow slot through which one could maneuver a sniper rifle. The back window opened into the crawl space where a Beretta M501 waited for him. Chato had acquired this particular Italian model at considerable expense, but believed that it was well worth it. The integral harmonic balancer contained within the stock sufficiently reduced the vibrations in the barrel, which improved his accuracy and complimented his ability to hit targets from great distances.

Life had taught Chato that the only way manhood is ever truly tested is through victory or defeat. And if a man is as profoundly gifted as Chato, defeat never establishes a sense of limits. Seeing a target and destroying it with a single bullet not only defines the entire world, it establishes the shooters dominion over it.

Chato had a clear view of the alleyway from where he was parked and there was nowhere for the targets to take cover once he unleashed his fury upon them. He had the entire event planned out. Juan Carlos would arrive in the back alley of Casa de Diana's in the company of his entourage. Chato would wait until everyone was out of the vehicle and in the open before he would immobilize Juan Carlos' bodyguards. He had a silencer that he had crafted himself from PVC pipe to suppress muzzle blast so that the targets would not even recognize the discharge as a rifle shot until it was too late.

After the crowd accompanying Juan Carlos had been thinned, Chato would immobilize his target by removing his kneecaps, or perhaps his shins. Then, as silent as a shadow, he would deliver to Juan Carlos the gift from Cárdenas, the black rosary, which would prove to be the last offering that the man known as El Cacique would ever receive.

Juan Carlos' black Mercedes turned down Calle Libertad and pulled into the parking lot adjacent to the alley behind Casa de Diana's. A primer red four-wheel drive truck with two men inside followed behind and disappeared down the alleyway. Chato crawled through the rear slider window and positioned himself so that he had the best view. The rifle rested patiently on a small tripod well hidden in the carefully stacked alfalfa bales. He pressed the stock into his shoulder and peered through the scope and guided the muzzle into the direction of the now parked vehicle until the crosshairs rested neatly on the rear driver side door. Now all that remained for Chato to do was wait.

The red brake lights faded and the parking lights illuminated the dimly lit parking lot, but still no one emerged from the vehicle. Chato could not make out how many men were in the vehicle through the dark window tint, but he knew that Juan Carlos often traveled with his brother and his bodyguard of whom little was known. With the driver, that was a minimum of four targets. He was certain that he could take all of them and be gone before anyone inside the brothel would notice, but he was growing nervous that they were taking so long to exit the vehicle. Then, there was the thought of the truck. Why would Juan Carlos permit it to follow him so closely, unless they were some of his own men, and where were they now?

A dark feeling swept over Chato. Something was wrong. He lifted his finger from the trigger and began to edge back toward the cab of the truck when he heard footsteps rapidly approach from outside. He heard a thud. Something was tossed into the narrow slit between the alfalfa bales. He heard a hissing sound and all at once the warren he had made for himself filled up with smoke and his eyes and lungs began to burn. He heard a second thud, followed by more smoke. He moved quickly toward the cab trying to remain low. He smelled gasoline and saw a flash behind him as he was hit with an intense wave of heat. He glanced over his shoulder and saw that the back end of the truck had begun to burn. He looked forward and through the windshield could see a figure standing in front of the truck. Chato pulled his pistol from his holster and fired one shot and the figure dropped. He fell into the cab of the truck when the ammunition boxes holding the shells for the rifle began to discharge wildly, ignited by the blazing inferno that the back of his truck had become. He could hear men shouting in confusion outside when he kicked open the passenger side door. His eyes were burning so badly he could barely hold them open. He heard footsteps to his right, he turned, fired and smiled when he heard the body hit the ground. His throat burned and his lungs ached as he wiped his eyes in a frantic effort to clear his vision. Chato knew that something had gone wrong. Someone had tipped Juan Carlos off to the hit, but of more immediate concern, he had to get away from the truck. Flames had overtaken the cab and he heard a loud pop as the glass from the windshield exploded, showering the parking lot with glass. He rose to his knees and onto all fours began crawling toward the shadows when he felt a sharp blow against the back of his head.

"¡Esta aquí! He is over here!" was the last thing he heard before the second blow swallowed him in dark silence.

5

When I was growing up, my father read the newspaper everyday. He made sure that I did too. He would use the headlines of the day in his sermons to illustrate how the whole damn world was going to Hell in a hand basket. I think he pretty much convinced nearly everybody in his congregation to take that as a fact.

As a kid, I was never too keen on having to read more than I had to, but he used to tell me that part of being an educated man meant knowing a little about what was going on in the world so that you could better determine your place in it. I remember coming across a headline about a couple of boys who lived over in the next town. They came out our way and decided that they were going to have themselves a little delinquent fun at someone else's expense. So, they stopped in at this little mom and pop gas station called The Gettin' Place sometime after dark and took to robbing it. Archie Mason owned the place and he was a nice enough fella, you could ask anybody and they'd tell you that, but he sure as hell wasn't gonna sit still for a couple of kids stealing from him. So, he confronted the boys.

His wife Anita came by later on that night after he didn't come home or answer the phone. She found the door to the station unlocked and him laying on floor in a pool of his own blood. Those two boys had beaten Archie to death and left him there and then helped themselves to the cash in the till. Archie was seventy-five years old; those boys were only sixteen. The same age as me at the time.

The Sheriff caught up with both of them and found the bat that they beat that old man with in the backseat of their car. Archie's blood and hair was stuck all over it. Turned out that the Sheriff didn't need any evidence to convict them. They confessed to the whole deal. I remember seeing their pictures in the paper. They were *all smiles, just grinning ear to ear like they was movie stars and just won a damn Oscar or something. Both of them ate up all the attention they were given by the papers from the day of their arrest all the way through their trial. I never did understand that either. What would possess two kids to kill a defenseless old man in cold blood and then be proud of it?*

My dad didn't have to use that story in his sermon on account of the fact that he conducted the funeral services. Everybody knew Archie and pretty much the whole town showed up for his funeral too. During the services, my dad said something that has stuck with me to this day. He said that we are all in trouble, every one of us, when the children in our community start living their lives as if there ain't no day of reckoning. I used to think a lot about that. I think about it a lot more nowadays.

I still read the paper everyday. Sometimes I think that I should quit. I read just the other week about how the Cartels are getting more and more vicious in their attacks on one another. It seems that some have taken up decapitation as a means of intimidating their underworld rivals and law enforcement officers as well. The writer of the article indicated that this year alone, at least thirty people have been beheaded in Mexico. Often the bodies are never found, but the heads end up stuck on fences, or hung in archways of town entrances with homemade welcome signs attached to them. Probably the most bald-faced strike occurred when five heads were thrown onto a nightclub dance floor in Tijuana. On one of the heads, authorities found a note attached to an ear with a safety pin that read:

So you will learn respect.

Three of the decapitated men were police officers.

Now, when I was a boy, I didn't pay attention to my dad as much as I probably should have, but I think that he may have been on to something. The only plausible reason why people do some of the things I've seen them do is because they think that there won't be any consequences, either in this life or in whatever comes after.

How do you reason with people who look at the world like that?
You don't is all I can figure.

Wednesday, October 1, 2008

G.H

The room was dark when they removed the stiff burlap sack off of his head. His skull throbbed and his mind swam in the pain caused by the blows he had received earlier that night. His right eye had swollen shut and he could feel the semi-coagulated blood sticky and thick, clinging to his hair. He felt nauseous. He hadn't eaten anything before going out that evening. That was smart. Things were bad. If he was going to pull through this by some miracle, he had to have a clear head. He had to think things through. But where was he?

The building was not completely sealed; he could feel a warm breeze dance through the room, bringing with it the smell of smoke from burning eucalyptus intermingled with the unmistakable aroma of *barbacoa* slowly cooking from somewhere outside. His mind drifted back to the town he lived in as a young man. He recalled once again, the beautiful young waitress at La Candelaria. He would save the money he earned from working on his grandfather's *rancho* and go there each week just so she would take his order and he could try to make her smile. Every week, he would order the same meal, *barbacoa de cabeza* with cilantro and onions, a side of black beans and hand made tortillas. On some nights, he would walk her home after work until these un-chaperoned escorts created a scandal and her father forbade her from seeing him again. That was so long ago. Before he left his grandfather's *rancho*. Before he joined the military. Before he signed on with the Zetas and pledged his life to Cárdenas. Before he was brought to this place. Now, he longed for the cool wooden benches of La Candelaria.

He could feel the room spin, his head felt heavy and he struggled to keep his chin from resting on his chest. He tried to remain focused.

Even in the darkness, he could vaguely make out the rough texture of the walls surrounding him. They were comprised of broken brick, concrete and mortar. He looked up and could see tiny specks of starlight twinkling through random holes in the metal sheeting that served as the roof. Steel rods ran the length of the room like rafters. He noticed hanging from them were several pieces of rebar bent into "S" shapes. The floor was dark and slightly damp, bearing the odor of bleach and old blood. In the center of the room he saw a drain and he realized that he was in a slaughterhouse.

The steel handcuffs bit sharply into his wrists and bound him securely to the chair that he was sitting in. He could feel his hands swell and tingle as blood struggled to force its way into his extremities. He had been hired to kill Juan Carlos Salazar, the man known as El Cacique. Not only did he fail, but he had allowed himself to be captured. There is no way that this is going to end well, he thought to himself.

He heard a click and a light pierced through the shadowy darkness and shined directly on his face. He was blinded temporarily until his eyes adjusted to the new conditions. He squinted and saw directly across from him stood a small camcorder with a sort of flashlight attached to it resting on a tripod. There were five men in the room and all except for one were wearing military issue camouflage suits and black bandanas hiding their faces. He could hear footsteps crunching on the gravel outside giving testimony to the presence of others—possibly three or four. Beyond that he could hear the familiar sounds of livestock and solitude. He was far away from Tecate. He was far away from any hope for salvation.

The man without the mask he knew. He was Juan Carlos Salazar, but to the world he was known and feared by another name. El Cacique. He had been tracking him for two months in an attempt to cash in on the contract that Felix Cárdenas had placed on his head. He was unsuccessful and now he was going to pay for it with his life.

El Cacique approached the chair and stood only inches away from him. He was a tall and striking figure, reminiscent of a movie star from the golden age of Mexican cinema. He was dressed in a dark black suit with a blue silk shirt. His black hair was thick and wavy and showed glints of gray and blue in the dimly lit confines of the slaughterhouse. He looked at him for a long moment, studying his face as though he might recognize him from some past encounter. He drew deeply from his cigarillo and tossed the unused end of it to the ground where its red coals hissed and smoldered when it came into contact with the wet floor. He took from his coat pocket a pair of black leather gloves and one after the other slowly pulled them onto his ring clad hands. His gaze returned to the man secured in the chair and his expression opened up with a broad, easy benediction and then as quickly as it appeared, the smile vanished from his face.

"¡El que se crea bien verga, lo mato a la chingada!" He drew back a gloved fist and let it loose striking him in the face with such force, his chair fell backwards and he felt the back of his head strike the cold wet concrete floor.

Two masked men moved quickly to pull him up from the ground and set him upright once again.

"How much did Cárdenas offer you? How much is my life worth to you I wonder?" El Cacique asked as he rubbed his knuckles and slowly circled him.

Chato kept silent. He would not give him the satisfaction of giving any response to this interrogation.

El Cacique reached into his coat pocket and pulled from it the black rosary that was intended for him as a final gift from his rival and carefully placed it around Chato's neck.

"I think that this was intended for me, but tonight, I return the gift to you cabrón," he said smiling.

He walked to the corner of the room and pulled a green canvas bag from somewhere in the shadows and then sat it on the ground in front of him.

"Surely you know that you are a dead man. Talking or not talking will not stand in the way of your meeting with God tonight . . . but it can have a great influence on how much you suffer on your way to see him."

Chato sat silent, squinting slightly in the light.

With his back facing the man tied to the chair, El Cacique squatted down low and unzipped the canvas bag. He reached inside and removed something from within and rose to his feet. Chato could not see what he was holding, nor could he see El Cacique's face, but he sensed his wicked smile.

"Pelón, I think that you should start the camera. We will want to remember this event, don't you think?"

One of the masked men approached the tripod and peered through the eyepiece and began pressing buttons until a red light above the camera lens turned on. El Cacique approached the camera and began to speak and it soon became clear that this was not a message to the press, to the public or to some government office, he was speaking to a specific individual.

"You disappoint me Patrón and you bring shame upon yourself. Look at you; you sit in prison because your mind, like your belly, became soft. You became consumed by your own lust and your own greed and you made poor choices as a result. Your bad decisions hurt not only you, but your extended family as well." He paced back and forth as he talked, which prompted one of the men to take a position at the tripod and began following his movement with the camera.

"The people in Northern Mexico suffer because many are greedy like you and think only of themselves and their own gain." He waved his hand in the direction of the man still bound to the chair.

"You use your Zeta thugs to incite fear and submission from everyone just so you can ensure your own wealth. You and your kind grow fat like pigs while the people starve and risk their lives trying to go north across the deserts and you do not even consider them. Unlike you, I think of the people. I am a patriot."

"Ok—that is enough. Stop the camera!" The man at the tripod pushed at a series of buttons and the red light turned off.

When he turned his back from the camera and once again faced Chato, he could now see what it was that El Cacique had taken from the bag. He approached him with a broad smile as the hay hook that he held in his right hand gleamed in the artificial light. As he drew closer, Chato could see that this hay hook had been modified to work beyond its original design. The inside curve had been ground and shaped until it formed a sharp knife-like edge.

Chato sat immobile and silent as El Cacique ran the pointed end of the hook across his forehead, gently brushing aside the damp, matted hair from his face.

"Now, I will ask you again cabrón, how much did Cárdenas offer to pay you? Surely you must realize that it was not enough?"
Chato could feel the hook slide down the side of his head past his ear and along his neck where it came to rest on his jugular just above the ebony beads of the rosary.

"I could tear open your throat right now since you do not seem interested in using it to tell me what I want to know. Have you ever seen a man die with his throat split open, cabrón? Have you heard them struggle to suck in air with a hole in their neck?" He leaned in closely and whispered in his ear, "When they scream it doesn't really sound like a scream at all. To the uninitiated, it would not be recognizable as a sound any human being would be capable of making, but you are a hired killer, aren't you? Of course you know what I am talking about."

Chato flinched slightly as the hook caught his collar and with a quick jerk of the wrist, El Cacique split his black shirt open from the neckline down to the waist. With his other hand, he grabbed the torn cloth and ripped it from Chato's shoulders, leaving him secured to the chair, naked from the waist up.

El Cacique again circled Chato in the chair, running the curved end of the hook gently across his bare shoulders and down his arm leaving the point to rest upon the discolored patch of scarred flesh that marked his bicep.

"I see that your flesh is not marked with ink. So you do not belong to any of the gangas, eh? You are a free agent?"

Chato stared blankly in the direction of the camera.

"You know what I think cabrón?" El Cacique hissed. "I do not think that you are a free agent at all. I think that Cárdenas owns you like a dog. I think that you are Cárdenas' bitch and when he calls you to do something you roll over and piss on yourself—just like all of his other bitches."

He spun on the heels of his shined black leather shoes and once again to the man stationed at the tripod. "Start the camera," he commanded. "Cárdenas and the rest of his bitches will not want to miss this."

The red light began to glow.

Chato twitched slightly as the sharpened hook bit into his chest and blood rose from his ruptured flesh. El Cacique smiled as he continued to work the metal into his brown, forgiving flesh, carefully carving the word: Puto.

He stepped back from the chair as if to examine Chato in the same manner an artist might admire his own work.

"Still you do not wish to talk to me, eh? Despite my appearances cabrón, I am a sensitive man, and you are beginning to hurt my feelings. But I think that I understand you. You and I are both men of discipline. You and I are both soldiers, no?"

Chato's eyes darted from the camera to El Cacique and then back again.

"Ah! You are a soldier . . . perhaps not in rank . . . not currently, but you were a soldier and now you work for Cárdenas. Now you are one of his Zetas, no?" He tossed the torn black shirt at Chato's feet and his smile widened at Chato's silence.

"Yes. You know it is true, you wear their uniform—the mysterious men in black." He smiled.

El Cacique returned the hook once again to Chato's flesh and made great sweeping gestures, which caused Chato to clench his teeth and gasp in pain. The man behind the tripod focused the camera on the letters carved across his abdomen: Zeta

Blood pooled from his torn flesh and streaked down Chato's torso and began to soak into the waistline of his black military issue pants.

"So tell me cabrón . . . where are you from? Where do you call home? Are you from Nuevo León? Chihuahua? Or perhaps Jalisco?"

Chato had begun to shiver. He knew that shock was beginning to settle upon him, he had to keep a clear head.

"Still you say nothing to me? I only ask you these things out of respect for your mother. Perhaps I will send her flowers along with my sympathies when she discovers that her son has gone to God. Or perhaps I will visit her personally . . . to offer my own tender consolations, eh?"

El Cacique reached once again into his canvas bag and removed from it a metal rod approximately six inches in length with a thin steel wire fastened to its center with a brass sleeve attached to the other end of the wire. At the center of the rod was a metal shank cut from a drill bit and welded into place at a ninety-degree angle forming a metallic "T."

Although the object varied slightly from the more traditional design, Chato recognized it immediately—it was a type of garrote. He himself had used similar devices numerous times and was intimately familiar with how they worked and what the fate would be of those on whom it was used.

"I see that you are familiar with the garrote, eh cabrón? But perhaps you only know of its usefulness in the field and are unaware of its rich connection to the past that you will soon become a part of."

He unraveled the cord to its full length of eighteen inches and pulled it tight.

"You see, the garrote has a long and proud history in dispatching wrongdoers. The mighty Romans used it to execute treasonous troublemakers. Even the Conquistadores recognized its usefulness. Francisco Pizarro used it in Peru to send the Incan emperor, Atahualpa, to meet his heathen gods. Now, I will continue the tradition and rid the people of Mexico of one more criminal and send you to your God for Him to pass judgment."

"This garrote is one of my own design, cabrón. It does not simply strangle the life out of its victim . . . it frees their head from their shoulders."

Chato's one un-swollen eye widened slightly as El Cacique removed from the canvas bag a yellow and black cordless drill. He placed the welded shank into the keyless chuck and pulled the trigger. The drill whined and the chuck ratcheted closed tightly securing the garrote in place.

"Ah! I see that your fate frightens you somewhat. I imagine that your heart is beating a little faster, your pulse is quickening and your mind is racing trying to analyze your options. Perhaps you think even now that escape may be a possibility . . . but I tell you that escape is not possible. You will die here tonight, but do not worry cabrón—death will come for you quickly."

He stepped behind Chato and looped the wire around his neck and slid the metal sleeve onto the center of the steel rod. Chato pivoted in his seat and strained against the handcuffs that bound him. El Cacique gently tapped the trigger on the drill causing the rod to spin quickly, twisting the wire tightly around Chato's neck and causing it to bite fiercely into his throat. Chato realized the futility of struggling and once again became still.

"When I was a boy, my father would have me butcher our chickens so that my mother could make for us her mole in celebration of Mexican Independence Day. I would take the machete to the chicken's neck and watch as the severed head lay on the ground with dust clinging to its bloodied collar and its eyes would stare up at me blinking repeatedly and its beak would open and close until finally it would lay still. I have always wondered if the chicken was still alive in those last moments or if it was just some kind of reflex. What do you think, cabrón? Did the chicken's life end at the moment the machete disconnected its head from the body? Or did death come in those moments afterwards as the head lay on the ground gathering dust?"

Tears welled in Chato's one un-inflamed eye as he struggled to breathe, staring silently at the camera.

"I have heard it said that the human brain remains in a state of consciousness for up to one and a half minutes after decapitation. Do you think that is true cabrón?"

Chato remained silent.

"Still no opinion? Perhaps you are silent because you do not know? That is okay, you will know for certain very soon, but it is a shame that you will not be able to share with me the answer to this little mystery."

Chato kicked at the ground and rocked frantically in a side-to-side motion in the chair. El Cacique secured the drill firmly in both hands and pulled up and back causing the wire to bite deeper into Chato's neck and once again he became still. El Cacique breathed deeply, pressed a switch on the drill and once again tapped the trigger causing the rod to spin in a counter clockwise rotation releasing the tension in the garrote slightly and continued his one sided conversation with the man in the chair.

"Do you like to read? I have read somewhere that in a heightened state of emotion such as elation or fear, that people are capable of speaking at the rate of one hundred and eighty words per minute. Isn't that interesting? That is precisely three words per second!"

He tapped the trigger again loosening tension of the wire a little further allowing Chato to gulp air into his lungs. When he calmed down somewhat, El Cacique leaned down close to his ear and whispered.

"Now you will not be able to speak because your vocal chords will be severed . . . but still, I wonder what words will be going through your head? Will you recall some happy memory from your youth? Will your thoughts call out to your mother for comfort like a child with a scraped knee? Or in your last moments will you be confessing your sins to your God? Only you and the Lord will know for certain."

Chato could hear El Cacique click through the gears on the drill.

"This drill has three settings. The first gives one the greatest amount of torque , thirty-five hundred RPM. You will realize how important this is in a moment. It would be unfortunate if I were to cut half way through your neck only to have the drill bind up, can you imagine?" His lips turned upward into broad smile.

He pushed a switch on the drill, and then once again tapped the trigger causing the rod to spin in a clockwise rotation. The wire wound quickly, tightening around Chato's neck. He jerked and twitched against the bindings but remained secured to the chair.

El Cacique held the drill securely in both hands and tapped the trigger once again. Chato gasped as the wire began to cut into his skin and squeeze his larynx closed. He felt a heavy pressure on the back of his neck that grew in intensity each time the rod spun. He pressed his feet against the wet floor attempting to gain some traction with the thick rubber soles of his boots. The chair began to slowly slide backwards. El Cacique once again pulled up and back on the drill and pushed his right foot against the back leg of the chair, effectively stopping its movement and pulling on the trigger again, only this time, without letting up.

Chato heard a sickening pop from somewhere in his head and he saw a dark crimson stream squirt across the room splattering the camera and the man behind it. For a second, a mixture of blood and air poured into his lungs as he attempted to inhale. His lungs spasmed violently, rejecting the invading fluid. He began to writhe wildly in his chair and attempted to scream but the only sound that he issued forth was a peculiar, muted gurgle.

The rod continued to spin winding the wire tighter.

Chato felt strange. A calm washed over him and he felt light as though his consciousness had become separate from his body. He no longer felt the stinging lacerations that El Cacique had carved into his chest and abdomen. He could no longer feel the pain in his wrists from the handcuffs that had bitten into them. All at once, the room seemed to spin inward and for a brief moment, he felt a sense of vertigo overwhelm him and he closed his eyes in an attempt to ward off the nausea. He felt a dull thud as though something hard had struck the side of his head. He opened his eyes and saw a pair of black boots twitching and jerking wildly as if attempting to dance some grotesque jig to a rhythm unheard by him. He realized that he was staring at his own feet. He could still hear everything around him. However with each passing second, the noises in the room seemed to become increasingly distant. He tried to breath, but felt nothing.

The smell of *barbacoa* cooking slowly in a fire pit somewhere outside was still strong in his nostrils and sent his thoughts racing back to when he was fifteen years old on the night of his first kiss outside of La Candelaria.

I finished the entire plate of barbacoa de cabeza.

I was certain that you had given me an extra large portion that night.

I felt like my belly would burst wide open, I was so full!

I waited until your work was done and I offered to walk you home that night.

I know that I had walked you home many nights before . . . but this night was different.

I could tell by the way the moon filled the sky as though it shined only for us.

I could tell by the way you smiled at me . . .

I could tell by the way the barbacoa just dissolved in my mouth.

I was clumsy in the way I offered you my hand, I let it swing loosely at my side and let it brush against yours.

You were braver than me . . . and you gently grasped my fingers.

We walked on . . . with our fingers entwined like lovers.

Your hand was so warm and felt so familiar in mine.

We came to the bridge that crossed the river leading into town.

We stopped half way across and watched as the moonlight shimmered on the waters below.

You told me how you wanted to one day paddle down this river in a canoe with a parasol shielding you from the sun and listen as your lover sang to you pretty songs like they showed in the movies.

I told you that I would take you down the river . . .

And I would sing to you.

I pulled you close to me.

You pressed your lips to mine.

You laughed and said I tasted like cilantro and onions.

El Cacique grabbed a handful of hair and picked up the head from the floor and studied the face for a moment, contemplating eyes so dull and black that it was hard to tell where the pupil ended and where the iris began. After a long silent moment, he spoke.

"You died honorably, cabrón. No begging, no bribe attempts. We are soldiers. Such actions do not become us."

His words found Chato's ears, but he could not make sense of them. A darkening gray veil began to spread across the room and the figures along with the voices that inhabited it began to fade away until they were consumed completely by the darkness and silence.

For the journalists and the rest of the employees of El Universal, the morning was anything but typical. When the morning crew arrived, they found all access to the building blocked off. No one was permitted inside the building and the ones who were already there were being questioned.

The janitorial crew had arrived that morning to prepare the grounds for the day when a black pickup truck with tinted windows drove up onto the sidewalk stopping just in front of the building and tossed a blue ice chest through the plate glass window. The chest bounced across the tile floor and came to a rest near the secretary's desk. The lid would have popped open spilling the contents onto the terracotta tiled floor had it not been sealed shut with gray adhesive tape.

The authorities spent a considerable amount of time weighing up the situation, trying to determine what might be in the container.

Speculations ranged from those who believed that it might be some sort of explosive that had failed to ignite to those who considered it to be a prank executed by teenagers with too much time on their hands.

A white flatbed Ford pickup truck with metal racks pulled up to the front of the building and stopped. In the back, four German shepherds whined and pawed anxiously at their metal enclosure. Two men wearing straw cowboy hats stepped out of the truck. The driver removed a pair of mirrored sunglasses and slid them into his shirt pocket and approached a group of uniformed officers who had congregated at the steps. The younger man stayed with the dogs and softly whispered words of consolation to them. They laid down on the truck bed and patiently watched the closed gate, waiting for whatever might come next.

After a lengthy exchange with the officers, the driver returned to the truck, accompanied by another man wearing a dark suit.

"Bring out Pepe," he said to the younger man. "He is the best one for this job."

He walked around to the front of the truck and pulled out a leather strap that would serve as a leash and then returned to the back of the truck.

He spoke in a harsh whisper, "¡Sientate!"

All four dogs immediately sat down.

He clucked softly, "Pepe. ¡Andale!"

The dog with the thick, solid black coat leapt to his feet and rushed to the end of the cage while the other three remained sitting, whining all the while. The man reached in and clipped the leather leash to the silver chain that looped around the dog's neck.

"¡Andale pues!"

The dog pulled at the leash creating a slight tension. The man tugged back and the leash went slack.

Two officers approached the man. One was carrying a black helmet with a clear shield that pulled down to protect the wearer's face. The other held a heavy black Kevlar vest.

"For your protection." The officer shrugged.

The driver took the leash while the man strapped on the vest and helmet.

The man took the leash from the driver and led the dog into the building and stopped just a few feet away from the blue ice chest. The man whispered something heard only by the dog. The dog's ears perked up and began to whine and paw urgently, its nails clicking wildly upon the terracotta tile as it stared intently at the blue ice chest that lay several yards before him. The man unclipped the leash and the dog sprung forward and slid to a stop inches from the container, circling and sniffing its perimeter. The dog spun around on its haunches and trotted back over to the young man and sat down by his side.

The older man advised the police that there were no explosives in the ice chest. After some deliberation, the commander ordered two younger officers to open the box. One held the chest secure while the other cut away the gray tape. When they lifted the lid, he smell hit them and the man holding the box nearly dropped it.

Inside, they found the head of a man. His eyes open and clouded over. Mouth agape in an expression of utter agony. The shallow pool of blood that had drained from the severed neck had gathered at the bottom of the chest had already thickened. Across the forehead was scrawled:

www.ejecucióndezeta.com.mx

When they visited the website, they were able to witness the entire execution along with a message from El Cacique appealing directly to the people:

"I am a patriot. Unlike Cárdenas and his Zeta thugs, I do not kill for pay, nor do I kill the innocent. The only ones who die by my hand are those who deserve to die, and all of the people know that this is divine justice."

At the close of the video, El Cacique stated:

"If you want to find the body . . . look for it."

Then longitude and latitude coordinates flashed across the screen before fading out.

The blackened, burned out remains of a Ford F-150 were found at the bottom of the ravine just south of Tecate. When the authorities found it, there was nothing left but the frame. The rubber from the tires were gone, steel belting from the radials and aluminum rims had melted and congealed into a twisted mass on the blackened ground. The windows had blown out from the heat sending safety glass hurling in every direction. What wasn't consumed in the fire sat sprinkled upon the ground glittering in the sun like confetti.

Just as the voice in the video had promised, in the burned out shell, they found the charred remains of a headless body.

The Federales moved in to shut down the website but not before the video was copied and distributed to the far reaches of the Internet.

PART 2

6

*T*here was a rodeo down here in September. It weren't all that big, but the whole town showed up for it, sort of a Labor Day tradition. Potrero is a small town and besides watching the alfalfa grow and the cows graze it, there ain't much else to do . . . so I went. I didn't know a soul but for Martin and Ester. They were the ones that talked me into going in the first place. I guess I am glad that I did.

I grew up around horses but never saw much of a need to try and ride wild broncs or bulls or any of that craziness, but I have to admit, it sure is one hell of a rush to watch others do it. I went to the concession stand and bought a soda and a corndog and came back to the arena. They was getting ready to start off the festivities with some pretty young girl singing the Star Spangled Banner, when I saw this little boy standing with his daddy—probably not more than three or maybe four years old. Blonde hair, blue eyes and wearing this little straw cowboy hat. He couldn't see more than the backs of folks' knees from where he was standing and I saw him tug at his daddy's finger. He didn't say nothing, he didn't have to . . . the man knew what the little boy wanted. He reached down and scooped that little bugger up in his arms and flipped him up onto his shoulders with the grace and familiarity of a motion often repeated. That little guy sat up there, perched on his daddy's shoulders and watched the whole procession with great interest and a wide-open smile.

I ain't anybody's daddy. I came close once. When I was a kid in high school, I got a girl in trouble. Only, I didn't know nothing about it until after there was nothing to do about it. She didn't figure that either of us was fit to be parents and decided to take care of things on her own and I had no say in the matter. I understand the whole idea about a person having the right to choose what happens to their bodies, she chose not to have the baby . . . and maybe she was right to do it, but I wonder what choice the baby would have made if it were given the option of determining what happened to it. We never even knew if it was a boy or a girl. I still am torn up about that, so I try not to think about it much.

There was something about seeing that little boy sitting up there on his daddy's shoulders that stuck with me. Something that gets to heart of what it means to be a human being and the hope that all of us hold for the future. When a father lifts his child up onto his shoulders . . . he is making a covenant, a promise of sorts, that he will raise and support his little one so that he can grow strong and find his place in the world. The way I figure it, if you are a parent and you are in your right mind, you want to see your son or daughter be successful. It ain't nothing you can help neither . . . it's just writ into us. Call it survival of the species or whatever you want to, but it's there, compelling you to care for your young and give them the best start that you can. So, you do your part to feed them and put clothes on their back. Maybe you take them to church or to temple or whatever to learn about God. You take time to teach them things that they need to know, like the importance of a firm handshake and keeping a promise. All the while, you hope that they become good people and that they go just a little farther, climb a little higher and see more of the world than you did. My dad never told me this and I'm pretty sure I never read it anywhere neither, so I am not even sure how I know it. But I know it.

When I left home, me and my dad didn't exactly part company on the best of terms. I guess that is part of the deal. You do all this raising, loving, and teaching and eventually your little one that held so firmly to your hand grows up into a man or a woman and they go out into the world and make choices that don't always meet your approval. My dad was a good man and anyone who knew him would tell you that. In more ways than I can count, he is my measuring stick for what it means to be a man. I never would've told him that when I was younger. I wish I would have, but I didn't and now he ain't around to tell it to. But I think about him every time I look someone in the eye and shake their hand .

. . and every time I make a promise. I was lucky to have him as a father and I am grateful to have been his son. I only wish I knew for certain if he knew it.

Monday, October 6, 2008

G.H

The Boxcar Grill is the only eating establishment within thirty miles of Potrero. For lack of any alternatives for dining, it is often alive with activity, frequented by local ranchers, truck drivers and Border Patrol Agents. This morning found the diner quiet. Garrett was lost in thought when the waitress approached and asked him if he had decided what to order. He sat at the counter looking down at his coffee cup. He poured in two packets of sugar and stirred in the cream and watched as it mixed with the black coffee, swirling and coalescing until the coffee lightened and turned the caramel shade of her skin.

"Hello . . . Earth to agent . . ." She leaned in to read Garrett's name. "Harrison, come in Agent Harrison!"

Garrett looked up from his coffee. "I'm sorry, what did you say?"

"Have you decided on your order?" The waitress smiled at him.

"Oh, yeah . . . I am going to have bacon and eggs . . . over easy, but I am waiting for somebody."

"She sure does have you tied in knots sweetie! I wish my husband got so lost in me like that every once in awhile." She laughed.

Garrett smiled. "It ain't that . . . I am thinking about my work."

"Don't give me that honey. I have been around men long enough to know when they are wrapped up in work and when they are wrapped up in women. That was definitely not an "I am wrapped up in work" sort of look. But, I am only here to pour your coffee and take your order." She winked and topped off his cup changing the color of the coffee inside from a light caramel to a darker brown.

The cowbell tied to the handle of the front door jingled as Brophy entered the diner. He sat down at the counter next to Garrett and patted him on the shoulder. "Morning bud!"

"Hey there Brophy." Garrett took a sip from his cup.

"You look pretty damn somber. If I didn't know that you was such a goddamn social butterfly, I'd swear you didn't have a friend in the world." Brophy laughed.

"What makes you think you know so much? You been reading my mail?" Garrett smiled.

"Hell, it don't matter, you don't need any friends in this line of work anyhow. Damned sure don't make any. You ready for another day of duty and diligence?" He grinned and waved at the waitress. "Irma, you know the routine!"

"Hey Brophy! Another heart attack special then?"

"Oh yeah. Country fried steak and eggs with a slice of ham on the side. Can't think of a better way to start my morning!"

"Sweetheart, you keep going like you are going and you will never make it to forty."

Brophy turned the white coffee cup upright on the counter. "Yeah, but when I die, at least I am gonna look dead."

Irma laughed and filled the cup. "True enough. You ready for them eggs and bacon now, Romeo?" She smiled at Garrett.

"Yeah, I guess so. Over—"

"Over easy. I know, I pay attention." She winked at Garrett and hollered over her shoulder to the cook behind the counter. "Jesus, give me a number three and an artery clogger with a slice of ham on the side."

Jesus waved his spatula acknowledging the order.

She returned the coffee pot to rest on the hot plate and disappeared into the kitchen.

Brophy and Garrett were the only two figures in the diner.

Brophy took a sip from his cup and let out a sigh. "Romeo huh? Are you making eyes at my girl Irma?" Brophy asked grinning.

"No, nothing like that."

"Then what was that all about?"

"She seems to think I have a woman on my mind."

"Do you?"

Garrett raised his cup to his lip in an effort to buy a little time. Brophy comes off as a wise ass, but he has a keen eye for detail and seldom misses a chance to invade someone's personal life, especially if doing so will give him something to laugh about. Garrett swallowed his coffee and turned to face Brophy.

"Okay, I'll tell you . . . but you have to swear to keep your flap shut about this," Garrett whispered through gritted teeth.

Brophy set his cup down. "Damn! This must be good!"

"I am serious, Brophy! Goddamn it! If you say anything—" Garrett hissed through clenched teeth.

"I won't tell anybody you son of a bitch, you can trust me." Brophy smiled.

"All right." Garrett leaned in close. "You know Ester down at the market?"

"Yeah."

"Well, her and I have had a thing going for about six months now. She has been giving me a break on the rent and I have been giving her . . . well . . . attention. I am just worried now that old Martin is getting wise to it. I think that her going to San Diego to visit the grandkids is just a cover. He knows that we have been doing the horizontal tango for some time and he wants to keep her from me."

Brophy's jaw dropped open as he sat in stunned silence for a moment. Then Garrett burst into laughter.

"Aw! Goddamn it Harrison!" Brophy shook his head. "You had me going for a moment."

"What the hell do you expect, Brophy? I mean, we're here in Potrero for God sakes. My pickings are pretty slim when it comes to eligible women in these parts."

"Still, Ester is a fine piece of woman. What is she? Sixty? Sixty-five? You ought not rule her out." Brophy smiled.

"Parker is right. You are a deviant. A certifiable nut job!"

"Speaking of Parker, have you talked to him lately?"

"Not since we got back from Tecate on Sunday morning."

"Oh! The night of the incident." Brophy chuckled.

"He ain't still all butt hurt over that, is he?" Garret asked.

"Oh no. Parker is, for the most part, the kind to just get along. He gets upset, airs out his lungs and then he's over it."

"Good to know it."

"So you haven't talked to him then?"

"No, not yet I haven't."

"Well, it turns out that he spoke to some people with the DEA about this El Cacique character that our Juan Doe was talking about before he checked out."

"Did he find out anything?" Garrett asked.

"Oh yeah. This El Cacique is involved in a whole shit load of bad karma. He is a drug dealer, drug smuggler, coyote and a pimp. He does a little bit of everything."

"A regular jack of all trades, huh?"

"You can say that. He is one vicious bastard though. You remember the women that we found gutted out there in Sycamore Canyon?"

"Hard to forget something like that."

"That is his M.O. He likes to use a hay hook to deal with those who piss him off. The coroner seems to think that those girls were cut open by something like that."

"Damn."

"No shit. In fact, the Federales in Tecate just found a body inside a burned vehicle. The poor bastard had been cut open from the pelvis to the sternum. Only it was missing its head."

"Goddamn. When?"

"Just before midnight this Sunday. The folks at the DEA are real interested. They think it might be the work of El Cacique . . . or Juan Carlos Salazar, if you want to call him by his Christian name."

"I have never heard of him. Is this guy with Cárdenas?"

"Not anymore. From what we can tell, he was with the Special Forces in the Mexican Army, a real bad ass. The irony is that we think that he was trained by our own to help Mexico fight the war on drugs and when he got out he started looking for a way to make some money. Word was that he had a few girlfriends that he met along the way while serving his country. He looked them up when he got out, promised to marry them, lured them to Tecate with the promise of a flowery wedding and a new life and then forced them into prostitution."

"Damn."

"Yeah. Cárdenas became interested in this ambitious young upstart and seemed to like him. He ended up hiring him to oversee and expand his operations into Baja."

"Hmmm . . ." Garrett sipped his coffee. "I guess Cárdenas figured that a man who is so business minded that he forces his girlfriends into prostitution has got to have some marketable qualities."

"Oh, it gets worse bud," Brophy replied in a hushed whisper. "He got one of his girls pregnant. I guess she thought that if she had his baby, it would get her out of having to work for him. After the baby was born, he told her that he had lost enough money on her, and it was time that she went back to work. Well, that didn't sit too well with her, so they got into this big argument in front of everyone. She told him that she would be content to continue working for him, if he was content in the knowledge that the mother of his daughter was a whore."

"What did he do?"

"Well, nothing right off. He didn't even make her go back to work, but a few nights later, he called all of his girls to the dinner table where he had prepared a meal of carne asada. They ate, they laughed and all seemed to be going well. He ate his plate clean, he even took seconds . . . then with everyone sitting there, he takes out his hay hook up and drives it right through the heart of the woman that was giving him all the trouble. He then announced to everyone at the table that he would not play favorites to anyone, not even a woman who claimed to be the mother of his child. If anyone else expected special treatment, he would be happy to treat them accordingly. He then expressed his hopes that everyone enjoyed their carne asada and he left the room. Two men came in and removed the dead woman. No one ever saw her little girl again. The girls think that the son of a bitch served the baby up for dinner."

"What?" Garrett gasped.

"That wasn't your regular carne asada," Brophy clarified.

"How do we know this?" Garrett asked.

"One of his girls is in protective custody with the DEA. She has agreed to testify against him if they ever catch the bastard. Word from the Federales is that Cárdenas corroborates her story."

"Yeah?"

"Hell yeah. Even the Cartel has some limits concerning brutality. Cárdenas kicked his ass out of the business. He didn't want any baby killers, let alone cannibals who eat their own children working for him, no matter how efficient they might be. Bad for morale I guess."

"Well, if what we saw in the desert and if what the Federales found on Sunday is the work of this El Cacique, it seems to me that he ain't all that interested in laying low."

"You are right about that. Our Juan Carlos has some ambitions of his own. After Cárdenas was extradited to the U.S., he figured that was the opportune time for him to take over the operations. In fact, there is some speculation that he worked as an operative with the Mexican government to help take Cárdenas down so that he could step in and fill the vacuum. He just didn't plan on Cárdenas surrendering." Brophy sipped his coffee.

"You mean that he didn't plan on him being taken alive." Garrett pushed his coffee cup away from him.

"Not at all, he figured that Cárdenas would go down in a blazing fit of glory. Turns out even bloodthirsty Cartel leaders have an instinct for self-preservation."

"So Cárdenas is here? In the U.S.?" Garrett asked.

"Oh, yeah, he's sitting in a maximum security prison somewhere outside of Victorville awaiting his trial. I hear that he spends his days reading the bible and making necklaces or something—rosaries I think."

"It's nice to know that even a fella like Cárdenas can find God as well as time to express his creative side with arts and crafts." Garrett's lips spread into a crooked grin.

"Well, our penitentiaries are doing their best to stem the rising cesspool of iniquity and produce the model Christian gentleman you know," Brophy shot back.

"So, is Juan Carlos running the show now?" Garrett asked.

"Oh, he is trying to. He brought his brother Santiago in to join him in his effort to take control."

"What does Santiago bring to the whole operation?" Garrett inquired.

"Well, for one thing, Santiago is just as crazy as his brother . . . and they're family, so Juan Carlos trusts him."

"I guess if you can't trust your own brother, who can you trust?" Garrett replied.

"Juan Carlos keeps Santiago close. They look after each other. In fact, they are the reason why we have seen so much bloodshed on the border lately. They're trying to establish the Salazar family as the new cartel and Juan Carlos as the Cacique."

"Juan Carlos has several men who are loyal to him and have left the Zetas. He has hired many more who are loyal to the money that he offers and he has intimidated or killed off everyone else. He is organized, smart and he is one cold-blooded son of a bitch. The DEA believes that there is not a kilo of narcotics or a pimp or a coyote that moves anywhere in Baja or into Southern California that Juan Carlos does not profit from."

"Is Cárdenas just sitting still for all of this?" Garrett raised his eyebrow.

"Oh, Cárdenas ain't sitting still for anything. He has put out a hit on Juan Carlos and Santiago from inside prison. So they both have a price on their heads, but whoever takes up Cárdenas' offer has got to be as psychopathic as they are."

Irma returned with two platters and sat them down in front of them. "Here you go boys, breakfast is served. Careful though, these plates are hot."

"I'm sorry Irma, I just lost my appetite." Garrett rose from the stool.

"What's the matter, hun?"

"I'm just not hungry anymore." He laid a ten-dollar bill on the counter top. "Keep the change."

Irma eyed him as he walked outside.

"That boy has got it bad," she said as she reached for his plate.

Brophy placed his hand on her wrist. "Leave it Irma. If he don't eat it, I'll finish it. Growing boy and all." He winked.

"Brophy, your doctor must hate you."

"Hey, give me some credit here. I am working hard right now so that my future cardiologist can pay for his kids' college. Do you have any idea how expensive tuition is these days?" He cut off a piece of chicken fried steak and used it to soak up some gravy and forked it into his mouth.

"Forget forty, you will be lucky if you make it to thirty." Irma took the money from the counter and closed out Garrett's bill on the register.

Garrett Harrison learned at a young age the power that absence can hold over a person. As a man, that lesson was not lost to him. Absence can be so vivid, so consuming that it can take on a presence all its own. Such was the case with Angelina Marguerite. She had not left his thoughts since the night he met her at Casa de Diana's. To him, she seemed to him to have everything. She was bright. She was funny. She was beautiful. She had an innocence about her that seemed rare to him. He wondered how she came to work at Casa de Diana's. He wondered if her conversations with other prospective clients were like the conversation they shared. He recalled the instance when he made her laugh and felt a residual warmth come over him. He wondered if he would ever see her again. He felt a stabbing pain in his heart when he considered that he might not.

He had completed restoring his father's old Indian Chief. It took time, but he finally returned it to its original glory. He had removed the rust damage from the fenders and frame and repainted it to the original Indian Chief Red. He had to special order the chrome muffler and the Indian head fender light. It was now ready for its first test drive. The 94 was the perfect road to break it in on, Harrison considered. He took a deep breath, climbed onto the broad seat, engaged the clutch, gave it a kick and the engine came to life as though it had been ridden only yesterday. The roaring engine vibrated through his entire body. It was a welcome feeling to him.

He remembered when his father brought the bike home and how excited he was to think that its restoration would be a father and son project. The bike was placed in the garage once his father found out that Garrett had enlisted in the Navy. His dad just didn't understand, with no way to pay for college, no real desire to go and no prospective job offers on the horizon, a man has to seek out other options.

His father did not believe in the military and did not approve of Garrett's decision to enlist. In fact, his father refused to talk to him after he signed on. Their argument over him enlisting in the Navy was the last time he spoke with his father. Garrett reasoned that he would definitely turn over in his grave if he knew that his only son was a Border Patrol Agent. Again, his dad just did not understand what desperate times will do to a person, Garrett thought.

Garrett's father was a minister. He participated in the Montgomery Bus Boycott, he marched with Martin Luther King in Washington. If you asked him what his political views were, he would wink at you and answer that he was the last of the true conservatives. He believed in fiscal conservancy, he also believed in conserving natural resources, conserving indigenous cultures, and above all conserving civil liberties. He believed that as a man of God, he, and other religious leaders across the country, should face off oppression and bigotry with their Bible, Koran or Torah in one hand, and the Constitution and Bill of Rights in the other. Few of his colleagues took him up on the challenge, but he continued to fight for the rights of others. In fact, he met Garrett's mother in Miami in 1976. She was born and raised in Cuba and had been working aboard ferry transport when it was hijacked by a group of Cubans seeking passage to the United States. When she arrived, all of the passengers were offered either amnesty, or the opportunity to return to Cuba. Garrett's mother chose to remain in the United States and met Garrett's father while she was working as a waitress in a restaurant in Miami. They married shortly after, and Garrett was born in 1984.

The stories that she told his father of Castro's oppressive regime gave him renewed sympathies for those who came to America seeking a better life. One of his favorite sermons to preach referred to the Bible's call for people to welcome the stranger and care for the needy.

He would tell the faithful that the biblical story is a migration story. The Bible begins with God's spirit migrating throughout the darkness and over the face of chaos and after forming the heavens and the earth, God migrated over the face of the water and after creating the birds, fish, and animals, all of which migrate, He moved throughout creation looking for a caretaker for this new world. Not finding one, God created Adam and Eve in His own image and gave them dominion over all the earth and told them to multiply and fill the earth. To do that, it was necessary for them to begin the human migration story. He explained that for anyone to deny others the right to migrate in an effort to find a better way of life is to deny the purpose that God designed for us.

Garrett recalled that occasionally, this would elicit groans of contempt from his parish. However, he never once backed down. He would admonish the naysayers reminding them of God's commandment for us to welcome into our homes the strangers and travelers and love our neighbors regardless of their status. He would remind his congregation of the fate of the cities of the plain. Sodom and Gomorrah were two of the wealthiest most beautiful cities in the land, yet the people of these cities became hardened and would turn away travelers who did not have sufficient wealth or education. As a result of their greed and hard heartedness, God destroyed these two cities and all of those who resided in them, saving only Lot and his family. Garrett's father would warn that if America ever did fall, it would not be because of the immigrants that come to our land, but rather, our own selfishness and greed that would serve to be our undoing.

His mother sat in the front pew every Sunday to hear his sermons from the time they were engaged until she was taken by an aneurism while driving to the store to buy groceries for dinner on November 2, 2000.

Garrett carried with him a sense of guilt and relief that both his mother and father passed away before he became a Border Patrol Agent.

He eased the bike toward the road, opened the throttle and headed to Tecate.

The Indian roared down the *calle*, rattling the windows of the buildings that lined the way. He eased up on the throttle and disregarded the collective gaze of those walking along the plaza. A small brown dog ran along side him, nipping at the chrome mufflers and barking a canine protest to the rumbling engine. He turned down an alleyway and pulled into a narrow dirt parking lot that rested behind the Hotel Tecate and shut the engine down. He pulled the bike back onto its stand and removed his helmet and strapped it to the seat. The little dog ran in a random circular path around the bike and its rider occasionally leaping into the air and barking all the while. Garrett squatted down low and extended his hand toward it. The dog stopped running and cautiously approached him sniffing at his hand. He spoke softly and patted the dog on its head, rubbing his fingers through coarse fur made so by living in the streets. A muffler backfired off of a passing truck, and as if on cue, the little dog turned and pursued the offending vehicle.

Garrett rose to his feet and headed toward the main street. The sun had set beneath the horizon and cast a brilliant glow of orange and purple across a darkening bourbon sky. As he approached the thoroughfare, his eye caught the familiar sight of the ancient tamale woman he had spoken to the weeks before. She sat on a small collapsible stool next to her unassuming white cart with the warm smell of spiced chicken and *masa* enveloping her like a mist.

"¿Buenas?" the woman whispered softly.

"¡Buenas noches!" Garrett smiled.

The woman looked up in the direction of Garrett's voice and fixed her milky eyes on him.

"Oh, it is only you mijo." The woman cast her eyes downward.

"Only me?" Garrett asked puzzled. "Are you expecting somebody?"

"I think so," she replied.

"Who?" he asked.

"I am not certain . . . I have had this terrible feeling that someone has been following me for the last several days. I have not heard him, but I can feel his presence, I know he is watching me. However, I am no longer afraid of him. Now he seems more like my companion than my enemy."

"You think that Death is following you?" Garrett asked.

"Perhaps so, mijo. I am old and I am tired. Maybe he wants me today or possibly tomorrow. Who is to say, really?"

"That is true, none of us knows the day or the hour of our demise," Garrett responded.

"That is not always so. Some who have resigned to end their lives know when Death comes. They summon him."

"Have you resigned yourself to ending your life, Señora?"

"Oh, no! Never. That would be an affront to God and a great imposition to Death. He has a busy schedule to keep with disasters, war and natural passing. Imagine one being so arrogant as to dictate to Death when he should come for you! But I do know when my light will go out. I saw it in a dream," she replied.

"A dream? When?" Garrett asked.

"I dreamt about my death when I was a young woman. I saw how I am to die, and I know that I go at dusk. But if you want to know about the specifics mijo, that is between him and me," she replied.

"I see," Garrett responded. "Some things are better left unspoken."

"No, it is not that I am afraid to talk about it. Here in my country, Death is not someone to be feared, he is not someone that we insulate ourselves from. He is part of life, and we celebrate him." The old woman continued, waving her hand in the air in taut robotic gestures as though she were ushering away some bothersome insect. "In fact, here we even set aside a special day for death, when we welcome him back into our homes and remember those whom he has taken. So you see, I am not afraid to talk about dying, I am just honoring Death and the trust he has bestowed in me. After all, he does not share with everyone the day and the hour that he will come for them."

He thought about that for a moment, and then spoke, "That is true, but do you suppose that any of us would act any differently if we knew when he was coming for us?"

"I do not think so. I think each of us are who we are, and knowing or not knowing would not make a difference," the woman replied.

"Has it made a difference for you? Do you think you have lived your life differently by knowing when you are going to die?"

"No. I have lived my life as I would have without knowing. I have made my mistakes. I have exercised acts of goodness, as well as those that have brought me shame," she said.

"Then you do not believe in a Judgment Day?"

"Why would that matter if there were a day of judgment or not? Either way, when you are dead, you are dead. The concerns and worries of the living are no longer yours, that includes worries over how one is judged."

"Then there are no rewards for the righteous or punishment for the wicked?" he asked. "Are you suggesting that the end is the same whether you have dedicated your life to helping others or helped no one but yourself and harmed others along the way? The missionary and murderer get the same treatment in the afterlife then?" Garrett raised his eyebrow.

She looked down at her sandals and crossed her legs at the ankles. "Yes," she retorted. "Death is not partial . . . eventually, he takes us all. The rich, the poor, the meek, the proud, the old, the young . . . those who do good and those who do evil."

"What about Heaven and Hell? Do you not believe in such places?"

She smiled. "Mijo, this is such a serious topic to have on an empty stomach. Would you care for something to eat?" She reached out and clasped his hand in both of hers.

"Yes, that would be nice," he replied patting her warm, wrinkled hand.

She rose from her chair and reached into the top of her wagon and pulled out two steaming tamales and placed it on a paper plate, handing it to him.

"I believe that you prefer chicken." She smiled a wide toothless grin.

"That'd be fine."

She spoke to him in a low pensive whisper, as if revealing to him some secret that might be startled and vanish into the night if she were to speak too loudly, "When I was a little girl, the Nuns taught me the principle of multiplication. After learning how to multiply numbers, I determined that it was not probable that Hell or Heaven are places that exist in the way that we have been taught to think of them."

Garrett peeled away the cornhusk from the tamales and asked her to explain her reasoning.

"Por supuesto," she continued. "Consider, if you will, that instead of spending eternity in either heaven or hell, one only were to spend one thousand years in either place. Now listen to me carefully mijo . . . and I will use mathematics to show you that a fair and just God would not allow any of his children to endure an infinite amount of time in either place."

"Okay." Garrett bit into the tamale. "I am listening."

"We know that there are sixty minutes in an hour. If we multiply that by the twenty-four hours that we have in a day, we find that each of us have one thousand four hundred forty minutes each day to do with as we please. If we multiply the minutes in a day by three hundred sixty-five days in a year, we find that each of us is given five hundred twenty-five thousand six hundred minutes each year. Now, the Bible tell us that the life of a man is seventy years, of course some live longer, some lives are cut shorter, but let us use seventy years as the basis for our argument. If we multiply the minutes in a year by seventy years, we find that each of us is given the gift of thirty-six million seven hundred ninety-two thousand minutes over a lifetime. Remember, in the universe that we have created for this argument, eternity is only one thousand years . . . or five hundred twenty-five million six hundred thousand minutes. Now let's suppose that a man in his imperfect state were to commit the sin of adultery or murder or any number of sins over the course of his lifetime. Is it reasonable to assume that a God who professes to love us would cast that man into a lake of fire to burn and suffer for five hundred twenty-five million six hundred thousand minutes when his time on earth only amounted to a fraction of that time? The punishment does not fit the crime. So you see, if God is truly a just and loving god, this would offend Him and He would not abide it."

"It is hard to argue with that," Garrett said as he swallowed the remainder of his tamale. "But you have forgotten something of great importance."

"What might that be?" the woman asked.

"What then about evil? What comes of it? You can't be suggesting that evil is not punished and good is not rewarded in some way? If that is true, where is the incentive for people to be kind, just and virtuous?"

"What are the incentives you ask? This life offers plenty. We are to be kind, just and virtuous because we reap what it is that we sow. It all comes back to us eventually."

"Do you really believe that?"

"I have considered the possibility," she replied.

"Even though I am now nearly blind, I have bore witness to some terrible events, and some wondrous things. For instance, about one year ago, I saw a man carried out of that very whorehouse by three men. They had beaten him and were trying to force him to get into the back of a car. The man cried and begged to be let go. He offered to pay them money if they would spare him, but the men persisted in their efforts to force him into the car. As he was being dragged to the car, the man managed to free his arms and grab a hold of the street lamp and would not let go. The three men struggled to pry his grasp from the post, when finally one of the men pulled out a pistol and shot him in the leg. Crying in pain, the man would still not let go, for he certainly realized that death awaited him in that car. Then another man pulled from his coat a hay hook and drove it deep into the man's shoulder and pulled him off of the lamp post and threw him into the car like a bale of straw. The car sped off, and I have not seen that man again."

"Are you telling me that you think that man was beaten, shot, stabbed and possibly killed because he was evil, and that was his punishment?"

"I am telling you that I have seen that very man sell drugs to young men and women. I have seen him beat whores here in this very alleyway. He died like he lived, in a wretched and wicked manner."

"What then about the men that killed him? Are they evil?"

"Yes, they too have done wicked deeds."

"Did you report them?"

"Why would I report them?"

"So that they can be brought to justice for their wicked deeds."

"Who would I report them to? The police? They are no better."

"Are you telling me that no one has stopped them? They have not been caught?"

The old woman smiled and shook her head as she spoke, "Mijo, what an innocent question! You can't look for a happy ending in this . . . it is a Mexican story, not an American one. The evildoers are not always brought to justice and the good are not always victorious."

"Does Death make such distinctions?" he asked.

"No, but your Hollywood does."

"You mean our movies?"

"Yes."

"Well, I would agree . . . but there ain't much substance in fiction."

"Who is to say what is fiction and what is real?"

"Reality is something that you can touch, something that you have evidence of existing. Fiction has no substance, there is no evidence, you can't weigh it and you can't touch it."

"Like the past, the present and the future?"

"That ain't the same thing. The past was here, but is now gone . . . but you can find evidence that it was here if you look around you. Today is here. Today is now and we are in the thick of it. As for tomorrow, well, it's coming whether we are there to greet it or not."

"I would only ask you to consider that even in fiction, there is truth. The stories we tell ourselves in books, movies or in spoken words, each simply are the narrator's efforts to name the world, to call it into existence."

"Like God?"

"Yes, like God."

"I don't agree."

"No?"

"No. If I were to tell you that in the sky above you there are two moons shining down on us, that would not make it so. My fiction is not reality. My words created nothing."

"How many moons are there in the heavens?"

"In all of the heavens, or just above us?"

The old woman laughed. "You make things more complicated than they have to be mijo, I am speaking of the heavens above us.

The one that holds that which you can see with your eyes."

"Well, there is only one moon of course."

"Well, there is the problem with your logic. I am old and I cannot see very well. When you told me that there were two moons shining down on us, in my mind, that is what I saw. Even though my experience tells me that there is only one moon in our heaven, in my mind, I saw two. Your fiction became my experience. You named the world and for an instance, I saw it as you described it. That is the job that our creator gave to us."

"To make up things that are not so?" Garrett raised his eyebrow.

"No. We are to name the world. It began with Adam's charge of naming the creatures of the earth and that responsibility is passed on to each one of his children."

"What then, if some calamity befell us and every man, woman and child were wiped from the face of the earth, leaving only the rocks, plants, animals, sky and water. Would there no longer be a world then?" Garrett asked.

"No, there would not. Because there would be no one around to say, behold, this is the world."

"What about God?"

"What about Him?"

"Does He cease to exist if there is no one around to invoke His name?"

"I think that God would know He exists; therefore, it would not matter if there were no one to call out His name. He would simply take His place among the many lonely gods of the civilizations before us that have vanished into the ether. There is no one left to call out their names, or to make sacrifice, or to sing songs of praise. But they watch over us just the same. They exist because they say that it is so."

"I don't know if I can accept the notion that if somebody doesn't say something exists, then it doesn't. That doesn't make much sense."

"I can only tell you, mijo, that reality is comprised of more than flesh and blood. It is greater than the tangible. Ideas are not just precursors to reality, they are reality. Someone had to conceive of an airplane before it could be built. If that were not so, we would still be shackled to the earth like the beasts of the field. Ideas are the reality of man. We are the only beings in creation that are aware of our own incompleteness, we have the capacity to realize that we are unfinished, and so is our reality. Consequently, we are also aware of our mortality. This awareness is exclusively a human manifestation and lies at the very heart of our reality."

"So our awareness of death makes us human?"

"Our awareness of death and our capacity to name it makes us human."

"What about the imbecile? Or someone who is brain damaged or in a coma. If they cannot be said to be aware of death, or if they have no capacity to name death, are they not to be considered human?"

"Those are interesting exceptions that you raise mijo, but no. They are but empty vessels, only shells of humanity. It is one's capacity to question, to know and one's potential to become, that makes us human."

"I don't know that I agree with your logic."

"You do not have to. Your agreement or difference of opinion does not make it more or less true."

The night had fallen, and tiny brown bats emerged from the eaves of the surrounding buildings and began their nocturnal dance around the lampposts, feasting on the insects that fluttered around them.

"You mentioned earlier that you have bore witness to wondrous events. I am beginning to wonder if that is true."

"Have I said anything to you so far that would make you think that I would lie?"

"No, it is just that you seem to have a very pessimistic view about the world."

"I told you mijo, you should not try to look for happy endings in a Mexican story."

"You have no happy endings to tell then?"

"I have seen wondrous events. They are not necessarily the same thing."

"I would like to hear about one of those events."

"I am watching one unfold right now."

"Where?"

"Sí, here, with you."

"With me?" he laughed.

"Yes. Would you like to hear about it?"

"I don't know, does it end with a visit from Death?"

"You know better than to ask that question. All stories end with a visit from Death, we established that already."

"Yeah, I guess we did."

"However, I think that you should know that she is not long for this world," her voice lowered to a whisper.

"Who is not long for this world?" Garrett asked.

"The girl to whom you will give your heart." Her milky eyes glowed softly as she squeezed his hand.

"What girl?" Garrett laughed nervously.

"Mijo, you know who she is. She is why you are here. She is why you have returned to Casa de Diana."

He pulled his hand away from the old woman. "You are telling me that a girl that I am going to give my heart to is set to die? How is that a wondrous event?"

"Do not let the knowledge of what will come to pass stop you from giving your heart. When it comes to love, we should not be concerned with time. If we are given five days or fifty years to love . . . isn't the simple fact that we had the opportunity to love enough?" she asked.

"If you are the one who is dead, I guess it doesn't make a difference. But if you are the one living with the loss, I think it would be a different matter entirely."

"That may be so, but remember mijo that in order to experience great love, you must be willing to endure the eventuality of great loss."

He thought of the two disemboweled girls in the desert. He thought of the man with the gunshot wound to the head. He thought of Angelina. "I better get going on."

"You do not believe that is so? You do not believe that risk is part of the deal we make with life?" she inquired.

"I just think that you and me take stock in two entirely different realities. I know that bad stuff happens to good people. Just as much as I believe that good things come to those who engage in evil deeds . . . but I think I will still look for the happy endings."

"Remember where you are mijo. You are a character in a Mexican story. If you are looking for happy endings here, you will most likely be disappointed."

"I think I will look for them just the same. Like I said, I best get moving on. How much do I owe you for the tamales?" he asked.

"You owe me nothing. Your company was payment in full."

"Well, I thank you for it."

"It was nothing. Go with God, mijo."

When he entered Casa de Diana, the cantina was bustling with clients. His heart beat rapidly as he scanned the room, looking for her. When he saw her, he felt his pulse skip and his hands began to tremble slightly. She was at the end of the bar holding a drink in her hand as a white haired man in a flower print shirt talked to her about whatever sort of things such men discuss with working girls.

He reasoned that he should try to pull himself together. It was pure craziness to think that he could have feelings this deep for a girl who may or may not be of legal age, for a girl whom he has only spoken to once, much less one who was employed as a prostitute in a Mexican brothel. He was about to turn around and leave when she noticed him. As the white haired man continued to talk to her, she smiled at Garrett.

He took a seat at the bar.

The barkeep asked him if he would like a drink. He indicated that he would like a Tecate and lime.

A whore in a low cut blue dress, eager to acquire a new client approached Garrett and slid one arm through his, and placed her other hand on his thigh and asked him if he would buy her a drink. She had so much powder caked onto her face that some of it had begun to crack and flake off. She smiled widely at him. Her lips were painted bright red, and some of the lipstick had begun to stain her yellowed teeth.

Garrett explained that he was not ready for company yet. But his good friend was. He pointed to the white haired man at the end of the bar and explained that he had been cornered by that girl in the black dress. He knew that she was not his type and he had been watching him trying to politely get away from her for the last several minutes.

She asked Garrett why his friend does not just walk away. Garrett explained that he was chronically polite and was incapable of rudeness and when he gets nervous, he tends to talk a lot. He lamented what a shame it was too. For his friend was a very wealthy, but busy man, and he only has one more night in Tecate and he was having to waste it with a girl that he was not remotely interested in.

The whore agreed that it was indeed a shame, but if his friend was too polite to walk away from the woman, what could be done? Garrett then asked her if she would do him a favor on behalf of his friend. He placed forty dollars in her hand and directed her to go over to the white haired man and introduce herself. This would give him an opportunity to get away from the other woman by distracting, and perhaps discouraging, her from taking up any more of his valuable time.

The whore grinned, prominently displaying her lipstick stained yellow teeth. She agreed that she would help Garrett's friend, turned and walked to the end of the bar.

Garrett watched the woman swagger up to the white haired man. She stepped in between him and Angelina, completely shutting the younger prostitute out of the conversation. The older prostitute pushed him onto the barstool and straddled his leg and began to grind her pelvis into his thigh. The man looked totally bewildered and tried desperately to make eye contact once again with the young girl. The woman on his lap grabbed him by his face and kissed him hard and deep.

Garrett made his way to the end of the bar and took Angelina's hand in his. It felt warm and delicate and he did not ever wish to let go of it.

She turned and saw that it was him, and shot him the same smile that turned him inside out just a few weeks ago.

She squeezed his hand and led him over to the red sofa where they sat down.

Garrett had thought about this encounter for weeks. In fact, thinking about her occupied pretty much all of his time. Now that the moment arrived, he was at a loss for what to say.

"¿Cómo está usted?" He smiled.

"Bien, gracias." She smiled back.

She began to giggle, breaking the awkward silence.

He asked her what was so funny. She explained that after the encounter with his sexually deviant friend and the food fight, she had not planned to ever see him again.

He laughed.

She told him that she knew of a place where his friend could go to get the service that he was looking for. There was a place with transvestites working there, but he would have to be careful because it is illegal in Tecate for men to dress up as women.

Garrett laughed again. He tried to explain that his friend was pretty normal and was not really a deviant at all. He admitted to her that he told Parker to say those things in order to teach him a lesson in humility.

She seemed puzzled and inquired why he would play such a mean trick on someone he called his friend.

Garrett explained that Parker has gone through life thinking that anyone who can't speak English is either lazy or ignorant. He simply wanted his friend to see first hand how uncomfortable and humbling it can be when one is not capable of speaking the language of the land.

She smiled and nodded. She asked him if it worked. Garrett told her that it did not, and Parker was just as stubborn and prejudiced as he was before the incident.

She remarked how shameful it was that some people have such a difficult time changing who they are. She asked him why he had returned to Casa de Diana without his friends.

Garrett looked down and realized that he was still holding her hand. He thought about what she said about how it is difficult for some people to change. He also thought about what his father said about how people eventually become who they are supposed to be and how the entire human experience involves movement, whether it is from a geographic place, or a spiritual or intellectual journey. We are all in a state of constant migration.

He turned to her, and took her free hand in his. He explained to her that he came looking for her. He came because she had been weighing heavy on his mind and he had not had a night's rest since he saw her last. He wanted to say more but words seemed inadequate and clumsy. He looked at the delicate features of her face. Her long eyelashes, her golden eyes, her olive skin. Her full lips. These images had been burned deep into his mind and had haunted his dreams for weeks. Now, his vision sat before him. No longer part of the ethereal world of dreams, but the world of flesh, bone and blood. He leaned in close to her lips and stopped.

"Yo también," she whispered as she leaned in and pressed her lips against his.

She held his hand leading him into her quarters. A diffused glow of green, red and white light from the passing cars and traffic lights shimmered through the small narrow window facing the street. Garrett could hear the constant hum of traffic floating in from outside. The room was small but clean. The wooden bed frame held a full size mattress with many overstuffed pillows and a crushed velvet comforter. The headboard was crafted from black wrought iron and consisted of several loops and curves in its design so that at first glance, it appeared to resemble a poorly conceived diagram of the female reproductive system. A wooden cross with a Christ figure hung above her dresser. The dresser top held a framed picture of the Virgin, a hand mirror, a tortoise shell brush and an open silver locket with a faded picture of a woman.

There was a knock at the door.

She explained to him that it was her boss coming to collect the fee. He asked her how much the fee was. She told him that it was two hundred pesos for twenty minutes. He told her that twenty minutes would not satisfy him. He asked her how much for the night.

"¿Por toda la noche toda?" she asked in surprise.

"¡Por supuesto!" He smiled.

She walked to the door and opened it slightly. He could hear her whispering to the man on the other side. The man's voice became louder. She whispered something back, and lowered her head, stepping away from the doorway. When the man entered, Garrett recognized him immediately. He was the man who accompanied Angelina to Casa de Diana when he first saw her the weeks before.

He did not seem as tall as when Garrett first saw him, but he was well dressed. Garrett figured the suit he was wearing alone would set him back a month's pay.

He passed the girl and walked over to Garrett smiling widely. "So, this is your galán?" He stopped in front of Garrett and looked him up and down.

"So my friend, you wish to spend the entire night with this girl?"

"That is my intention." Garrett eyed him suspiciously.

"Well, that can be a very expensive prospect, you realize." He spun on the heels of his Italian leather shoes, and walked back to Angelina. "During a typical night, she can bring me in as many as twenty customers." He curled a ringlet of her hair around his finger, held it up to his face and breathed in.

"I'll pay you what they'd pay you," Garrett replied.

"Hmmm . . . that is very generous of you galán, very generous indeed." He rubbed his chin with his ring-crested hand.

"Let me see . . . twenty customers by two hundred pesos . . ."
"That'll be four thousand pesos," Garrett said as he pulled out a roll of bills and began counting them out.

"Did you realize that it is the whore's birthday today, galán? Or perhaps that is why you want to be with her tonight? Because you think you want to give her a present?" He smiled.

Garrett looked up from his bill roll. "No, I did not know that today is Angelina's birthday."

"Yes, it is. When I have my whores work on holidays or on their birthdays. I charge their patrons double." His eyes narrowed as he smiled at Garrett.

"I don't have eight thousand pesos on me. But I can get the rest to you in the morning."

"Am I to take you at your word, galán? That if I let you spend the night with my whore, you will pay me what you owe me in the morning?"

"Yes. You can take me at my word."

"Shall I trust this galán of yours, whore?" he asked the girl.

"You don't have to talk to her like that," Garrett growled.

"Oh! I have offended you. My apologies. I am so used to using, how do you say, professional jargon, I sometimes forget that it can come across harsh," the man replied.

He turned to face the girl. "Very well then, I will allow your galán to stay the night with you. And to show you that I have complete faith in your integrity galán, I will not even collect the partial payment tonight. You will pay in full tomorrow morning, after the bank opens."

"That's all right," Garrett replied. "I don't want to owe you anything more than I have to. Here is half, four thousand pesos. I will square up the rest in the morning."

"Very well," the man said as he walked towards the girl.

"Happy birthday mijita," he whispered as he kissed her on the forehead. He opened the door and left the room.

Angelina collapsed onto the bed, burying her face into the mountains of pillows and began sobbing.

Garrett sat next to her, not certain where to place his hands. He finally resolved to place his hand on her head and gently stroked her hair.

"Lo siento," she cried.

He told her that it was okay, that she had nothing to be sorry about.

She indicated that she did have much to be sorry about. Her life had never been easy, but it had become one huge tragedy after another since she met him.

He asked her who he was. He told her that he had seen him before, but did not know his name.

She explained that his name was Juan Carlos Salazar. But he was known everywhere as El Cacique.

"¿Qué?" he asked.

She explained that he was involved in many things. He was owner of the Casa de Diana but owned brothels all over. It was believed that he even had some in the United States. Juan Carlos sometimes helped people cross the border. But his prices were very high, and most of his customers ended up working for him to repay their debt.

Garrett asked her how she came to meet Juan Carlos.

She explained that she had believed that Juan Carlos was somehow placed into her life for a purpose. Only now, she was not certain what that purpose was. She explained that her family was from the small fishing village of Yelapa, Jalisco. Her mother and father were very happy together. Her father was a fisherman and owned his own boat and had several villagers working for him. She explained that while her father was gone, she would play with and learn from her mother. Her mother taught her how to cook, sew and pray the Rosary. She described how she and her mother would dance in the rain and sing childish songs. She described these moments of her childhood as living with God's Grace. She felt very loved, very safe and very content, until one day, her father's boat capsized at sea and he and all the men that worked for him were lost. She explained how that was the last time she heard her mother sing and that her mother grieved every day she lived, until she no longer had the will to go on living.

She described how she came to live with her grandparents in the village of Yelapa. She told him about the little church near their home that had a statue of Jesus out front. The figure was adorned in a purple robe and wore a crown of thorns upon his head. She was not certain if there was blood painted on the Christ figure's face, or if she had only imagined it, but she was drawn to it. She explained that to her, the statue was beautiful and terrible all at the same time. She feared it and loved it all at once. She told him how she would write little notes, and place them at his feet when no one was looking. Some of her notes were prayers and some were messages that she wanted God to give to her parents in heaven.

She explained to him how the statue and the little church always provided her a point of origin. Not her childhood home with her parents, not her grandparents' home, but that little church seemed to whisper to her, "this is where you are from", and how that brought her comfort.

She told Garrett that as she grew older and started on her path to becoming a woman that she began to feel lost. She described how difficult it is when you feel God's grace, even for a moment, and then have it taken from you. The absence of God's grace, she explained, leaves you with an emptiness that cannot be filled. She told him how each night she would pray that God would remove the emptiness from her and allow her to once again feel like she had a home, to allow her to feel whole again.

She told him about the day Juan Carlos arrived to her village. How charming he was. She explained how he had pretended to fall in love with her and convinced her grandparents that she could go and work as a housekeeper in the United States and earn more money in a single day than she could in a whole month in Yelapa. He promised her that once they saved up enough money, they could be married and move her grandparents to live with them in San Diego. She told Garrett that she loved Juan Carlos and thought that he loved her too. She believed that by following him to the North, it would be the answer to her prayers that she had been seeking for so long.

She described how she was taken by Juan Carlos to Tecate, and while she waited for him to arrange for her to be crossed over the border, she discovered that Juan Carlos was truly a wicked man. He forced her to prostitute herself at the Casa de Diana with threats that her grandparents would be killed if she refused to do his bidding. She explained to Garrett how the trip to the United States never came and she realized that the prayers she had prayed for so long were never answered. She told him that she has since changed her prayer. Now, she asks God to help her to understand His love. If she is meant to suffer with this emptiness gnawing at her, if she is forced to work away her youth, giving her body to different men night after night, she asks Him to at least help her understand how He loves her and how to find peace with that.

The two continued to talk into the early morning hours. He laid on her bed with his hands folded behind his head. She laid beside him, resting her head upon his chest listening intently to his voice, his breathing and the beating of his heart. He shared with her the story of his mother and father. How his mother was taken from them suddenly.

How he enlisted in the Navy hoping to escape his own emptiness and then was sent off to free Iraq from tyranny. He detailed for her the conflicts he had with his father and how his father had died before they could be reconciled. He told her that he worked as a Border Patrol Agent and how he loves the job and hates it at the same time.

He asked her if it really was her birthday today. She told him it was and that she would turn eighteen in only a few hours.

She lifted her head from his chest and looked into his eyes.

"Diga mi nombre," she said.

"¿Qué?" he asked.

"Diga me," she said again.

"Tu nombre es Angelina," he replied.

She smiled wide. "¿Angelina . . . qué?"

"Angelina Marguerite," he whispered, focusing his eyes fiercely on hers.

She pulled herself close to him and kissed him hungrily. She pulled back slowly, gently holding his bottom lip between her teeth.

"¡Que rico!" she whispered through slightly clenched teeth, and then slowly released his lower lip.

She gathered up the skirt of her black dress and climbed on top of him. Her knees straddled his waist and her long raven hair hung low, tickling his face. She pulled her hair back, and slowly began to unfasten the buttons on his shirt. She saw a glint of silver from a medallion that hung around his neck, which reflected the light in the dimly lit room. She gently ran her fingertips down the length of the chain and wondered if it might bear the image of some forgotten saint.

She unbuttoned the clasp on the neck of her dress and then pulled the zipper down the back, keeping her eyes fixated on him all the while. She gathered up the dress and pulled it over her head, tossing it toward the dresser. The light from the occasional passing car would pass through the narrow window, dancing along the walls and cascade gently across her bare shoulders, illuminating her body and shimmering off of her hair like some heavenly thing.

Her skin was brown, a deep bronze color with so many wonderful shades like the richest of soils. Her warm body stretched out before him like the world and he wondered if she might be Mother Earth made into flesh. Her every movement was graceful and strong, demonstrating purpose with each gesture all the while seemingly innocent and unaware of her incredible beauty. She smiled down at him and shrugged her shoulders as her long, dark hair continued to caress his face and her round, soft breasts lay suspended above him like magnificent caramel teardrops awaiting their fall into oblivion.

He lifted his hands to touch her face and ran his fingertips gently across her lips. She was warm yet shivered slightly at his touch. He moved his hands down her neck and across her bare shoulders with the slow deliberation of a blind man trying to capture the essence of an object by touch. He closed his eyes and slid his hands down the contours of her body. He wished to memorize every curve of her perfectly formed figure and create a map in his mind of her fleshy terrain. He opened his eyes and his hands rested upon her narrow waist. He felt a delicate rise in her skin slightly below her naval where a thin fishhook shaped scar gave testimony to where her appendix once had been. He caressed it with his thumb, gently tracing its path. She leaned down and pressed her naked body against his, kissing him impatiently with her full lips. She pulled back and looked him in the eye, smiling so radiantly that he almost lost his breath. How he loved her eyes and her mouth, seemingly filled with fire and gentleness all at the same time. She laughed and he heard music. She was a stranger to him but he found himself all too willing to become lost in her voice, reasoning that she was a safe harbor for him, and from her perspective, he never need fear, hurt or unkindness.

As she moved her hand across his chest and down his stomach, he felt his skin burn and his heart pound somewhere deep within him. He pulled her close and put his lips against her skin and his tongue hungered for the taste of her. As the twinkling lights of the living night passed through the window and shined on her clean, soft skin, he was fascinated by the subtle tints of gold, yellow and all the browns that flickered up at him.

He pulled back and looked into her eyes, fearing for a moment that she might vanish like a dream. A cloud of uncertainty and haunting memories moved across her face and stirred the lovely golden pools of her eyes. He began to kiss her deeply and held her close. As he felt her flesh beneath his, he wished that he could pull her right into his heart. He looked into her eyes again and the cloud had passed and her face was radiant. He wondered if the cloud had ever been there at all or if it was something imagined by him. He felt a fire rise within him like he had never known, a feeling akin to a kind of fear of God and joy of life all at once. She bit softly upon his ear and he listened to her cries, wondering what retribution he might face for being so presumptuous as to dare to mingle with the gods by loving one of their own.

As the two lay on her bed tangled in the thin silk sheets, the soft glow of morning began to creep in. He awoke, staring up at the cracked plaster ceiling and watched silently as the morning sky commenced to redden and cast a strange glow through the lace curtains, illuminating the room where she slept. He listened to her breathing. He knew that she was in trouble. Juan Carlos, the man known as El Cacique, was dangerous and held little stock in life. He and all of his kind only understood two things, money and death. Garrett knew what he had to do.

He felt a strange disquiet stir within him, as though whatever he resolved to do at this moment would define him and set the course for every moment that followed. At that instant, lying in twisted sheets on a bed in a brothel with his arms wrapped tightly around a young woman he barely knew, Garret realized that he did not know who he was. He was far away from home, exhausted from a night of deep conversation and wild passion, haunted by ghosts of loved ones he felt he had betrayed. He could hear the sounds of morning stirring outside as if there was nothing in the world out of place. He was not fearful of this strange new realization—he was simply somebody else. He felt up until now, his life was a haunted existence where he dwelled within it like a ghost. Now he found himself in a Mexican border town just a few hundred yards south of the crossing. The border served as a dividing line, a demarcation of sorts. To the north lay his past and present responsibilities, both ordered and predictable, while to the south lay his future, uncertain and wild.

She began to stir from her sleep. She stretched her arm out and he gently brushed the hair from her face with his hand. She smiled at him. He told her that he had to go. He wanted to tell her other things. He wanted to share with her secrets that his heart knew. He wanted even more to share the day with her. He wanted her to know the simultaneous euphoria and ache that he was now feeling inside.

He told her that he would be back. He kissed her several times, walked to the door, and returned only to kiss her again. Finally, he backed away towards the door, she smiled at him, and he pulled the door closed, and he walked out through the empty cantina and into the street. The morning air was cool. A gray sky loomed above him like it might open up at any moment with rain. There was a scent of burning creosote in the air. A boy pedaled past him on a bicycle delivering the morning edition of El Universal, the local newspaper.

He arrived at the bank, which was still closed to walk in clients, but the ATM machine sat in a glass booth just outside the entrance. He stepped inside, swiped his card and withdrew what he owed to Juan Carlos. He took a deposit envelope and stuffed the money inside.

When he returned to the cantina, a man in a black suit was sitting at the counter smoking a cigarillo and clicking the lid to a silver Zippo lighter repeatedly in his hand. He turned to face Garrett when he heard the door open.

"Ah! You are the American that owes my brother money." He smiled.

"Yeah. Is he here? I need to talk to him," Garrett replied.

"I regret to say no. My brother is a very busy businessman . . . very busy. That is why he asked me to come in his place," he replied.

"And who are you?" Garrett inquired.

"I am Santiago." He extended his hand.

Garrett shoved the envelope into Santiago's hand.

"I would rather do business with the man himself. You tell your brother I want to talk to him. I have a business proposition that he will definitely be interested in."

"I will tell him, but I can make you no promises. Like I said, he is a busy man." He drew heavily on the cigarillo, tilted his chin and blew smoke into the air.

"Busy and smart ain't the same thing. There is more where that came from." Garrett jutted his chin at the envelope. "A lot more. If he doesn't meet with me, I can't see that he is a very smart businessman at all."

Santiago crushed out the red coals of his cigarillo on the countertop and spoke gravely. "You Americans are all the same. Always mixing your business with pleasure. A very volatile combination."

"I will be back here in two weeks. You tell him that." Garrett pushed open the cantina door and for a second time that morning, walked out into the streets of Tecate.

7

I have done my share of traveling, but I can't say that I have had the luxury of taking many vacations. This is largely on an account of me not having sufficient money nor time to properly dedicate myself to the proposition. I imagine that if I had much of either, I would probably just go fishing. No need to rush from one place to the next, no postcards to mail, no need to pack along a camera or other such non-essentials; just a rod, a reel and a shady place to cool my heels and make the world right. Uncomplicated I know, but I guess when you're a simple man your needs are just as simple.

The closest thing I ever had to a vacation came just before I graduated from high school; the senior class planned a weeklong trip to Mazatlan during our spring break. We stayed in one of them five star hotels; the kind that provide you with bathrobes, room service, the whole bit. The drinking age was eighteen and even that seemed more like a guideline than a hard and fast rule to be followed. Since most of us were seventeen, we welcomed this relaxed attitude towards enforcing such social conventions. I spent a full six days on them warm Mexican beaches and I didn't spend a single moment of it fishing, but I did share every spare moment with Julie Davis. That fact alone made me the most envied guy in Mazatlan. Julie and me passed the days with our toes in the sand, drinking Margaritas and exchanging salty kisses while the warm breezes drifted in from an ocean as big as the world. At the time, I figured that I was about as close to heaven on Earth as a man could ever hope to get.

When we came back to the states, it was all over the news about how some high-flying businessman named Jean Nadeau was arrested for money laundering and his ties to organized crime. He was accused of being the head of a group of prominent men who sexually abused young children around Mazatlan and put it all to *film. A reporter had done an exposé and alleged that this fella had taken poor children from the surrounding area, had sex with them and filmed the whole damn thing. She investigated and documented ties between Mexican politicians, prominent businessmen and a child pornography ring that literally spanned the globe. She claimed that Nadeau alone had been responsible for violating over 200 young girls. The youngest of the bunch was only four years old. Nobody had paid her much attention until she died in an apartment fire. Amnesty International intervened and put pressure on the Mexican government to investigate her death and her allegations against Nadeau.*

Turned out, she was right. The authorities found in his possession hundreds of videos and thousands of photographs of grown men violating young boys and girls . . . babies really. Nadeau was the kingpin of a child pornography ring that stretched from the Americas to Europe. The rules were simple. In order to be a member of his little club, you had to submit material to the group library. To qualify, the images had to show a child being sexually assaulted by an adult. The images were prized more if they showed the child in visible pain. The more images and videos you contributed to the library, the higher up the hierarchy you were placed. The rank of Superstar was reserved for members who submitted pictures or videos of themselves having violent sex with children. Nadeau ran the whole damn thing from his hotel.

All of this was going on right under our noses while we were there and didn't hear word one about it. I realize that we was all a bunch of wide eyed teenagers immersing ourselves in as many of the seven deadly sins that we could wade into, so we might not have been paying close attention to begin with. But you would figure that a story about a murdered journalist and well known politicians and businessmen being wrapped up in a child porn ring in a popular tourist town would get a little airtime. But it didn't.

In my line of work, I encounter all kinds of folks who break the law. Most of them are nothing more than poor hardworking souls who are seeking out a better life in the North. But there are some that are just plain evil. I mean, there is a darkness upon them that is unmistakable. The problem is . . . I don't see it getting any better. What do you do when the very people that are responsible for upholding the law are violating it in the worst possible way? I suppose the right answer is that you stand up to be counted. You either decide to stand on the side of what is good and right or you stand in the shadows. The shame of it is, I don't think very many of us take the time to distinguish the difference, let alone do anything about it.

Monday, October 13, 2008

G.H.

Reverend Caffrey sat cross-legged on the faux leather seat with his slender white fingers clasped above his knee. The rain outside pattered steadily against the window. A deep purple vein rising just above his gray eyebrow and ending near his temple twitched spastically beneath his pale, diaphanous skin. His bright blue eyes blinked in wide rapid repetition as though he were trying to focus on the face of the woman sitting behind the desk directly across from him.

At the other side of the room sat a dark haired little girl clad in a navy blue skirt and a white blouse embossed with a bright yellow cross and lantern, the emblem of Grace Christian Academy. She observed the two adults with silent interest, staring at them with a deep sadness welling in her great dark eyes.

"Yesenia!" the woman whispered harshly. "You are not here to observe. You are here because you were disrupting your class. Put your head down! I am very disappointed in you and I do not wish to see your face right now!"

The girl folded her arms and buried her face into the folded crook of her elbow. Her ebony hair spilled over onto the tabletop and her deep brown eyes looked on with meek curiosity from beneath her curls.

Judith Sanderson smiled at the reverend and glanced down at her daily planner. She picked up her pen and crossed "Reverend Robert Caffrey 11:30 a.m." off the sheet. She looked up and studied him for a moment. She hated these meetings. The reverend had always been a generous benefactor to her school, even before her appointment as director. The charitable donations he gifted to Grace Christian Academy had made it possible for her to bring computers into the classrooms and renovate the playground. She knew that this next donation would bring a new library to the school, along with a resource center for the adult education program that she longed to provide for the parents of the community. But there was something about the reverend's demeanor that made her wish for the company of just about anyone else in the world but him. She did not trust him but could not put her finger on just why. Perhaps, it was an accumulation of all the little things. His cold sweaty palms, his weak handshake, the way his watery, pale blue eyes would stare at you but seem to not be looking anywhere at all. The way he would embrace children. His insistence upon taking children from impoverished families to his church for weekend youth leadership retreats. His smile. Any one of these taken alone might not be enough to make one feel ill at ease but when placed together in one individual, it set off a series of warning bells in her head. She tried on numerous occasions to reassure herself that she was simply overreacting. No child or parent ever complained about the reverend and his support of the Academy was legendary. However, she could not still the cautionary voices inside of her head. His words broke the silence.

"Aww! Miss Sanderson!" Caffrey's pale eyes widened and he motioned for the girl to come to him. "See this poor child. She is so thin, and as brown and as lovely as the earth from the garden." He pulled her onto his lap, and gently caressed her hair.

"Just look, the clothes on her back. The uniform of this fine Christian Academy are most likely the finest clothes she owns." He kissed the top of her head.

"This check, this gift from my church, will make certain that she can continue receiving a fine education. One that will be vastly improved with the construction of your new library, will it not?"

"Yes, Reverend, without a doubt." The woman rose from her chair, walked over to the reverend and extended her hand to the girl, gently clasping her tiny brown fingers and smiled down at her.

"Yesenia, you may return to class now. Just promise me that you will pay attention and not disrupt the classroom anymore. Do you promise?"

The girl nodded silently.

"Okay. Off with you then."

The girl climbed off of the reverend's lap and ran to the door.

"Perhaps that little one could benefit from participating in the next youth retreat that I am hosting. The theme is on obedience and respecting your elders," he said licking his narrow, chapped lips.

"Yes, well, about that . . ." She returned to her side of the desk and lowered herself into the chair. "I just do not see that having a weekend retreat for the students at the church is entirely necessary. I mean, most of my students have never slept a night away from their parents before. An entire weekend away from home might be a bit much for them."

"Oh, don't be ridiculous!" He rose from his seat and slapped his open palm on the top of her desk. "Half of the students that come to your school have endured nightmarish hardships to get here. Freezing nights, blistering heat, cramped in dark spaces like animals with the smell of sweat, urine and feces filling their nostrils. A weekend at church away from their parents hearing the word of God is a gift!"

"I just don't think that taking them away from the familiar is a good idea," she replied.

"Oh! Quite to the contrary! I think that it is a splendid idea. These children are a blessing to us and I would like to provide them every opportunity for growth, both intellectual and spiritual. Besides, wasn't it our Lord who said, Let the little children come unto me . . . for the Kingdom of God belongs to such as these?" he questioned.

"Yes, Reverend. The Lord did give that command."

"Well then?"

"Can I ask you a question Reverend?"

"Of course child."

"What if the Academy were to respectfully decline your offer . . . if we were to cease official sanctioning these Youth Leadership Retreats?"

His brow furrowed into a frown as one in deep concentration.

"I mean . . . you . . . the church could of course invite families to participate. The Academy would no longer be in the middle." She laughed nervously. "It might even be better to cut out the middle man."

"In the seminary, I learned a great deal about human nature through the application of the hypothetical. It seems that this is only the first part of a two part question. Why don't you ask what is really on your mind my dear child?"

She stammered slightly and then tried to regain her composure. "If I were to end my students' participation in the Youth Leadership Retreats that your church sponsors . . . would you still want to . . . I mean . . . would the First Congregation Church still be interested in funding the construction of the new library?"

"Well my dear, one is always interested in things which they feel a vested stake in. We have a connection, a viable partnership between my church and your academy. It would be a shame to see something come between such an intimate relationship, would it not? Imagine what such a loss would mean to the school and to the community."

"I am not suggesting that we end our partnership, Reverend." She lowered her eyes.

"Oh, I cannot tell you how pleased I am to know that. I have been so excited at the prospect of breaking ground for this library . . . and the Youth Leadership Retreats are something I always look forward to." His thin, dry lips broke into a wide smile.

"I am sure that you do, Reverend." She felt nausea sweep over her.

"Besides, I have already made arrangements with the Salazar Brother's Construction Company," he replied.

"Made arrangements?" she asked.

"Yes. I have worked out a wonderful deal with the Salazar Brother's Construction Company. They are willing to donate the materials for the construction if the church will cover the cost of the labor."

"I did not know about this . . . are they licensed? What about our advisory board . . . this didn't go through them? Did it?"

"I have already made the necessary arrangements. The advisory board is aware of everything and they support it, why wouldn't they? The school is going to get a state of the art library and it will not cost them a penny!" He smiled proudly.

She adjusted the hemline on her skirt. She could not shake the feeling that she had just sanctified an unholy agreement. His smile always made her uneasy. His bleached teeth contrasted obliquely against his wrinkled, translucent skin. The thick lens on his wide framed glasses made his enormous pale blue eyes look even more immense. He sat across from her, blinking beneath the fluorescent lights of her office like a caricature sketch of some cave dwelling creature that had never before seen the sun. She wanted to scream.

Once again, his voice broke the silence. "Judith?"

"Yes?" she replied, pulling herself from her thoughts.

"I believe we have an audience waiting for us."

"Yes, we do. Shall we go?" She smiled weakly.

"Of course. It would be a shame to keep the children waiting."

When they entered the auditorium, the students were sitting cross-legged on the floor in neat rows beneath the watchful eyes of their teachers. The younger students were seated in the front rows in closest proximity to the stage and the older students were positioned towards the back. Behind the students were rows of chairs provided for parents and members of the community who wished to attend the event. Nearly every chair was filled with camera wielding parents and family members who eagerly waited to document their child receiving whatever award their teacher deemed them worthy of receiving. There was also a reporter from the *North County Gazette* present to cover the story of Reverend Caffrey's generosity.

She had always loved public speaking. She had given dramatic poetry readings and delivered speeches in front of crowds since she was in high school, but these award ceremonies always made her nervous. She looked forward to them and dreaded them all at once. The children were great. They would always come to the stage to claim their certificate before the crowd of their peers and loved ones; they would flush red as their teachers' words of praise filled their ears. They were both timid and bursting with pride at the same time. They were the epitome of sweet innocence and promise. But there was always one parent who would become upset over something and ruin the moment. Their child's name was misspelled on the program, the room was too hot, the room was too cold, or the seats were uncomfortable . . . it was always some damn thing or another. So much so that she could never feel completely at ease. Her stomach would twist into knots upon each parent's approach as she wondered if words of praise or complaint would issue from their mouths. She had plenty of practice in shrouding her anxiety and she was certain that it would not show today. She only hoped that she could conceal her contempt for Reverend Caffrey as well.

She stood at the podium and began to speak. She greeted the children and the guests in both Spanish and English, but more for the benefit of the parents than the children. She explained that this time of year always provided a challenge for the teachers; the selection of students to honor was always difficult when presented with a school of such outstanding students. She praised the parents for their support at home, acknowledging the importance of unity between the family and the classroom. She then explained that other partnerships have helped make Grace Academy a rich learning environment as well. Through the generous donations from their community partnership with the First Congregation Church, they had been able to renovate the playground and to purchase computers for each classroom, and now, thanks to the continued support of the church, they are able to begin construction on the new school library. The auditorium filled with applause.

"The man responsible for these generous endowments is not a stranger to most of you. Many of you are familiar with his Saturday vespers at the beach and Sunday sermons." She felt a cold nausea sweep over her. "Many of your children have benefited from his weekend leadership retreats as well . . . I would like to welcome to the stage Reverend Robert Caffrey who will tell us about the plans for the library and assist me in handing out our award certificates."

The auditorium once again erupted into applause.

Reverend Caffrey rose from his seat, smiling. He clutched a large rectangular cardboard cutout that was crafted to resemble a check. He approached the podium and scanned the audience. She could not be certain of his gaze but he seemed to be looking for someone. A flash from the reporter's camera compelled him to blink. He ran his tongue across his thin, dry lips and breathed heavily into the microphone.

"Thank you, Miss Sanderson. Parents, I cannot tell you what a blessing and a privilege it is to be here before you today. Your children, as the book of Psalms reminds us, are a blessing from the Lord. And we have been commanded to raise them upright in the way that is pleasing to God. We must help them to become wise and I can think of no better way to accomplish this than by helping them to develop a love of reading. In fact, the great writer Elizabeth Hardwick, tells us that the greatest gift one can give is a passion for reading." He smiled. "Boys and girls, how many of you love to read books? ¿A quién le gusta leer libros?" he asked the students.

As if on cue, children's hands left their laps and rose into the air.

The reverend smiled down at them from the stage. "How nice. I have here a gift to give to all of you. Something that I think will help you with your passion for reading . . . Do you know what this is?" He grasped the cardboard check in both hands and thrust it high into the air above his head.

Mixed cries of recognition and confusion filled the room.

"It's a big card!" called out one child.

"It's a check!" cried another.

"Ah! What is your name, little one?" the reverend asked.

The room fell silent.

"You, with the pretty yellow ribbon in your hair. What is your name?"

All eyes turned and began seeking out the object of the Reverend's attention until they came to rest on a girl dressed as all of the others in the auditorium, made distinct only by a single yellow ribbon tied into a bow that served to pull her brown hair back from her eyes.

"Yes, you." The reverend smiled.

"Eva," the girl replied meekly.

"Eva, you are correct. It is a check from my church for your school. A check for two hundred and fifty thousand dollars so that all of the boys and girls at Grace Christian Academy can have a new library."

The auditorium once again exploded with applause.

"Eva. Are your mother and father here today?" the reverend asked.

The girl shook her head no.

"Eva, have you ever in your life seen a two hundred and fifty thousand dollar check before?" The Reverend smiled.

"No," the girl replied.

"Never?" he asked in mock surprise.

She shook her head.

"Would you like to . . . touch it?" he whispered into the microphone.

A smile spread across her face and the girl lowered her head shyly.

"Oh, don't be like that," the Reverend pleaded. "Come on up here and see what real money feels like. Come on . . . you can do it. You know that you want to!"

The girl slowly rose to her feet, resulting in another barrage of applause from those in the audience.

"That's a good girl." The reverend's smile widened.

She shuffled over to the podium and stood quietly before him with her back to the crowd.

"Go on," he encouraged. "There is nothing to be frightened of . . . touch it." He held the check at waist height in front of him.

She extended her hand toward the check and her delicate brown fingers gingerly touched the lettering when the reverend suddenly pushed the check toward her and let out a loud bark. The girl jumped back in startled surprise and the whole crowd erupted into laughter. Reverend Caffrey grasped the child tightly in one arm and laughed out loud.

"I am sorry little one. I promise, I won't bite! Go on mija. Touch it."

She touched the check with her trembling fingers.

He kissed the top of her head. "What about the rest of you. Have you ever seen this much money before?"

"No!" the auditorium resounded in a uniform, negative response.

"Well boys and girls, would you like to touch it too?" the reverend shouted.

The auditorium echoed with a thunderous, "Yes!"

Reverend Caffrey smiled. "Then you know what to do!" He waved his arm signaling the children to charge the stage.

The auditorium exploded once again into cheers from the children. A few older students from the back stood up and rushed down the center isle toward the podium. A few students in the middle rose to their feet wanting to move forward but uncertain if they should. Several children sitting near the first few rows clambered over those sitting in front of them and rushed toward the stage. Electric flashes from several digital cameras popped randomly from somewhere in the back of the room. A dozen or so children had made it to the stage before one of the teachers blasted her whistle. Miss Sanderson rushed to the front of the stage, extended her arms with her palms pressed forward and shouted to the students to stop and return to their seats, causing the tide of children who had not yet reached the stage to freeze in their tracks.

Amid the chaos and riotous applause, Reverend Caffrey danced on the stage laughing with gleeful abandon as several children crowded around him clutching wildly at his waist. With his pale cheeks flushed red and his great amphibious eyes wide open, he held the cardboard check high above his head beyond the reach of the children's tiny hands as he hopped from one foot to the other in a sort of carefree, drunken jig.

It was ten in the morning when Jordan entered the Sacred Grounds coffee shop. This was where they had both agreed to meet. They would have a cup of coffee, engage in the requisite small talk and then Mitchell would share with her the story that would, as he put it, make her career.

Mitchell was a business minded man with a medical background. Like Jordan, he had grown up in Oceanside and left to attend college and like Jordan, he came home. They had attended the same high school but did not meet until college. Jordan was completing her internship at the *Los Angeles Times* with graduation on the horizon and the world at her feet when she crossed paths with Mitchell. They had serendipitously bumped into each other at a coffee shop in Los Angeles, where they had spent the rest of the evening laughing and catching up on events, familiar people and places from home. She told him about her internship and how she felt as though her life was finally coming together, how she finally felt like an adult. He confided in her that he was barely passing his classes and was beginning to believe that he probably was not cut out to be a doctor. He took a copy of the Times off the table and began rattling off an impressive list of movies that was printed in the entertainment section, smiled at her and asked if she had contributed to writing any of the movie listings.

For the last part of the semester, their relationship had developed into an uncomplicated, on-again off-again, friends with benefits sort of propinquity. She had always regretted how things between them ended. The fact was that they didn't actually have an ending. When they graduated, they drifted away and lost contact until several years later, Jordan had been assigned to report on the opening of a new community clinic, which turned out to be owned by Mitchell Stevens. Suddenly, a routine news story became something of a personal reunion.

After completing one year of med school, Mitchell had dropped out and drifted a little before entering the Physician Assistant Program at Riverside Community College. He later returned to Oceanside and opened up his first community clinic where he provided medical services to those living on the fringes, many who were unable to afford health insurance or qualify for assistance due to their citizenship status. He would take what his patients could afford to pay, and for some, he would even work for trade. He had accumulated numerous containers of goat cheese, handmade tamales and even had work done on his car in exchange for services provided. This had elevated him to the status of a saint for some in the community, for others he was accused of placing the undocumented and the dregs of society at the front of the citizenship line by offering them affordable and sometimes, free, healthcare. He defended his position by declaring that healthcare was not a luxury or a privilege to be afforded by those with means, but it was a basic human right that should be offered to all.

While in college, Jordan had never thought him an unattractive man. He was tall with broad shoulders and on those nights that he held her, she felt safe, which was at conflict with every belief she held as a young feminist. When she covered the opening of his community clinic for the *North County Gazette*, she discovered that both her position and attraction to him had remained unchanged.

After the first year, he was so successful that he took on a physical therapist, a registered nurse and a family practitioner as full time partners to help him meet the demands. He was in the process of opening a second clinic that would be ready to serve patients by the end of the year.

He entered the coffee shop with the same broad and easy smile that caught her attention in that Los Angeles coffee shop those many years ago. He was carrying the *North County Gazette* tucked neatly under his arm when he sat down in chair across from her.

"What?" she demanded.

"I was just thinking that you are too beautiful for anyone to have to tell you that you should get out more." He beamed.

"What makes you think that I don't?" she shot back.

"Nothing would make me happier if that were true. But look at you. You live in a beautiful Southern California city, literally only a few hundred feet from the beach . . . and you have no tan." He grinned.

"Perhaps you have never heard of sunscreen," she replied.

"When was the last time you went to a concert?" he asked.

"More times than you think."

"One that wasn't assigned as an entertainment news assignment?" he pressed.

She closed her eyes and shook her head. "I . . . I go to concerts."

"What about movies? What was the last movie you went out to see? Quick . . . five seconds . . . four . . . three . . . two . . . one . . . beep! Times up!"

"You make way too many assumptions about me Mitchell." She laughed.

He was teasing her, but his words stung just the same. Here she was, twenty-nine years old. Since she had taken on with the *North County Gazette*, she worked ridiculously long hours, she was not seeing anyone, nor had she any promising prospects. She did not answer his questions simply because she couldn't. When was the last time she had been to the beach? When did she go to a concert last? What was the last movie she had seen? Good God, when had she last held a lover? He was right on so many levels. She needed to get out more.

"If this was going to be a guilt ridden conversation about how I need to work less and try to find a nice man, I could have just as easily met my mother for coffee. I thought that you had a juicy, 'stop-the-presses' kind of story to share with me." She shot him a crooked smile and took a sip from the cup.

"Same old Jordan. Always strictly down to business." He sat the paper down on the table in front of him.

"Well, how do you think I found myself working as a freelance reporter at such a prestigious, internationally known newspaper?" She nodded at his copy of the *North County Gazette*.

"Your sarcasm isn't lost on me." He winked. "What I have to tell you Jordan will at the very least let you sit at the table with the big boys and girls. But I think it will do more than that."

"You think it is that big of a story, huh?"

"Yes, I do."

"Then why give it to me?" she inquired.

"You work hard Jordan, you always have. I have admired that in you."

"Ok Mitchell, you can stop it with the flattery. I am beyond caring about what you think. If you have a story to give me, then you should come out with it. Otherwise, I have better things to do with my time."

"Okay. I will. But you have to be careful with this, it involves some powerful people on both sides of the law and on both sides of the border."

"Okay, you have my attention."

"Well, you know just as well as anybody the community my clinic serves." He paused.

"Yes, those who need it. You're a great guy. Your halo is blinding me."

"If you would like me to stop, just say it," he replied sharply.

"Okay, go ahead." She stirred her cup.

"Many of my patients are undocumented, some are seeking residency too. So about a year ago, I took on Dr. Johnson because he's a registered civil surgeon. Patients can see him to carry out their medical examinations so that they can submit them to the U.C. Citizenship and Immigration Services to adjust their citizenship status."

"Okay . . . not a real page-turner so far," she replied.

"Jordan, believe me, there's more, so much more . . ." he continued.

He proceeded to tell her that one of Dr. Johnson's patients who had worked at the First Congregation Church doing light handy work on the grounds had confided in him that he witnessed some bad things take place there. According to this patient, the reverend was doing business with a very cruel man who smuggled drugs and people across the border. He told him how many of the people were children, young girls who were forced to lay down with men for money. The man explained to Mitchell that many of the girls would come to the church first and stay with the reverend for many days. They would conduct housekeeping at the church and in the reverend's house during the day. But at night, they would retire to the bedroom and give themselves to this "man of God."

The man went on to explain how after a few days, the girls would disappear and would not be seen again. He was very afraid, but he could not bear the thought of the evil things that visited these children, so he waited one night to try to discover what became of them when they would leave the church. He told Mitchell how in the early hours of the morning, a black Mercedes followed by a white van came to the church. Several men met with the reverend and one man gave him an envelope and then the girl was placed into the van that held several other women. The man watched as the van drove away and turned off the main road, heading down toward the river. He explained how he was too afraid to follow, but the next day, he retraced the path of the car and found himself at the edge of a forest of thick reeds. He found a narrow path tracked with footprints, so he followed them. What he found was a small encampment populated by women of all ages, guarded by two armed men. He explained that the only reason that he didn't vomit at the sight was because he skipped breakfast and had an empty stomach. He watched from the reeds as these women, most only girls, serviced man after man, laying down on the earth, sheltered only by the brush.

"My God. Is this reverend the same Reverend Caffrey? The one who just donated money for the construction of a new library at Grace Christian Academy?" Jordan gasped.

"The same," Mitchell replied.

"I just submitted a human interest story to the Gazette about him and his church's philanthropy. The community loves him," she retorted.

"My guess is he has some unseemly people making generous contributions to the offering plate on Sundays," Mitchell replied.

"What did you do?" she inquired.

"Well, I investigated it. And he was right . . . at least about the reeds. It was truly a grotesque and unimaginable thing to witness."

"So what, you just walked into this camp?"

"Yeah. I was in my hiking gear. I posed as a weekend adventurer. It made them nervous but having the occasional uninvited guest was not something entirely unexpected by these guys. I let them know that I ran a health clinic. I asked them if these girls ever received any medical attention, physicals and such."

"You offered them your services?" Jordan asked in surprise.

"Well, yes."

"And they took you up on it?" she replied in disgust.

"I told them that it was none of my business what they did here, but it was my duty to make sure that the people I served in this community remained healthy and if any of my patients were clients here, it was my business that the women who serviced them did not have HIV or AIDS or some other venereal diseases, so I left them my card."

"Wait a minute, aren't you supposed to take some Hippocratic Oath to do no harm? How could you in good conscience offer your services if you know that it will help these men continue to exploit these girls?" she whispered harshly.

"Look, I wasn't happy about it but I knew that if I was going to be any help to these girls, or to the girls that came after them, I had to develop a relationship with the men who profited from them being there. I had to transform myself into someone who didn't make judgments, who didn't express opinions—"

"Someone who didn't have ethics," she growled.

"Don't you think for a moment that I enjoy any of this!" he shot back.

"I bet those pimp friends of yours made it well worth your while Mitchell. How much did they pay you for your services? How much did they pay you to keep quiet?" she pressed.

"You really have no idea what it is like out there, do you? If I was going to help anyone, I had to get close and you don't get close to these kinds of people by carrying your morality pinned on your chest like some goddamn medal. The fact that I am talking to you risks a price being put on my head. I want to bring these bastards down, that's the only reason we are having this conversation. If you don't want to help me, I'll find someone else who will," he said.

Jordan saw that he was hurt by her words and immediately regretted using them.

"I am sorry Mitchell, it is just a little much to take in. Go on, tell me the rest," she said softly.

He continued to tell her how he eventually gained the trust of the Salazar brothers and the women and the girls that he treated. He would go to the reeds to offer his services and the things he bore witness to while he was there. He saw men from all walks of life enter into the reeds seeking their time with the girls that the Salazar brothers offered. Old men, teenage boys, men of means as well as men who had little to offer the world. On one occasion, he told her how two Border Patrol Agents entered the reeds and were welcomed with open arms by the men, each disappearing into the caves with the girl of their choice.

"What about Reverend Caffrey?" she asked. "Is what the groundskeeper told you true?"

"There is no way to tell for sure. He has never been down to the reeds, at least not while I've been there, but I don't have a reason not to believe him."

"So, what do you want me to do with this information Mitchell?" she asked.

"You are a reporter, investigate it. Bring it to the public."

"If I do, you will be exposed too, your clinic is already under enough public scrutiny. Do you want it known that in addition to serving the tired and poor huddled masses that you also serve primps and prostitutes? That is a career ender right there."

"I have done nothing wrong. I only got involved to help these girls. I only contacted you because I want to end it," he insisted.

"Okay. I will help. I'll expose these guys . . . but you need to bring me there. I need to see it. I need to talk to these girls."

"It doesn't work that way. This is not some rotary club meeting where I can just bring in guests. It's way too dangerous for you to go to the reeds, besides, these girls won't talk to a journalist, they're too afraid." He paused. "You will have to come to the clinic."

"The clinic? Why would they talk to me there? Do I check my journalist credentials at the door?"

"They might talk to you if they thought you were a nurse or a doctor. You're like a priest then. They can confess without fear of reprisals."

"So, this is going to be an undercover investigation?" She grinned.

"All of the best stories are."

"Do I get to wear a stethoscope and one of those white lab coats?" Her smile broadened. "Because I would look so hot!"

"Jordan, this is serious. These men are dangerous. If they knew I was talking to you, we would both be dead. They come from a place where the truth is something to be exterminated, not illuminated. You know what happens to journalists south of the border. Guys like the Salazar brothers are the reason for it. If we are going to do this, we have to be careful," he professed solemnly.

Jordan felt it in her gut. Mitchell was right on both accounts. This was a career-making story but it was also a dangerous one. If she took it, she would be laying everything on the line. She looked at Mitchell sitting across from her and saw the profound sadness in his eyes. He was a good man who by the virtue of his own kindness found himself in a very dark place.

"It is true," she mused to herself. "No good deed goes unpunished."

She reached her hand across the table and clasped the end of his fingers and spoke softly, but with a steel in her voice that emboldened her.

"I'm with you. Let's go after these guys."

"Okay." He welcomed her touch.

"I have an appointment with a group of the girls next Thursday. They don't come by during regular operating hours."

"I guessed that much," She said smiling.

"I will contact the Salazar brothers and let them know that I have a new nurse working with me. It'll make them nervous but I'll tell them you are my cousin and that I trust you."

"I'm a nurse. We're cousins. Got it."

"Another thing Jordan." He spoke gravely and his broad smile was gone.

"Yes, Mitchell?" she asked.

"Don't talk to anyone about this. Not family, friends, your editor . . . no one. If the men I am working with suspect even for a moment . . ."

"Mitchell, you act like this is my first investigative reporting gig. Don't worry so much, I know how to protect my sources. I'm a journalist."

"It's not me that I'm worried about."

"You don't have to worry about me, it turns out that in addition to being a world class investigative reporter, I'm a big girl too." She winked.

He laughed.

"All right, Jordan. Keep your dance card free for next Thursday morning—early! I'll be in touch." He rose from the table and started toward the door.

"Mitchell," she called after him.

"Yeah?"

"We are going to bring these bastards down."

A smile spread wide across his face as he walked out the door and disappeared into the crowd.

8

A while back, I went to San Diego to attend some kind of mandatory training that was supposed to help make Border Patrol Agents more sensitive to the plight of the individuals we might encounter in our work. There was an instance before I signed on where a couple of old boys were unprofessional in their dealings with a few undocumented migrants and the coyotes that were with them, resulting in a lawsuit against the agency. I guess this was Uncle Sam's effort to prevent that from happening again by engineering a kinder and gentler Border Patrol. I spent three days listening to speakers at the San Diego Convention Center go on about stereotypes, bigotry and use of force. Three days seemed like a long time to impress the Golden Rule upon us: treat folks the way you want them to treat you. But I guess some people are a little slow and need more time to process.

During one of the lunch breaks, I found myself sitting at a table with a group of women that were discussing with considerable excitement about this book written by a famous journalist and economist that uses statistics to make sense of the world. I had never heard of neither of the authors, but they evidently held some acclaim at the table I was sitting at.

One woman was pretty excited over an argument that the book made about abortions being the reason our crime rates were so low as of late.

"It makes complete sense if you think about it," she asserted. "Since Roe v. Wade, women have had control over their bodies and can decide for themselves when a baby is wanted in their lives and when the optimal time for having a child is. God knows I could not have raised a child at eighteen!"

Everyone at the table nodded in agreement. I normally make it a point to never miss an opportunity to keep my mouth shut;

especially when it involves things I have no expertise in, such as having a uterus. But it seemed to strike me odd that here we were, officers of the law, attending a mandatory training on how to be more considerate towards the criminal elements we encounter in our daily activities, actually contemplating the argument that killing an unborn baby reduces crime. So I had to ask the question.

"How do we determine who the dangerous fetuses are?"

"Wh . . . What?" the woman stammered.

"How do we know what fetus is going to become a criminal mastermind and what fetus is going to cure cancer?" I expanded my question.

"Well," she said. "There is no science to it, but it makes sense to me that after Roe v. Wade was passed, women in America had the opportunity to decide if they wanted to have a baby or not."

"So wantedness makes you a good person, and un-wantedness makes you a criminal then? That's your argument?"

She laughed at my question. "The numbers don't lie! The fetuses that were aborted after Roe v. Wade would have been more likely to commit crimes had they been born and reached adolescence than the youth who developed from fetuses and were carried to full term . . . because their mothers wanted them and were probably better equipped to care for them."

"So, a parent's ability to care for a child would make them less likely to become a criminal? So rich families don't raise criminals and poor families do? That's what you are telling us?"

The woman got real hot then and accused me of being a mindless Fox News watching Republican or something along those lines. So, I rephrased my question.

"If I am hearing you right, you're saying that a child's wantedness by their parents influences their inclination toward criminal behavior?"

Then she started speaking to me really slow and loud as if I was both delayed and hard of hearing.

"What I am saying is that we don't do a good enough job as a society in supporting mothers once their children are born. Especially *impoverished, unwed teenage mothers. These children who are born into poverty don't have the support they need to become productive adults, so crime doesn't even seem like crime to them—it is a method of survival."*

I told her that there were two hitches in her argument. The first was that she was looking at these poor, unwed, teenage mothers as a social problem, while the poor, unwed teenage mothers in all likelihood don't see themselves that way at all. Instead, they probably think of themselves as human beings facing the age-old challenge of just getting along in the world and, if they're lucky, passing their genes on to the next generation. The second hitch was found on the headlines in today's paper. There were three teenage boys in Orange County who were going to trial for gang raping one of their classmates and videotaping the whole ordeal. According to the reports of law enforcement officials who had viewed the tape, before raping this girl, the boys violated her with a cigarette, a pool stick and an empty liquor bottle while she was unconscious. These boys weren't your stereotypical "thugs from the hood" either. Each one of them came from families of means. They were all honor students and the father of one of them was a County Sherriff.

The woman sat in stunned silence for a moment and then accused me of using a single anecdote to argue against hard data. She then stated that she would not stand for raising her daughter in a country where she didn't have the right to an abortion if she chose to have one.

I told her that I didn't think that she would need to worry about that. I believed that the way I saw the world heading, her daughter would not only have the right to have as many abortions as she wanted, she would probably be able to hire a goddamn videographer to document the procedures for one of them reality television shows.

That pretty much concluded our conversation. I ended up eating by myself for the rest of the convention.

Thursday, October 16, 2008

G.H.

Jordan arrived on the steps of the Ocean View Community Health Clinic at 6 AM holding two cups of coffee with steam rising out of the narrow openings from the plastic lids. Mitchell greeted her at the door with a weary smile. She was barely awake herself, but he looked exhausted and it occurred to her that this was a strange look for a man with the endless amount of energy that Mitchell was famous for. He motioned her inside to the clinic's waiting room. She handed him a cup and sat down on one of the chairs lining the wall.

"Have you even slept?" she asked.

"Nope. I have been prepping." He tossed her a white lab coat.

"Sweet! Do I get a stethoscope with this thing?" She smiled as she pushed her arms through the coat sleeves, one at a time.

He reached into his pocket and pulled out a tangle of orange tubing fixed at the end with a copper colored bell.

"I was given this my first year of medical school." He smiled, handing it to her.

She took it from him and placed the ear tips into her ears, tapping gently on the diaphragm.

"As I recall, you weren't such a successful student." She grinned.

"Perhaps it will bring you better luck than it did me!" He sipped his coffee.

"What, you can't even get me sugar with my coffee? What sorry excuse for an intern are you?" He smiled.

"Touché! What's with the packing, are you going on a trip?" she asked, jutting her chin toward the dozen clear plastic storage bins filled with medical supplies stacked neatly on the floor.

"We both are. The Salazar brothers want to expand their business partnership with me."

"What does that mean?" she asked.

"When I contacted Juan Carlos to advise him that I was training my cousin to help take over one of my clinics and informed him that I would like to have her assistance in treating the girls from Los Carrizales, he told me how he didn't trust outsiders. I told him that you were blood and I trusted you with my life. He then suggested that Los Carrizales was too small of an assignment for us and that he wished to expand our partnership."

"So, we are not going to the reeds?" she asked.

"No. He wants us to treat the women who work for him at a brothel he runs in Tecate. I know it isn't the story I promised you, but—"

"So, you are taking me into the belly of the beast?" she interrupted.

"You can say that."

"Well, one thing's for certain Mitchell, you haven't forgotten how to show a girl a good time!" she grinned.

Outside, the headlights of an approaching car cast shadows on the clinic wall. Three sharp blasts from a horn announced the arrival of another visitor.

He peered through the window and looked back at her.

"Our ride is here." He smiled faintly.

On the second Thursday of every month, the women of Casa de Diana have a day off, of sorts. The brothel and bar are closed for business and the women assemble in the cantina and line up for inspection. The doctor—a short, heavy man with thick, sweaty fingers and thinning, jet black hair, meets with each woman and conducts physical examinations. He administers shots of depo provera to prevent any unwanted pregnancies and treats infections and any other occupational hazards that the women might encounter in their work with heavy doses of antibiotics.

Angelina had disliked him from their first meeting. He was not a cruel man, merely indifferent; as though he were not working at all with women born of flesh and bone, but passive, insentient things. It seemed to Angelina that his bedside manner had long ago been bartered in exchange for a commitment to process and proficiency. He did not flirt with nor give preference to any of the whores he treated. Young or old, pretty or plain, each woman was met with the same cold, mechanical efficiency. None of the women trusted him, for it seemed unnatural that a man in his position would not demonstrate the slightest interest in them. So, it had become widely rumored among the whores of Casa de Diana that El Cacique had him castrated, like the biblical eunuchs who cared for the concubines of kings. Angelina did not throw in her lot with the women she worked with on many things, but her distrust of the doctor was in perfect alignment with theirs.

She always dreaded these monthly examinations and the way he probed her with his sweaty, sausage-like fingers as if she was some farm animal being prepared for auction. More than that, she feared him and what he would tell Juan Carlos along with the consequences that such a disclosure would bear. She recalled her first days at Casa de Diana—there was a woman who had contracted syphilis from one of the men who had paid to be with her. She had violated one of the house rules by allowing a man to have unprotected sex with her. It was well understood by the women of Casa de Diana that such a privilege was reserved for only Juan Carlos and the consequences of breaking this rule were severe. The infection had progressed to the point where she had developed painful, bleeding ulcers on the palms of her hands and the bottom of her feet. She would rub ointment on the sores to no avail and each night Angelina could hear her softly weeping in her room next door. The doctor told her that the disease had reached a point where he could not treat it. He told her the ulcers would continue eating at her until she was either driven mad or her heart stopped beating. Early the following morning, Angelina could hear the muted curses of a man's voice followed by silence coming from the hallway. The woman was never seen again. Her absence was the manifestation of every woman's fear at Casa de Diana: that El Cacique would find her no longer profitable and then cast her aside like something to be forgotten.

Today, Angelina's anxiety was exceptionally high. She could not quite put what she was feeling into words, but she knew her body. Some people lived in their heads entirely and did all that they could to be detached from their bodies by ignoring its quiet susurrations. However, Angelina was fully in-tune with hers. As a girl, in the days preceding her transition into womanhood, she knew what was coming. No one had to tell her anything. She simply knew. What she was experiencing now was in many ways similar. She felt different and that terrified her.

When the Dueña announced that El Cacique had brought in a new doctor and nurse to conduct the examinations that day, it was met with great curiosity. Questions were raised about the new doctor regarding whether he was handsome or single. If anyone wished to inquire the fate of the balding doctor with the fat, sweaty sausage-like fingers, no one voiced it. When Santiago escorted the two strangers into the cantina within the sight of the waiting patients, a quiet but enthusiastic murmur rolled down the line of women, like a wave pushing intensely toward the shore.

"¡El doctor. Él es muy guapo¡" one of the women giggled.

"¡Callete!" the Dueña hissed. "You are not whores today! You are patients. Do not disgrace yourselves or cause our guests to feel uncomfortable!"

"Do not worry Señora, we will make the doctor feel most comfortable!" a woman shouted from the back of the line and the entire cantina burst into laughter and catcalls.

The Dueña glared in the direction of the woman who spoke and her gaze remained unflinching until the room was once again quiet.

"The procedure has not changed," she proclaimed. "You will remain seated at your tables until your name is called. If the doctor believes that he requires a urine sample, you will be given a container that you may take to the washroom. After you are finished here, you may have the rest of the day to do as you please. Just make certain that you return in time for your duties this evening."

The women shuffled to the four corners of the cantina and took up residence at the various tables that were available to them. Angelina picked up a magazine and thumbed through the glossy pages, pretending to read as she closely watched the two strangers prepare for their patients. They looked to her like something from the novellas that some of the women watched on television. The doctor was indeed a handsome man and the woman with him was beautiful. She was tall and pale and her long blonde hair reminded Angelina of how she imagined angels to be when she was a child. She continued to observe the two as they conversed with each woman that approached them for examination, and the more she saw, the greater comfort she felt. She sensed a kindness in them that was noticeably absent from the fat fingered doctor and anyone else she had met that worked for Juan Carlos.

When her name was called she approached them. The doctor smiled and introduced himself in fluent Spanish as Mitchell Stevens and introduced the woman accompanying him as his cousin and assisting nurse. Angelina smiled and nodded. He explained that he was going to ask her a series of questions and some of them might be personal, but she should answer them honestly and share with him any concerns that she might have.

She told him that she did not have any concerns and immediately felt guilty for lying.

He smiled and told her that he hadn't arrived at that part of the examination yet. He placed a large blue sleeve on her arm and asked her if she had seen it before. She told him that she had not. He explained that it was called a pressure cuff and it would squeeze her arm a little, but it wouldn't hurt. It would help him determine her blood pressure and give him an idea of how healthy her heart was. She smiled.

He asked her how old she was while squeezing her wrist slightly between his thumb and fingers. She told him that she had recently turned eighteen.

"One eleven over seventy-one," he said smiling.

The woman wrote the numbers onto a chart.

He asked her if she had an estimate of how many men she had sex with since her last examination. She thought for a moment and trembled slightly. She shook her head and told him that she did not know.

He saw the tears welling up in her eyes and patted her on the shoulder and lifted his voice a little higher, assuring her that it was okay. He then asked her if she had unprotected sex with anyone since her last examination.

She paused and told him that she did know the answer to that question. There had only been two men. Juan Carlos would call upon his favorites at Casa de Diana whenever he wished and would never use protection. The other was Garrett. When he came to her the night of her birthday, she was heartbroken and so taken by his compassion that she had lost herself in the moment and forgot to insist that he cover himself.

"Dos hombres," she whispered.

He asked her if she could recall the last time she had unprotected sex with either of the men. The last time Juan Carlos had called on her was the evening that the Americans had been thrown out of the cantina and the night that she first met Garrett. The second time was with Garret a few days later. She sat staring at her feet for a long moment and told him that she had been with a man unprotected ten days ago.

He asked her if she had experienced any discomfort during urination.

She told him that she had not.

He asked her when she had last menstruated.

She told him that she thought it was about twenty days ago. He then began conversing with the woman and looked around the room nervously and then began sorting through his bag until he retrieved a plastic bag that contained a long, white cylinder and three white pills and he placed the bag on top of the magazine she was reading. He whispered to her that the bag contained a simple pregnancy test and if she should need it, three pills that would terminate the pregnancy.

She told him she didn't believe that she could be pregnant because she had been taking the injections like all of the other women.

The man explained to her that nothing was one hundred percent effective and that there was always room for error. He asked her if she had taken a pregnancy test before. She nodded her head. She had purchased one from the local *farmacia* shortly after she was first forced to lay down with Juan Carlos for the first time.

The man told her that she should take the test right away and explained that if she were to test positive, she should take the larger white capsule before going to bed and in the morning, take the two smaller pills. He explained that they would induce menstruation within a few hours and expel the fetus out of her body.

"¿Aborto?" she asked softly.

"Sí," he replied.

He emphasized that she should wait to take the tablets until she knew that she had at least twelve hours to rest, but not to wait too long because chemical abortions are only effective and safe if they are done during the first nine weeks of conception. He went on to tell her that if she experienced any nausea, diarrhea, or stomach pains afterwards it was completely normal that she shouldn't worry. He assured her that he would be back in a month to evaluate her but if she felt that she needed to speak with him before then, she could call and then he handed her his business card.

She rose from that table folded the magazine in half, hiding the plastic bag from the view of other women in the room, wiped a tear from her cheek and thanked him. Angelina did not need a test to confirm what she already knew to be true. She was confident that she was pregnant before she exited the cantina, she just did not know for certain who the father was.

It was dark when the black Mercedes pulled into the gravel driveway of the clinic. Both passengers were exhausted from the emotional and physical toil of the days long unfolding. The legion of women she had encountered that day had marked her. She wondered deeply what had brought them to that end. She always believed that everyone had choices to make. That every moment was composed of a choosing and a turning and like a piece of music, the time signatures created by those choices defines the melody perfectly. Depending on the repercussions of decisions made, our melody takes on an upbeat or melancholy timbre. However, the women that she encountered, in spite of their attempts to hide behind weak smiles, played a melody that was far beyond melancholy.

For the first time since she was a young girl, she felt like crying. Despite her efforts to hold back, sitting in the shadows of the backseat, tears welled up in her eyes.

They had sat in silence until the car rolled to a full stop at the entrance. The driver glanced back at the two passengers through the review mirror.

"We're here." Mitchell smiled.

"Yeah." Her reply sounded weak in her own ears.

"Come on. Let's get cleaned up and I'll buy you a drink." He patted her shoulder.

When they entered the front door, Mitchell flipped the light switch, illuminating the waiting room where El Cacique was sitting at the receptionist's desk waiting for them. Jordan dropped her purse and gasped slightly. Mitchell's hand dropped from the light switch on the wall. El Cacique did not move and all three remained immobile, frozen in the room like some life-size diorama. Finally, Mitchell spoke.

"I figured there was more to our trip to Casa de Diana's than simply broadening our partnership."

"You are indeed a smart man."

"Jordan doesn't have anything to do with your problem with me," Mitchell asserted.

"And what problem would I have with you, eh? Unless you are making reference to your attempt to deceive me," El Cacique replied flatly.

"She has nothing to do with you and me," he reasserted.

"I need to sit down," Jordan whispered.

El Cacique nodded toward one of the chairs lining the wall. She picked up her purse from the floor and sat down and held the bag to her abdomen.

"It is too late," El Cacique replied. "She is involved now. She is a liar by trade and a liar by association. Her fate became bound with yours when she agreed to become a participant in your effort to betray me. But in truth, her fate was determined long before that."

"Juan Carlos . . . we can work this out." His voice took on a desperate tone.

"That time has passed. Did you think that I would not know who she was? Did you think that I do not investigate those that I take into my organization? I do not put my head to the pillow without knowing for certain that I am at least three-steps ahead of my adversaries!"

"You don't have to hurt us," Jordan spoke up. "I won't tell anyone. We won't."

"I see the journalist has found her voice," El Cacique said. "But sadly, you use it to lie once again."

"I am not lying. I won't say anything," Jordan insisted.

"That would be wonderful, were it true. But to remain silent would be to go against your very nature, to oppose the very purpose for which you were designed. How could I ask you to do that? It would be an affront to God." He laid a revolver on the desk with a gloved hand.

"But you are not God. You can't just decide who lives and who dies," Jordan raised her voice.

"No, I am not God, but I emulate Him and more importantly, I would not act in a manner that would offend Him. To ignore your treachery would dishonor my design. It would be in conflict with the very purpose for which I was made and that would be an insult and a far greater offense to Him. Even as a non-believer. I would not risk that you understand."

"I never did any wrong to you. I'll swear my silence to you. We both will."

"There are two occupational hazards to being a man in this world. One is that you learn that you can never trust the words spoken by a woman and the other is that lesser men will betray you."

"You son of a bitch!" Mitchell growled.

"Harsh words from such a pathetic, little man. But what's done is done. The time for talk has passed."

El Cacique lifted the revolver from the desktop and fired a slug into Mitchell's head, leaving a nearly perfect, nickel sized crimson circle just above his right eye, splattering the wall behind him in a soup of blood, hair and gray matter. In that instant, the form that once was Mitchell Stevens collapsed to the ground in a lifeless heap of flesh, blood and bone.

Jordan began to shake uncontrollably in her seat. She wanted to scream. She wanted to run, however her body refused to respond to even the simplest command ushered by her brain, so she remained seated and sobbed.

"You might be distressed to know Jordan, that this man that you trusted had every opportunity to keep you safe. He could have prevented your early departure from this world, but he did not have the courage to act alone. He was a coward. He needed an accomplice in his betrayal, so he asked you—a woman—to help him."

"You are going to kill me too, then?" she asked.

"I am sorry, but yes. You see, I am in the process of building an empire and there are many challenges in doing so. I can guarantee you that the center will not hold if I forgive treason."

"No one will know," she sobbed.

"Even if all of the world were deaf and dumb to your actions and mine, I would know, and wouldn't that be enough?" he asked.

"I don't know."

"I do," he said. "Is there anything that you would like to say?"

"About what?"

"Some people ask for forgiveness in their last moments," he said.

"Forgiveness? From who?" she cried.

"Besides you, I am the only one here," he said.

"I have nothing that I want to say to you."

"Very well." He rose from the desk and walked over to the chair where she sat and leveled the revolver, pointing it to her head.

"Oh God," she said, "Oh my God."

Oceanside Police Investigate Apparent Murder-Suicide

OCEANSIDE, CA—Police said a North San Diego County woman fatally shot her estranged boyfriend and then fatally shot herself at the Ocean View Community Health Clinic late Thursday evening.

Oceanside police responded to the 1700 block of Oceanside Avenue to investigate an anonymous report of a shooting just before midnight.

Officers said they found the victim, Mitchell Stevens Jr., 30, and

Jordan Sandholtz, 29, inside the clinic with gunshot wounds to the head.

Both were pronounced dead at the scene.

Sandholtz has worked for the last two years as a reporter with the North County Gazette and Stevens owned the Ocean View Community Health Clinic that serves low-income residents.

Investigators said they believe Sandholtz shot Stevens before turning the gun on herself.

Anyone with information about the case is asked to contact police at 760-555-4925 or Crime Stoppers at 866-555-TIPS.

9

I'd never admit this to anyone, but I watched one of those daytime television talk shows awhile back. In my defense, it wasn't one of the train wreck variety where some guy finds out his girl used to be a man or anything like that. It was a human interest piece on the subject of forgiveness.

There was a panel of people who had been wronged in about every way imaginable. One woman was going through a divorce after her husband had an affair with her sister, another had been molested by a family member as a child, and the third panelist had lost her husband when his plane was rerouted from its Los Angeles destination into the North Tower of the World Trade Center on September 11th. However, it was the fourth woman who told a story that hit me the hardest and stopped me from changing the channel. This woman lost her youngest daughter on a family camping trip in the high Sierras several years back to a kidnapper.

She told how she and her husband woke up in the night to check on their two daughters who were sleeping in the tent next to them. When they peeked inside, they found their oldest daughter sleeping soundly, but their youngest was gone. They found that a slit had been cut into the back of the tent where she had been sleeping. She recounted how they desperately searched the campsite, calling out her name. When it became apparent that she was nowhere to be found, her husband and brother in-law drove into town to get the Sheriff. As she continued to tell her story, she talked about how for one year the FBI could find nothing. No clues. No ransom demands. No body. Whoever took her daughter disappeared like a ghost.

Then one night, a year after her daughter's abduction, she gets this call from some guy who claims that he was the one who took her little girl. He confirmed this by describing a birth defect that her daughter had, which was never made public. The man torments her.

He tells her how it was him who had taken her daughter and that he killed her and how there was nothing that she or anyone else could do about it. The woman explained how she had responded in a manner that surprised her as much as it did her daughter's killer. She told him that she had been in a living hell the past year, not knowing if her daughter was dead or alive and at last now she knew that her daughter was at peace. She thanked him for telling her and then told him that she forgave him for what he'd done.

After hearing this, the guy softens up a bit and stays on the phone with her for an hour talking about how he was worried that the phone call was being traced but that he needed to talk to somebody about what he'd done. She asked him if there was anything that she could do for him and he broke down crying, talking about how he wished this burden could be taken from him. He finally just hung up and the conversation was over. The woman explained that the police weren't successful in tracing the phone call but she had her wits about her enough to record most of the conversation. The guy gave up enough details about himself and his whereabouts that the FBI tracked him down and arrested him.

The woman went on about how that year, she went from absolute paralyzing fear to blind rage and finally found it in her to forgive the person who killed her baby girl. She explained how in God's eyes, the life of this wretched, mixed up man was just as precious as her beautiful little girl. The guy was up for the death penalty and probably would've got it, but not for this woman who actually asked the prosecutor to offer the lesser alternative—life without the possibility of parole. The prosecution honored her request and that guy is sitting in jail right now.

When someone in the audience asked her how it was possible that she did not want this monster's head on a stake, let alone find it in her to forgive him, she explained that her daughter was too beautiful of a soul to tarnish her memory with a state sanctioned execution in her name. It would be a far better thing to memorialize her by making the statement that all life is precious and deserving of preservation and respect. Then she quoted Ghandi and said *something about being the change that you want to see in the world.*

I have sat through enough of my father's sermons to understand that, depending on what scripture you are reading, the Almighty is a god full of forgiveness and mercy and He expects us to follow his example. I also know enough about human nature to realize that some folks look at things like mercy and forgiveness as signs of weakness. Forgiveness is for sissies. But I have got to hand it to this woman. She was a mother who had lost her baby at the hands of some psychopath and found the will to not only forgive the man, but to plead on his behalf and save him from a certain execution. That's something I don't think many of us could do. If you ask me, that wasn't weakness. That was an act of unimaginable strength.

It seems to me that forgiveness ain't for sissies at all. Forgiveness is hard work.

Friday, October 17, 2008
G.H.

Garrett had always felt compelled to travel. To him the road always held intrigue. The promise of something new and wonderful lay just beyond the next bend. This restlessness had resided in him for as long as he had memories. Even before he had the words to name it, he was a spirit on the move. For him, Sunday mornings had always presented a special challenge. When he was a child, every Sunday was spent at church with his mother, listening to the Word as it passed from his father's lips and washed over the congregation like an antiseptic for the conscience. His father would speak of society's evils in general terms and then drive them home. He would make them personal and he would compel his parishioners to act. His father's approach would often offend some and result in those whom he had offended, leaving his church never to return. His response was always the same.

"I would rather be a servant of God and lose the whole congregation than to be a hypocrite and hold services before a full house."

As a boy, he would sit in the pew, listening to his father speak, but all of the while, silently wishing he could be somewhere else. He couldn't help but believe that a world of adventure was passing him by while he sat inside, listening to his father's admonitions of sins that his young mind knew little about. Since his father's death, Garrett found that he was un-tethered to Sunday service. He was, in fact, a man without a religion. When this determination would well within him to wander, he discovered that he had nowhere to go and no compass to guide him, only this drive deep within his soul to simply be elsewhere.

On this Sunday, it was different. He rose in the morning, like many mornings before, with the desire to be someplace else. Only now he could give that place a name. However, the place that beckoned him was country without geography. No cartographer could create a map to guide him there; there were no coordinates, no lines of latitude or longitude. Only a longing to once again know the fire he felt in the tips of her fingers. This yearning within him pulled at his heart like the great magnetic north and called him again to the road, compelling him to follow it like some ancient migratory path leading to her. The sun had not yet risen when he climbed onto the leather seat of the newly restored Indian and turned the ignition. He thought about his father as the engine roared to life. When he had brought the rusted out shell of this bike home to Garrett, he recalled a gleam in his father's eye as he explained to him that an Indian was something of far greater importance than mere transportation.

"If you just want to get from point A to point B, you might as well take a bus. But if you want to be something more than a passenger; if you wish to become part of the landscape, if you want to bind yourself to the tapestry of the journey, then riding on the back of an Indian, with the gravel under your feet and the wind in your hair is the only way for a man to go."

One of the things that Garrett enjoyed about living in the desert was the quiet blackness of night. The stars were not muted by the glow of city lights and instead blazed in the sky like jewels laid out upon an inky velvet blanket. The stars of the Milky Way spread out above him seemed so close that he felt as though he could touch them. He recalled camping beneath the stars as a boy gazing up into the speckled heavens and feeling as though he were transported into the immense vacuum of space. He would engage his father in conversation about whether or not it was possible to count the stars in the sky. His father would entertain his curiosity by suggesting that they try and they would lay on their backs counting from one until Garrett drifted off to dream.

Beneath skies such as these, when the stars were immense and the world seemed transparent, his father would tell him the story of the Calle de Santiago. He would explain to Garrett how the stars of the Milky Way served as a map, revealing to everyone who gazed upon them, the way to Santiago. Garrett would listen to these stories and decided that one day he would set out and make a pilgrimage to Saint Ignacio de Compostella. His father told him how in the darkness of night so long ago, a young shepherd saw a bright light appear in the field that revealed to him the very spot that St. James was buried. Some time later, a cornerstone for the foundation of the church was laid on that very spot along with an altar honoring Apostle James the Great, the man that was considered to be Jesus' closest friend.

Garrett imagined what sights he might behold on such a journey and what sort of people he would encounter along the way. But most of all, he wondered if the stars that led travelers to the final resting place of Christ's friend somehow looked different blinking down at him from another sky. Now he made a pilgrimage of another kind: the stars above served as a thin celestial path leading him once again to her.

The sun had been up for only a short time when he parked the bike outside of the church. When he entered, he saw her kneeling before the Altar of the Virgin. Her hands were clasped together so tight that the skin on her knuckles had whitened. Her head was bowed and she was whispering a prayer in such a low murmur, that he could not understand the words coming from her lips. He took a seat three pews behind her and remained there for quite some time listening to the rhythm of her prayer before he rose to his feet. She was so beautiful that he hesitated to touch her, fearing that she might vanish upon contact like some ethereal being. He waited until she finished praying. She was still kneeling when he placed his hand upon her shoulder. She turned her face toward him and smiled.

"What are you doing here?" she asked in pleasant amazement.

"Well, if you would like me to leave, I can go. Ni modo." He smiled.

She rose to her feet and smiled back at him. "I am glad that you came. But, I think that we should leave this place," she whispered as her eyes darted back and forth, nervously looking around the nearly empty church.

"I know," he whispered pulling her closer to him. "Run away with me. Let's leave Tecate."

She pulled back from him. "Do not joke like that!"

"I am not joking, Angelina."

"Do not say things that you do not mean. Empty words can be cruel."

"Look at me." He held her delicate face in his hand. "I don't say things that I don't mean."

She turned her head away from his gaze. "You make jokes all of the time."

"I don't joke about things like this," he replied. "I mean what I say. Angelina, leave with me."

"Do you think it is as simple as that? Do you think that I can just walk away from here?"

"If you want to, you can."

"Then what would I do? Sneak away with you across the border?"

"Yes."

"Then what?"

"Marry me."

"What? Marry you? You are crazy!"

"Why? Because I love you?"

"No. Because you do not understand the consequences."

"The consequences?"

"Yes. If I leave this place, El Cacique will look for me."

"He won't find you."

She explained to Garrett that El Cacique had told her once that if she ever left him, he would find her. She told him that he was a relentless and evil man who would not rest until he tracked her down and punished her for her disloyalty. He had promised her that if ever there were such a place on this earth that she could hide and he could not find her, he would simply return to Yelapa and pay a visit to her grandparents where he would kill them. But not before making them suffer so greatly that they would beg for death to ease their torment.

"Those are only threats, Angelina. Only empty threats he is using to frighten you," he replied, but even as he spoke them, he took little stock in his own words.

"You do not know him," she replied.

He asked her why she was in the church if she was so afraid. He asked her why she was not in Casa de Diana's. She explained to him that Tecate established an ordinance that prohibits the bars and certain restaurants from operating until the evening on the Sabbath so that people may honor the holy day. As a result, El Cacique permits the women to have Sundays off unless they are otherwise needed.

Garrett pondered the irony of this. Here was a man who pedaled flesh for profit. This was a man who was responsible for the deaths of many people on both sides of the border, both directly by his own hand and indirectly through drug smuggling and who knows what else. Yet he was so righteous as to honor the Sabbath.

"I spoke to his brother," he said.

"What?"

"I spoke to Santiago on the morning I left you."

"For what purpose?"

"I told him that I want to meet with Juan Carlos—face to face."

"Why?"

"I'm gonna ask him to let you go. I'm gonna tell him that I love you and I want to take you away from this place."

She wanted to laugh and cry all at once. "And you think that he will just let you do that?"

"I will make it worth his while. I have some money saved up. I will compensate him for his losses."

"What if he refuses?"

"Then I will take you anyway. That is, if you want me to, I will."

"Mi amor, you are so beautiful and so naïve." She ran her fingers through his sandy blonde hair. "You do not even realize that such things are not possible."

He squinted and looked up at the bright blue sky above them. "It is a beautiful day. Let's not fight over what we think is possible. I love you and I want to take you somewhere. Let's go." He smiled as he took her hand.

"¿A dónde?" she asked.

"We're gonna have ourselves a picnic."

"Mande?" Her brow furrowed at his English.

"Trust me." He took her hand and his smile widened.

The Indian rattled up a narrow dirt road and came to a rest on a dusty hilltop overlooking a small mango orchard below. Her hands were clasped tightly around his waist and he did not wish for her to loosen her grip. He remembered how his father had told him when they begun the restoration work on the motorcycle, that there was never a bike made with a soul like an Indian Chief and that he would be hard pressed to find anything in the world so magnificent as a 1947 Indian with a beautiful girl riding on back. The leafy trees appeared before them as cool oasis of green amidst the brown rocky landscape. The engine idled loudly and vibrated beneath them like a living thing, breaking the morning silence and announcing to the world their claim on the day before them. With her arms still wrapped around his waist, Angelina rested her head lightly against his shoulder. Garrett turned off the engine and realized that his father, like so many times before, was right.

"We are here." He smiled.

"Where is here?" she asked.

"Can you think of a better place for a Sunday brunch?" He waved his hand slightly over the landscape. "Mademoiselle, welcome to Chateau Coyote. We have a spacious dining area with a wonderful view."

She laughed.

"Yes, it is very beautiful. I can think of no other establishment in all of Tecate that is its equal!"

"Only Tecate? I think that you would be hard pressed to find its equal in all of Mexico!"

"What is on the menu, mi amor?" she asked playfully.

"Well, we have no need for menus here at Chateau Coyote. For we serve only one thing . . ." He reached up into the branches and grasped a tight hold of an oval shaped fruit and snapped it free from the branch. "We have the sweetest mangos in all of Mexico."

She laughed and all of the worries that Garrett held began to evaporate. Nothing in the world seemed more pressing to him than keeping a smile on her face. He handed her the mango and returned to the Indian where he pulled a blanket from the saddlebag. He spread the green and blue-checkered bedcover on the ground and she emerged from the grove carrying several mangos cradled in her blouse. Her brown navel peeked out at him from just above the waistline of her skirt.

They passed the morning untroubled. They fed each other fruit; talking and laughing as though everything in the world was right and made only for them. Garrett carefully crafted his words so not make the smile leave her face. He wanted to tell her so much more. He wanted her to leave with him but knew that she would not as long as El Cacique was a threat.

"Do you believe in God?" she asked.

"Well . . . my father was a minister . . . I really had no choice," Garrett replied.

"Being raised as a child to know God and believing in Him as an adult is not the same thing." She rested her head on his shoulder.

"Well, of course I do. I ain't exactly sure what team he's on, but I believe that God is out there somewhere."

"Do you think that he punishes the wicked?" She squeezed his hand.

"I really don't know anymore."

"I think that he does. He punishes us. In this life and after," she whispered.

"I don't know if I believe that he has a hand in punishing us in this life. I have seen people do some pretty bad things and get along just fine."

She raised her head from his shoulder and looked into his eyes. "I don't agree with that. I think that all of us receive our due punishment eventually in this life. I think God gives it to us as a warning of things to come. If we don't redeem ourselves or come to him seeking forgiveness before our death, then we are punished again in the afterlife."

"You think that God punishes us twice then?"

"Well, He is our father. Like a loving parent who wants to correct an errant child, He may scold us at first and if we don't change the offending behavior, then he uses the rod."

"Hmmm . . . interesting perspective. So we all receive compensation for our wicked deeds in this life. If we don't pay attention and repent, then we get the lake of fire later?"

"Sí."

"Seems to me that the Almighty is a pretty harsh disciplinarian by your view."

"Sí. But, He is not cruel, discipline is a form of love."

"But are we all disciplined?"

" Sí. Even you and I."

"Us? Why?"

"Well, we are both committing grave sins. I am prostituting my body for money. You have paid to be with me."

"But right now, what we are doing now. It's not the same thing."

"Is it not?" She lifted her head and looked in his eyes.

"No. It ain't. Least I don't believe it is."

"You might not be paying to be with me, but we are both committing the sin of lust. We are fornicators."

"Listen to me. I love you, Angelina. I can't believe that our love is a sin. You are my heart."

"I have done so many wicked things. You would not say such pretty words to me if you knew." She turned her head away from him.

He placed his hand beneath her chin and tilted her face toward his. "Listen to what I am telling you. I don't care what you have done in the past. We ain't our mistakes. We've all done things that we ain't proud of . . . myself included, but I love you and when I look at you, I see a beautiful woman who loves her family so much that she will suffer any injustice to protect them. That ain't sin, that's a virtue. If God can't see what a beautiful soul you are, if God can't forgive you . . . well . . . then, Hell, I don't want his forgiveness either."

His words sent a shiver throughout her body.

"Don't say that!" She pressed her fingertips against his mouth and he saw clouds stirring once again in her golden eyes. After a long pause, she spoke.

"I do not believe God will judge me for what I have done at Casa de Diana. I have no choice in that. But what I do with you, I do on my own free will. You are a gift, mi amor. God has blessed me with you and I have repaid his generosity with sin."

He took her hand and gently kissed her fingers. "We are both making choices and there are risks with the choices we make. But the way I see it, I don't want to be anywhere that you ain't. Even if it means goin' to Hell."

She placed her hand against the side of his face. He could feel the warmth in her fingers radiating against his cheek. "Do you love me? Will you love me all of your life?"

"Angelina, I have no life if you ain't in it."

Tears welled up in her great golden eyes as she struggled to find the strength to look at him. "Mi amor," she whispered. "I no longer have the luxury of worrying about your life . . . or my life alone."

He sat taller on the blanket. "What are you telling me?" He asked.

Tears flowed from her eyes, streaking her face in a mad race to the tip of her chin where they quivered and remained suspended until their volume and gravity freed them from their perch to fall into the abyss.

"I am pregnant," she whispered.

He remained silent for a moment as his mind processed the information she presented to him. She told him how El Cacique arranges for a doctor to visit the women at Casa de Diana once a month to conduct physical exams, check the women for disease and administer shots that the doctor claimed would prevent them from getting pregnant. She told him that an American doctor that she had never seen before did the last examination and that when the pregnancy test came back positive, she was not surprised. She had felt different over the last couple of weeks and the doctor merely confirmed her suspicion.

Garrett tried to reconcile the conflict welling within him. He imagined her belly round and taut and her face warm and radiant in a glow that only motherhood could produce. Then he recalled the horrific tale Brophy shared with him at the diner. He could not be sure that El Cacique was a cannibal, but he was certain that he was dangerous. He knew that her pregnancy was a liability to his profits and that placed Angelina in danger.

"Say something!" she pleaded.

He took her hand in his and squeezed it gently. "Are you certain?"

"As I breathe." Her voice quivered, "The only thing of which I am not certain is who the father might be."

He listened as she told how she had always taken extra care to protect herself with all of the men she had been with while working at Casa de Diana's with the exception of two men. His blood burned as she told him how El Cacique would visit her room on certain nights, like he would all of the women that worked for him; and come to know her without covering himself, insisting that the injections the doctor gave her would protect her from any unwanted pregnancy.   His rage was met and nearly equaled by the sense of shame that filled him when she reminded him that on her eighteenth birthday, they had given themselves to each other throughout the night without any thought of consequence.

She rose from the blanket and took her purse from its resting place on the handlebars of the motorcycle, removing a plastic bag from inside and returned to the blanket.

"The doctor told me that I was still early in the pregnancy. If I took these pills, it would wash the baby out of my womb as though it had never been." She sat on her knees and laid the small, clear plastic bag down on the blanket in front of him like an offering.

"You haven't done it then?" he asked.

"No, I thought that I should tell you first," she said, wiping the tears from her eyes. "Please understand mi amor, nothing would make me happier than to be the mother of your child. But Juan Carlos will not abide it. And even if he did, how could I know if the father would be you or a monster?"

He thought about her words for a moment before he spoke. "I don't think you should take them then."

"No?" she asked in surprise.

"It ain't the child's fault that it was conceived. Whether I am the father or Juan Carlos is, we can't none of us choose our parents."

"What am I to do with a child?" she pressed.

He cupped her face in his hand and looked intently into her eyes and smiled. "You don't have to do anything that you do not wish to do and whatever you do, you won't have to do it alone. I just thought that if the child was a boy, we could name him Samuel, after my father . . . and if the child should be a girl, we name her Marguerite, after the mother of my beloved."

They made love into the hot stillness of the late afternoon. Then, like two weary figures from a renaissance painting, they lay beneath the shade of a mango tree drifting silently in and out of sleep. She wore his shirt and rested her head against his chest. She had curled up close to him and her brown legs tangled around his, contrasting deeply against the green and blue-checkered blanket that they lay upon. His lips still bore the sticky sweetness from the mango she had fed him earlier. He lifted his eyes above him and saw among the thin wisps of white clouds a hawk floating in grand circular motions against an immense blue sky. The sun warmed his face while a balmy breeze rolled in from the east and caressed them gently. He softly stroked her hair with his fingers, smoothing out the ebony strands that had become tousled by the wind. His eyes became heavy and his breathing became deeper and more rhythmic. He thought that this day was perfectly formed and if he were God and given the charge of creating it, he could think of nothing to add to or take away from this moment that would improve upon it.

Garrett found himself often losing himself in thoughts such as these. He would forget for a time that he was a Border Patrol Agent for the United States of America and that Angelina was a prostitute. When he touched her skin and breathed deep her scent he was lost in a place from which he did not wish to be found. He looked down at her face, resting silently on his chest. Her long eyelashes would occasionally flutter with her twitching eyelids as she slipped deeper into her dreams. In that moment, something stirred within him and Garrett felt like everything of consequence in the universe was about to arrive and visit him. He knew that everything had been decided and the fate of Angelina, the unborn child growing within her, as well as his own had been written and committed to the stars.

10

I guess everyone remembers their first love. That exhilaration, the shortness of breath, the warm ache. The great longing. It has a way of leaving its mark on you. I was in the sixth grade the first time that I fell in love. Now some folks might not call it that on account of me being so young. They'd call it a crush or some other such thing that diminishes what it was. But I was there and I know what it was. What it was, was love.

It was late April when she entered our class for the first time. She was new in every sense of the word. She was a new student, she was new to the town and from the moment that I saw her she stirred in me strange new feelings of wonder and desire. The thing about being new, whether you're the new kid in town or the new guy at work, is you have no history to speak of. You stand before your new peers a blank slate and as such, you have a tiny window of opportunity to leave your past behind and begin anew. Now she was only twelve years old, but I think that if circumstances would've permitted it, she would've re-invented herself.

Her name was Regina White and she was beautiful. I remember when the teacher introduced her to the class. She wore a pair of olive green slacks, brown boots and a white blouse. She had long, thick sandy blonde hair and these great sad blue eyes that you could just swim in. She was quiet and kept to herself at first and the other kids let her do it. Rumors began to circulate about who she was and where she came from. But that's what they was, rumors, because when it came down to it there weren't nobody who knew anything about her.

It took me three days to get the nerve to talk to her. On the third day, I was so lovesick that I thought I would lose my fool mind. She sat at one of the benches in the outdoor lunch court eating an apple that she'd taken from a brown paper sack. I sat down at the bench across from her while the whole courtyard was a buzzing with conversation and all the energy that only a crowd of adolescents can generate but as far as I was concerned, she was the only person there.

I sat there for a good five minutes trying to work up the courage to walk over to her and say something. I sat there like a crazy person, talking to myself, playing out the same conversation in my head.

Get up and go talk to her! Do it now! Get up and say something—anything! Do it or you are going to go home and spend another night feeling sorry for your fool self. Ain't you tired of that yet? And before I knew it, I got up and crossed the walkway and I talked to her. I can't for the life of me remember what I said, but I'm glad I said it, 'cause I can't imagine life without the memories that followed as a result. If I never spoke to her, I guess those memories would've been replaced by a dull feeling of regret. But I'm here to tell you, that ain't no kind of substitute for first love.

She had a broad, easy smile that made you feel all warm inside just to see it. And if there is one thing that I will remember about her right up 'til the day that I die is that I would do just about anything in my power to bring a smile to her pretty face.

There was only four weeks of school left before they let us out for the summer. I wasn't ever much of a scholar, but during those last days, I never loved going to school so much. We spent our lunches together and grieved because they passed too quickly and in class, we would pass each other notes risking the merciless rebuke of the teacher. When the school year ended, we promised each other that we would find a way to see each other everyday. This was a romantic notion and posed a problem. She lived in town, roughly nine miles from my father's house.

When I got on the school bus that last day and watched her as we pulled away, I felt a stabbing pain in my heart and I resolved then that I would find a way to see her, and I did. Each morning that summer, I would eat breakfast, finish my morning chores, and hop on my ten speed and head into town. I pedaled nine miles in *and nine miles back out. My heart a pounding and burning with the anticipation of just seeing her face. For sixty-one days, I pedaled out to her house and back. You would figure that at some point it would get old and I would lose interest. But I never did. Each time I pedaled down the blacktop across the silvery bands of heat that would shimmer up from the surface and each time I was rewarded with the gift of her. Her broad smile and great shimmering eyes. Her golden laugh and her long warm hair. When I grew weary and would feel like stopping to rest, I just imagined her smile, and I would pedal faster.*

We never stayed at her house. She would meet me out front and then we would venture into town where we would pass the time at the park laying on our bellies on the soft green grass counting the clover, or at the library browsing the stacks and trying to suppress our giggling so as to not invoke the wrath of the librarian. On other days, we would bring our portable CD players along and share music. She introduced me to Nine Inch Nails and I introduced her to Credence Clearwater Revival. She teased me about listening to geriatric melodies but I eventually brought her around. One afternoon, we got caught in an unexpected summer downpour. We grabbed our backpacks and ran to one of the shelters and sat atop of the picnic bench listening to "Have You Ever Seen The Rain?" as we looked out upon a wet and empty world.

It was then that she finally told me that the family she lived wlth was not her real family. She confessed that she was in foster care because her father had done some bad things to her and her mother had let him. She cried as she told he how her old man was in jail and her mother was in counseling and how the court had ordered her to counseling too. As she told me her story, I felt a little piece of me die with each sob that escaped her beautiful mouth. I wanted to hold her and somehow make things right. I hated her parents and I had never met them.

We sat there for a time just listening to the quietness. She rested her head against my shoulder and placed her warm, delicate hand on top of mine. She looked up at me, this little girl who had endured so much and I understood the sadness that I saw in her eyes, even when she smiled. Then, without coming to any particular agreement, on that warm summer day sheltered from the rain, we kissed.

I walked her home that afternoon like I had so many others before. When she got to her doorstep, she hugged me tightly and I buried my face in her hair, wishing to God that I didn't have to let go.

I rode out to see her again the next day, filled with the same exhilaration and new feeling that intensified when I thought about the kiss we shared. My calves burned as I pedaled those nine miles as fast as I could go. When I arrived at her driveway, she was not there waiting for me as she had in the past. I knocked on the door and a middle-aged woman with bottle-bleached hair opened the door. A cigarette dangled delicately from her index and middle finger as she told me that Regina had left the night before. When I asked her where she went, she told me that it weren't none of my business.

Up until that point, I had never felt pain that intense before. I could neither eat nor sleep for three days. My mom worried that I was sick, my dad just got irritated. On the fourth day, I got a letter. She had explained that her mom finished her counseling and took her out of foster care and that they were leaving to go live with relatives somewhere back east where her dad wouldn't find her and could hurt her no more.

We wrote letters back and forth for a few months. Her address kept changing along the way. Eventually, she stopped writing back. The last letter I got from her didn't have no return address on it. Her mama said it was too dangerous for people to know where they was. The post office seal pressed across the postage stamp read: Boston, MA. She told me that she was doing fine and that she missed me. She said that there was this old record store near her apartment where she bought a Credence Clearwater Revival's Greatest Hits CD and listened to "Have You Ever Seen The Rain?" in her room over and over until her mom made her use her headphones. I wrote her back, three more times, but I never heard from her again.

I know that I probably have idealized her and that summer we spent together a bit. But what else would you expect with your first love?

I have dated since. I was even engaged once. None of them ever lasted. The problem wasn't with them, it was with me. The thing is, with every woman I ever held, I was searching for the woman who could resurrect that feeling in me that I knew when I kissed Regina in the rain, that summer when I was twelve years old.

I was starting to lose hope of ever finding her.

Sunday, October 19, 2008

G.H.

It was dusk when Garrett had dropped her off in front of the church. She had insisted that he take her there instead of Casa de Diana for if Juan Carlos saw them together, it would be dangerous for both of them. He told her that he didn't care about his safety, that he could handle Juan Carlos but out of respect for her and to keep her safe, he would honor her request.

She loved him as she had never loved a man before. She knew this from the very night that they spent talking on the red plush couch in Casa de Diana and with each passing moment her love deepened for him. There were times when she thought that she would like to surrender herself to the waves of emotion that washed over her when she was with him and simply let herself drown. She admired his romantic notions. He expressed his love fearlessly as a boy who never had his heart broken. She loved that innocence about him and she wanted to keep him safe, she wanted to protect him and told him that to do so would mandate that she never see him again.

He had told her that he loved her fiercely and would lay down his own life if it meant keeping her safe. He told her that if she loved him as well, she would understand that to never see him again would be an act of cruelty and that she not shut him out even as a means of protecting him.

As they sat on the steps outside the church, he asked her if she loved him and she told him that she loved him to the moon and back, that she loved him more than she loved life. He told her that he was happy to hear that and then shared with her the details of his plan to meet with Juan Carlos and to buy her contract.

She told him that he would never consider selling her contract; that Juan Carlos believed that he owned all of the women who worked for him and only one thing would end their obligation to him—death. Those whomever tried leaving met with his unimaginable cruelty. He told her that he would meet with him. Regardless of whatever else he might be, Juan Carlos was a businessman and a greedy one at that. He would try to negotiate with him and offer him compensation. He told her that if he could not appeal to his business sense, that he would take her anyway and the two of them would run away to Yelapa and take her grandparents to a safe place and they would begin their lives together far away from Tecate.

He cautioned her to not tell anyone about the child. Juan Carlos was far too unpredictable and there was no way to know how he would react. The only way to insure her safety and the safety of the baby was to keep her condition unknown. He then removed a silver chain from around his neck and laid it across her shoulders. He explained to her that it was the image of San Cristóbal, the patron saint of travelers. It had been a gift from his mother and that she had believed that it would keep him safe on his journeys. She told him that she could not take something so precious from him. He told her that she could not give back a gift and that his mother was right about this as she was many things. San Cristóbal had kept him safe through all of his travels, and that now he would keep her safe as well.

She kissed him deeply, made the sign of the cross and watched him climb onto the Indian. She walked quickly down the *calle* in the direction of Casa de Diana looking back several times at him as he revved the idling engine watching her go. She smiled, waved her hand and turned the corner.

She sat at the foot of her bed brushing her long ebony hair with a brown and green turtle shell hairbrush that her father had made for her mother as a wedding gift long ago. It was the only physical reminder that she had of either of them. When she ran the bristles through her hair, she would feel as though her mother and father were in the room with her wrapping her up in their love like a warm blanket.

Since she had come to work at Casa de Diana, she felt ashamed and she had thought of giving the brush away on many occasions, for she could not bear the thought of her mother and father seeing their daughter in such a place. But each time she would brush her hair, she felt as though they were with her and she would imagine them taking her up in their arms in a warm embrace and whispering to her that they loved her no matter what. Until Garrett entered into her life, these quiet moments in her room brushing her hair with her mother's hairbrush was the only time she had felt as though someone could love her.

She heard a series of taps at the door and the blood drained from her face as she recognized the knock. Whenever Juan Carlos desired the attention of any of the women who worked for him, he would come to their room and tap their door in a rapid succession of knocks, seven to be precise. All of the women at Casa de Diana knew his knock and understood what it meant.

Her pulse had quickened and she felt light headed as she tried to catch her breath. She could not bear to lay down with him again. Not after today. A deep, primal fear began to rise within her and she felt as though something inside of her might break when she felt a sudden calm wash over her. It was a serenity that she had not felt since she was a little girl attending her grandparents church in Yelapa. She heard a reassuring voice speak to her from somewhere inside of her head. It was warm and kind and unmistakable. It flooded her mind and it sounded to her what she imagined sunlight would be if it had a voice: He is not worthy of you. I have a greater love in store for you. Do not be afraid.

Her hand trembled as she returned the brush to its resting place on top of her dresser. She ran the palm of her hand down her abdomen and cast her eyes upon the wooden cross that hung on the wall before her and she knew what she must do. Tonight, she would deny him and she would not fear the consequences.

She turned from her dresser and walked to the door and let it swing wide open. He stood before her in the entryway, holding a single red long stemmed rose in his hand. This was the gift that he brought to all of the women that worked for him on such occasions. He smiled broadly at her. He was dressed in a black custom-made suit with a burgundy silk shirt. He smelled faintly of cologne. Juan Carlos was a remarkably handsome man. She considered the irony of how his outward beauty effectively masked the cruelty that dwelled within him.

"Buenas noches, mi cielo," he whispered softly.

"Buenas," she replied as she returned to the dresser and once again took the brush in her hand before sitting down at the end of her bed.

She was wearing a white silk robe that covered her shoulders and was cinched at the waist by a thin belt cut from the same cloth. The hemline fell just above the curve of her knee.

He walked over to her bed holding the rose by the stem and caressed her calf with the soft red bud. "You are a vision." He smiled. "More beautiful than the Virgin that you prayed to at the church today."

"You are very flattering Juan Carlos, but do not say such things. It is blasphemous." She continued to pull the brush through her thick black hair.

He laughed. "I think that God knows what he made when he formed you and if it is possible that the Holy Mother surpassed you in beauty . . . is no wonder that He chose her to be the vessel for his son." He ran his ringed fingers through her hair, pulling it to one side revealing the angular curve of her neck. He leaned in close to her and caressed her skin gently with his lips.

His touch offended her to such an extent that it took every ounce of strength that she could muster to suppress the convulsive reflex that her body demanded of her. She rose from her bed and walked over to the dresser and sat the brush down. Her lips mouthed a silent prayer as she made the sign of the cross. She pleaded with God to provide her with the strength to honor the gift that He had given to her. She prayed that He would soften the heart of Juan Carlos so that he might release her from the shameful servitude that he had forced upon her.

He rose from the bed and placed his hands upon her shoulders, massaging them slightly. "Why do you fight me so much, mi amor? Why do you not surrender your heart to me?"

She was silent for a moment, drew a deep breath and then spoke.

"Juan Carlos, I know that you do not love me."

"That is not true. I love you as I love all of my girls. In fact, you are one of my favorites." He smiled. "Do I not demonstrate this to you with the fine clothing I give to you? Do I not show you my love by providing you with a room with silk sheets and good food? Have I ever left you wanting for anything at all?"

"It is true that you provide me with things that sustain my body, but your notion of love and mine are not the same," she whispered.

"Love is such a romantic notion! Don't tell me that you have fallen prey to this idea? Do you mean to tell me you want to wear white, swear eternal vows to a single man, allow your body to be ravaged by the pangs of childbirth and die an abuelita rocking in a chair on some porch with a husband who will more than likely express his passions on women young enough to be his daughters? Is that what you are seeking that I am not providing you?" A familiar harshness in his voice began to stir.

"You have given me much Juan Carlos, but you have not given me love. The portrait that you painted is not the love that I have been given."

"Ah! My little one thinks that she is in love!" He burst into laughter so loud it sounded like a gunshot and caused her to jump from her perch.

"Ah mija . . . who is he? One of our clients?"

Her head lowered and she spoke not a word.

"He is! Ha! You have given your heart to a man who exercises his vices in a whorehouse? Mija, have you learned nothing of the nature of men while working here? You cannot give your heart to a man who pays you to fuck him. Such a thing is not love, it is commerce!"

"You do not know him. He is not like the other men that come here."

"You do not think so? Who is he then? Ah! I know. He is the gringo, your galán who bought you on your eighteenth birthday, yes?"

"Sí," she whispered.

"Mija . . ." He laughed. "I have come to know many, many American men in my life. And I can tell you as surely as I am standing before you in this room that he does not love you. He pays for your affections. He is a man seeking to live out his passions and you are nothing more than a whore to him. Such men do not fall in love with whores; they fuck them. He may have told you all of the pretty things that you wanted to hear. But at the end of the day, he will not marry you. That I can promise."

"You do not know him." She could feel the tears beginning to well in her eyes and she struggled to hold them at bay.

"These American men lay down with whores and marry virgins, that way, their marriage bed is pure and without reproach. You cannot offer your galán this." He shook his head whispering softly.

"Juan Carlos . . ." Her voice trembled slightly. "I know that you know the minds of most men but this man is different. He loves me and I love him. I cannot offer you evidence of this right now, but I can tell you that he is a gift given to me directly from God. How can I possibly lay down with you or any other man knowing that God has sent to me the one man that I have waited my entire life to love? To do such a thing would be an offense to God and a greater transgression than all of the sins I have committed under this roof combined."

He considered her words for a moment. He walked toward her dresser and stared at the simple wooden cross that hung above it. He stretched out his hand and caressed the Christ figure with his index finger and then turned to face her.

"Do you really believe that God sent this man to you mija?" he asked.

"I do, with all of my being."

"How can you know for certain?" He raised an eyebrow.

"Because he told me so . . . and I think that you know this to be true. He told me that he spoke with your brother Santiago about meeting with you to discuss a business proposition."

"He wishes to buy you from me, mija?" He smiled.

"He wishes to honor you as the Cacique by offering to compensate you for any losses that you might incur due to my departure."

"A man will say all kinds of things, mija. Him telling you these things is not evidence that he is your gift from God. It could be quite the opposite."

"I know that he is meant for me. God spoke to me and told me so. I have been praying to him, pleading with Him to help me to understand His plan for me . . . to help me understand how He loves me . . . and He finally answered."

"And you think that your galán is the answer that God gave to you?"

"Yes," she whispered.

"And for that, you refuse me and you tell me that you no longer wish to work here?"

"I do not wish to offend you Juan Carlos . . . for you have taken care of me. You have fed and clothed me and provided me with a place to live, but I would rather die than to give myself to another man and to sin against God."

She noticed that the vein on his forehead slightly in front of his left temple began to pulse. The muscles in his jaw clenched tightly as he looked at her. His gaze made her feel uncomfortable and she felt something inside of her begin to tremble. He did not appear to be looking at her directly, but at something that resembled her seated in some deep nether region of her soul. His face seemed almost childlike in the expressionless way that he looked at her, as though he were not a man at all, but a boy lost in a daydream. She had never seen him this way before. She tried to comprehend his silence. She examined and catalogued every blink and facial gesture no matter how slight in hopes that it might reveal something that would make known his thoughts, but she could anticipate nothing.

After a long moment he spoke.

"Mi cielo . . . I love you . . . and perhaps one day, you will understand how much. I think that you are making a terrible mistake with this galán of yours. But if you believe that he is a gift from God, who am I to argue? Besides, death seems like such an extreme option to laying down with me. I could not in good conscience ask you to do something that would elicit that kind of response. I would much rather you decide to give yourself to me on your own free will."

"Then you understand me?" she asked.

"Oh, I could never presume to understand the complex mind of a woman mija." He smiled. "But if you are telling me that you are in love with your galán, I will not stand in the way of your happiness. If he comes to me, and makes to me the offer that you tell me that he intends to make . . . I will honor his request and send you both into the world with my blessing."

"He will come, Juan Carlos," she replied with boldness in her voice that he was unaccustomed to hearing.

"I am certain that he will. I tell you what . . . Friday evening, I am going to throw a fiesta for you to celebrate this newfound happiness you have found. I will close down Casa de Diana for the day. I will give everyone the day off so that we can all rejoice with you." He smiled.

"That is very generous, Juan Carlos . . . but it is not necessary."

"Oh, but it is mija. I insist upon it."

He handed her the long stem rose and she hesitated to take it. He once again boomed with laughter. "Oh, mija! Please take the rose, it is my gift to you. I do not expect anything from you in return."

She took the rose in her hand.

He took her face and held it between his hands. After staring into her eyes for a long moment, he kissed the top of her head and walked out of the room. She could hear his footsteps fade down the hallway.

When he got out of the shower, Garrett still had soap on his neck. He always thought that taking a shower in an Airstream trailer is not the easiest of tasks. You are crammed naked into a space roughly the size of a phone booth and the tank on the hot water heater provides warm water just long enough to get you wet. He quickly rubbed the towel over his head and then wiped the steam from the mirror and examined his reflection. He frowned at the damp hair that hung slightly over his ears. He thought about her and reached into the drawer beneath the sink and withdrew a pair of scissors.

He emerged from the tiny bathroom with his brown hair trimmed neatly above his ears, wearing a crisp new shirt which still bore the creases from being folded in its packaging. The coffee maker sat resting on the narrow counter and sputtered the remaining drops of its steaming brown liquid into the pot. He took a cup from the sink and filled it.

Garrett spent the rest of the morning on his laptop computer attempting to decipher the mysteries of eBay. He had borrowed Brophy's digital camera and had taken several pictures of his newly restored Indian Chief. He had Googled the cost of Indian Motorcycles from that era, and cross-referenced his searches with estimates from a Kelly's Blue Book. He determined that his was worth twenty to twenty-five thousand dollars to serious collectors. He had worked tenaciously over the last several months to restore it and it was now in show room condition. He reasoned that he would have no trouble fetching that dollar amount.

He finally succeeded in opening an account and uploading the pictures of the bike. He set the minimum bid for twenty thousand dollars, and figured now all he had to do was sit back and wait.

Garrett began to shut down his computer when he heard a knock at his trailer door. He peered out the window. It was Brophy.

"You ain't using my camera to take any unseemly pictures of your ugly ass are you?" Brophy shouted.

Garrett opened the door.

"I don't want to be an unwilling participant in your demented amateur porn fetish," Brophy said as he stepped inside.

"You never know." Garrett smiled. "I might make it to the big time, and if I do, I will have you and your little camera to thank for it."

"I figured the whole eBay thing was a cover anyway. So, you can be honest with me," Brophy whispered with a grin. "You are making your debut into gay porn, ain't you?"

"Of course, that is where the money is." Garrett smiled. "If you think that a movie about gay cowboys in the mountains was such a box office smash, wait til they get a piece of gay Border Patrol Agents in the desert. All I have to do is just sit back and wait for the Oscar nominations."

"I wasn't aware that they even had a gay porn category in the Oscars," Brophy said.

"They might not. I think I may be breaking new ground here." Garrett grinned. "You want any coffee?"

"I'll take some."

"You take anything with that?"

"Why would I ruin coffee by adding anything to it?" Brophy asked. "Just so long as it is hot, black and strong—like my women."

"With lines like that Brophy, just why in the hell hasn't some woman swooned over you and hauled your sorry ass off to the altar yet?" Garrett asked as he poured the coffee.

"Oh they have tried, but this ol' cowboy is just plain selective." Brophy grinned.

"Oh yeah, that's the reason you're still single all right." Garrett smiled as he filled the empty cup.

"Thanks buddy. Hey, did I ever tell you the story about the cowboy and the Muslim?"

"I can't say that I remember it," Garrett said as he returned the pot to the stovetop.

Brophy stretched out his legs extending them from beneath the small table, crossing one boot over the other.

"Well, it seems that there was this cowboy, this Indian and this raghead sitting in an airport waiting to catch their planes to their respective destinations. The Indian was on his way to a statewide Indian Pow-Wow. The cowboy was on his way to sell some cattle at a stock show and the raghead, well he was some fundamentalist Arab student on his way to study engineering at college.

Their flights were delayed due to poor weather, and well, before long, they began talking to each other.

The Indian looked a little somber and said that he was looking forward to getting back to the reservation, but lamented how his people were fading away like the stars in the morning light.

"Once, my people populated this land and were many like the stars in the night sky, but now, we are fenced in on these small reservations and my people are now few."

Then the ol' raghead spoke up. He was pretty much full of himself too and he started boasting about the accomplishments of his people.

"Once, my people were few, and we were relegated to the deserts of North Africa and the Middle East. But Allah is great, and as his word spread, so did my people, and now we are many. Muslims populate every corner of the world. Islam is growing faster than your Christianity! Now, the numbers of my people are great! What do you have to say about that?" He chided pointing to the cowboy.

The cowboy was leaning back in his chair with his hat pulled down low over his eyes. When he heard the question, he lifted his hat just a bit so his eye could fix itself on the old raghead and he replied in a slow, Texas drawl—

"That's only cause we ain't played cowboys and Muslims yet . . . but maybe we're about due."

"Ha!" Brophy laughed. "Hot damn! That one cracks me up every time I tell it!"

"Yeah." Garrett smiled. "To think that the government is spending all this money on homeland security to make us safer. And all we need really need to do is cowboy up and dish out a little ass kicking, John Wayne style!"

"Yeah, you got that right brother. Hot damn!"

"Between you and me though," Garrett whispered. "You probably ought not take your little comedy act of yours on the road, cause you just ain't that funny."

"Oh, I am sorry, I forgot that you are half Cuban and you don't really have a sense of humor to speak of. So I reckon I am wasting my talent. Say, you never explained to me exactly why you are selling the Indian," Brophy said sipping at the coffee cup."

"Well, I need the money," Garrett replied.

"What in the hell for? I mean, you ain't exactly living the lifestyle of the rich an famous here. What kind of expenses have you got?" Brophy asked.

"I have some things I need to see through is all," Garrett replied. Brophy leaned in across the table and squinted his eyes. "Something is different about you. Are you wearing a new shirt?"

"I have some business at the bank today, I hear that they have a strict policy regarding topless customers."

"It's nice. The green brings out the color in your eyes."

"You asking me out?" Garrett grinned.

"I'm serious here bud. Something ain't right with you. You're . . . happy."

"Careful now Brophy, you don't want to go saying something that you can't take back."

He reached across the table and carefully removed freshly cut strands of damp light brown hair from Garrett's collar pinched between his forefinger and thumb.

"You went and cut your hair too, didn't you?"

"I don't see what you're getting at. You want more coffee?"

"Don't change the subject. You're selling your bike, you're wearing a new shirt, you cut your hair and have this goddamn zippity do dah change in attitude. . . . Oh, goddamn. It ain't a woman is it?"

"What makes you think that?"

"Oh, Christ! There are only three reasons a man would sell his cruiser or convertible. Either he is dying, or he owes the mob and will die if he doesn't pay up . . . or a woman is making him. Oh man. Irma was right, wasn't she? You are in love!" Brophy barked.

"I haven't seen you much outside of work lately either. Who the hell is she Garrett?'

"All right. If I tell you, you ain't going to go all Oprah or Dr. Phil on me, are you? Cause I don't need talked out of this," Garrett replied.

"I think I'll reserve judgment. Now tell me you sly ol' son of a bitch!" Brophy grinned.

Garrett told him about Angelina. He told him about her connections with El Cacique. He told him about what the tamale woman had said. He explained to him that he was in love with her and was selling the Indian so that he could buy her out of her contract and bring her back with him across the border. Brophy listened intently and did not speak for a long time.

He sat looking at his cup, then looked sternly at Garrett.

"Just what in the hell is wrong with you that you go off falling in love with prostitutes?" Brophy shouted.

"She ain't like that," Garrett hollered back.

"Jesus tap dancing Christ! Garrett they are all like that! That's why they're whores. You are supposed to lay 'em, you ain't supposed to fall in love with them!"

"I don't need no commentary from you," Garrett growled.

"Mary and the Shepherds. Goddamn! I blame myself. This is my own goddamn stupid fault. I should have never brought you to that whorehouse in the first place. I should've known that you was soft in the head. I think that all of this time in the desert sun has baked your brain."

"It ain't your fault. This is my decision."

"Just how much do you think it will cost to buy a woman? I mean what? Is it like buying a car? A boat? What?" Brophy yelled.

"I ain't buying her; I am going to buy her contract," Garrett snapped back.

"You think that you will walk in and pay for her like you would a set of tires at the Wal-Mart and she will be free to walk out—just like that?" Brophy asked.

"I don't suspect it will be like that at all," Garrett replied.

"Do you really think that this pimp is going to sell her contract to you?"

"Do I look like a goddamn gypsy fortune teller? I don't know what will happen until it happens," Garrett shot back.

"What if he don't? What you offer him the money and he tells you to kiss his greaser, pussy pedaling ass?"

"Then I'll take her."

"You will? Just like that."

"Yes, I will. Just like that."

"Look. I am going to say this loud and slow so that it is easy for you to understand. You are a Border Patrol Agent. You are an officer of the United States government. She is a Mexican prostitute. Even if this bastard El Cacique takes you up on your offer, as soon as you get her across the border, she is an illegal. If you help her or house her, you are an accomplice. Do you realize the deep shit you are about to go wading into?" Brophy pressed.

"I am already in it," Garrett replied. "Angelina's pregnant."

"Oh damn, bud," Brophy muttered shaking his head. "What makes you think it's yours?"

"It don't matter if it's mine or not. I love her."

"You know what people are gonna say. They're gonna say she is throwing one of them anchor babies and that you have lost your fool mind!" Brophy shouted.

"I don't care what anybody says."

"Sure you don't. You are going to get your ass fired . . . or worse."

"I know it," Garrett whispered. "I can't help it."

"Horseshit!" Brophy shot back.

"I guess that I just ain't cut out to be a Border Patrol Agent." Garrett shook his head.

"It don't make no difference whether you think you are cut out for it or not. This is the job that you applied for. This is the job that you were hired to do. So long as you wear the uniform and that badge, you are sworn to duty!" Brophy shouted across the table.

"I know it." Garrett swallowed hard. "But my obligations have shifted."

"You can't just go about making compromises with law and order. The law has got to be kept. Now you have got to stop for a moment and think about this carefully bud. You are standing at the point of no return here. What you do now is going to determine the rest of your life."

"I understand what you are saying. I might have even agreed with you before Angelina, but I see things a little differently now." Garrett rotated his wrist and watched the coffee swirl in his mug.

"What I think is that you ain't seeing things clearly at all. All of the goddamned blood has rushed from your head to your penis and you can't think straight on account of the fact that your brain is all oxygen starved. I am beggin' you here . . . don't fuck up your career bud. Not over a piece of ass."

"You know Brophy, I have always considered you my good friend. If you could quit trying to be right for just a goddamn minute, you might consider being my friend too."

"Yeah, well, I am your friend . . . and I am telling you that you are being mule headed and ignorant!" Brophy slammed his coffee mug on the tabletop, causing the remnants from the cup to spill over onto the table and drip onto linoleum floor.

"I am telling you, you need to think about this long and hard bud. I will say no more about it." Brophy rose from the table, walked out of the trailer and slammed the door behind him.

It took less than three days for Garrett to receive the high bid of twenty-three thousand dollars from a collector in San Francisco. He was a software engineer who happened to be visiting friends in San Diego. He drove out to Potrero to inspect the bike and gave Garrett a Bank Check for the full amount. The software engineer loaded the bike onto the back of a rented trailer, strapped it in and drove away. Garrett felt a slight heaviness in his heart and wondered what his father would think.

When Garrett walked into Valley Independent Bank in Tecate, California he told the teller that he was going to be cashing a check and closing out his savings account. She had asked him if he had been dissatisfied with his service. He explained that the service had been just fine, he was just in need of the money. She asked him if he would be interested in talking to a representative about a signature loan or a mortgage. He told her that he wouldn't.

She asked him if he would like to leave the two hundred dollar minimum in his account so that he could keep it open. He again explained to the girl that he would be needing all of his money and he would have to close out his account.

"You have two thousand dollars in savings, Mr. Harrison." The teller smiled. "How would you like that?"

"I'll take it in hundreds," he replied.

She offered him a withdrawal slip and some other papers to sign, indicating that he was closing his account.

"Would you be interested in taking a few minutes to complete one of our exit surveys?" she asked.

"What?"

"An exit survey," the teller repeated.

"What I would really be interested in is getting my money," Garrett replied.

"The exit survey is really important Sir, it helps us identify areas for improvement so that we may provide better customer service." The teller smiled.

"Oh, the customer service was great. Don't worry, I will be sure and tell all of my friends. Now can I please have my money?" Garrett groaned. "I have an appointment to keep."

The teller counted out twenty new one hundred dollar bills and slid them through the door in the window.

"Is there anything else I can do for you today?" she asked impatiently.

"Yes, as matter of fact." He signed the back of the bank check and passed it over to the teller.

When she saw the amount on the bank check, she told him that she would have to refer him to the manager. He said that would be fine.

The manager was a tall narrow faced man with thinning hair. He examined the bank check and Garrett's driver's license.

"Twenty three thousand dollars is a lot of money," he remarked.

"Are you sure you want to take out such a large sum in cash? We can wire it someplace if you would like," the banker suggested.

"That's all right," Garrett responded. "I will take the full amount, in large denominations please."

"Of course, Mr. Harrison. Can I offer you any coffee in the meantime?"

"No, I'm all right."

"Very well, if you will have a seat over at that desk, I will be with you shortly." He pointed to a desk in the rear of the building.

Garrett sat and waited.

The banker returned with a teller and the bank security guard. Here you go, Mr. Harrison. He sat a canvas bag on the desk that was full of neatly stacked, banded bills in one-hundred, fifty and twenty dollar denominations.

"Would you care to go into the vault so that you can count it?" the banker asked.

"Do I have any reason to think that you shorted me?" Garrett lifted his eyebrow.

"No, not at all Sir it is just that—" the banker stammered.

"That's okay. You all look to me like stand-up people. I'll take you at your word." He placed the canvass bag into his backpack and headed out the door.

PART 3

11

*I*n the America that my father grew up in, a man knew his own mind. The icons of manhood back then, from Gene Autry to John Wayne to my own red-blooded father, weren't ever confused. Right and wrong was clearly demarcated and it was easy to tell the good guys from the bad guys. The good guys always did right by those around them and weren't never afraid or at least they didn't let fear get in the way of doing what needed to get done. In fact, back then it was the patriotic duty of every American to be brave.

My old man was a preacher and he was fond of using quotes from famous people in his sermons. One of his favorites was from Franklin D. Roosevelt's first inaugural address: "the only thing we have to fear is fear itself." Here was a man with a broken body, called forward to lead the country out of a great economic depression. He reminded Americans that the nation's difficulties concerned only material things. He reassured everyone that the country would not only endure, but would prosper. He spoke with conviction and the country believed him. This was the kind of fearless certainty that in my mind was the very epitome of manhood.

Nowadays, things seem a lot less certain. The line between right and wrong is blurred, our heroes regularly check in and out of rehab, our leaders get prison sentences for a whole laundry list of wrong doings and our Presidents' don't call on us to be brave anymore. In fact, it seems that it has become our patriotic duty to be fearful. Hell, we even color code our fears and broadcast them from sea to shining sea. Ever since September 11th, we can't even celebrate holidays or go to sporting events without being reminded that some bad guy is out there, lurking in the shadows and if we ain't careful, he'll get us. Our leaders warn us to be watchful of suspicious individuals and advise us to protect our families by keeping on hand plenty of duct tape and plastic sheeting.

I don't think this happened all of a sudden. There are some things that you can't peg on terrorists. Some things we done to ourselves.

I remember a few years back, you couldn't turn on the radio without hearing this woman mournfully sing out the question, "Where have all the cowboys gone?" She sang about how she wanted her John Wayne and her happy ending. I didn't think much about it then, but I think she sang about John Wayne on account of him being a man's man. He was the good guy. He respected women. He was tough. And he knew what the hell he was doing.

I look around now and I have to wonder what in the hell is happening to the American man? I read somewhere that by the time boys get into high school that they are behind girls in reading and writing. This same article went on to say that boys are more likely than girls to drop out of school or get expelled. Boys are ten times as likely to get diagnosed with some kind of hyperactivity disorder and put on behavior modifying medication. Girls outnumber boys in college classes too. I think that might be right. I remember sitting at my high school graduation, waiting to get my diploma and they was giving out awards for academic excellence to twenty-five graduating seniors. The awards included a little money to help with college expenses such as books and what not. Twenty of them awards went to girls. If that ain't enough proof that our young men are losing their way. The writer went on to list other statistics as well. Nearly ninety five percent of all prison inmates are men, more than two-thirds of the drug addicts and alcoholics are men and every nine seconds a man somewhere in America commits a violent act against a woman.

Why are men deteriorating? I think partly because boys have lost their role models. There are more and more single mothers trying to play both roles and it just don't work. I don't mean to disrespect the moms out there who are going it alone, but it takes two parents to raise a boy. It takes a mother to civilize us, but it takes a father to teach us how to be a man. I believe that too. The writer of that article pointed out that boys raised in homes without a father are more likely to have behavioral problems, more likely to drop out of school and more likely to join gangs. So when I look around at the disintegration of the American male, I don't blame the schools or the media or the movies or the video games or music. I blame the fathers who are ducking their responsibilities and giving up their boys to the abyss. As the saying goes, a woman is—but a man must become. I worry that there aren't enough fathers out there showing boys how to become men and if that trend goes on long enough, we're gonna have us some serious problems. Hell, we have serious problems now. Sometimes I think that the only thing stopping the whole country from disintegrating into total anarchy ain't design, it's habit.

I used to love watching the old westerns on television and I would go to sleep dreaming about what it would've been like if I was born a hundred years ago. That's why it killed me when my old man wouldn't allow me to play cowboys and Indians, or cops and robbers or anything that involved a gun. My dad was a pacifist. A preacher who advocated something he called liberation theology and he rejected the whole myth of the American cowboy. And he didn't care much for the police neither. He would tell me that the West wasn't won by noble hearted cowboys with a code, it was stolen at gunpoint and John Wayne and Jesus sure as Hell weren't the same people. This didn't mean a whole lot to me when I was eight and all of the other kids were running around firing off their cap guns defending the Alamo or chasing down bank robbers or whatever it was that kids did and I was stuck inside reciting scripture.

In spite of this, I somehow still held onto the notion that cowboys somehow had it all figured out, and that certainty and courage were the hallmarks of a man. When John Wayne decided to make a stand against Santa Anna at the Alamo and drew that line in the sand, he never backed down from it. Even though the odds was plainly stacked against him. And when my dad made up his mind about something, the Almighty Himself would be hard pressed to change it. My mom said that he was the most strong headed man she ever met. The amazing thing about it was that my dad was *usually right about most things, even though I never would admit it to him. My dad was John Wayne with a bible and when he spoke, he was unwavering in his conviction and people paid attention to what he had to say. Some might not have agreed with him either, but they respected his conviction. So by the time I set out in search of my own fortune and fate, I had pretty much sold myself on the notion that a man is knighted by his fearlessness and christened by his certainty.*

Looking back, I know that at eighteen I didn't know much. Except that I had graduated from high school, I had no immediate plans for my future, and my little slice of small town America wasn't the world. So I was itching to see what else was out there. I didn't have the brains to go away to college, and I was pretty sure that even if I did, that it wouldn't do nothing for me anyhow. I saw some of the guys who went away to college when they come back home, they was nothing more 'n a slightly older version of what they was before they left. But, when I saw the guys who joined the military come back . . . they was different. There was an edge to them, a certainty that proclaimed to the world that they met the test and passed.

Then one day in early July, I sat down with a Navy recruiter. I took a few tests. He took me out to lunch. He told me that I could earn money for college. I told him that I wasn't the college going type. He told me that I could learn a trade. I reminded him that I just turned 18 and that I wasn't too hot on trying to figure out what my life long career was going to be right at the moment. Then he told me that I would see the world and I believed him.

Friday, October 24, 2008
G.H.

It was late in the afternoon when the summer skies over Tecate had given up some much needed rain in an all too brief shower that served only to bring about a hot and sticky humidity to the residents rather than offer them any comfort from the heat. The tamale woman was tugging at the weather beaten canvass parasol fastened to her cart in an effort to close it when the white washed roll-away door steel slid open and three well-dressed men stepped out into the open air of alleyway. They approached the black Mercedes E63 that had been splattered by the shower.

"I am not going North in that car looking like that. Pelón, make this car look presentable," the taller man commanded.

A short, stocky bald headed man went back inside the building.

"Juan, do we have time for this? We have a meeting with the Reverend," the third man pleaded.

"Santiago, my brother. The first rule of business is, presentation is everything. We are not going to a business meeting driving a dirty car. The good Reverend will wait for us, because we are bringing him money, and a little gift. Besides . . ." He jutted his chin in the direction of the old woman. "I am hungry. Come, I will buy you some tamales."

The bald man emerged from the building carrying a bucket followed by a skinny boy wearing jeans and a t-shirt carrying a hose.

"Quieres tamales Pelon?" Juan Carlos shouted.

"Sí, gracias," the man replied.

The boy stretched out the hose and connected it to a spigot and began to fill the bucket as the man poured in some blue colored liquid soap.

The two men approached the tamale woman. She disregarded them at first as she was still struggling to close her parasol. The two men stood silently watching as her wrinkled, gnarled hands worked to close the umbrella and wrap a long yellow piece of twine around it, securing it closed. When she was finished, she turned and folded her chair.

"I am sorry. I am closed," she said without looking at the two men.

"I am sure that you have earned a rest at the end of such a long day abuelita, but surely you would not deny two hardworking men something eat?" Juan Carlos smiled.

"I do not believe that I am your abuelita nor do I believe that you are all that hard working." She lifted the collapsible stool and hung it on the two wooden pegs protruding from her wagon. Her heart began to beat faster, causing her to pause and take several deep breaths.

"Ha! So you choose to insult me? A man you know nothing about?" Juan Carlos laughed.

"I know who you are. You are known and feared by many as El Cacique," she replied. She felt strange. A burning sensation appeared just below the left side of her breastbone and grew with intensity.

Juan Carlos leaned in close to the tiny old woman, so that their two faces were close enough to feel each other's breath. "Since you know my reputation old woman, then perhaps you should be a little more agreeable."

She could feel her throat begin to ache, but she spoke firmly, forcing the words out.

"I know your reputation . . . but I have no fear of you. Others call you El Cacique, a title reserved for tribal chieftains, but you are no chieftain. You are an unfortunate son, a man without God."

"You presume to know my soul, old woman? By what authority do you profess to know so much?" Juan Carlos snarled back.

Santiago placed his hand on his shoulder. "Come on Juan, let's just go. She is a crazy old woman."

The tamale woman looked at Santiago with her milky white eyes and for an instant, he felt a shudder run through him.

"Your brother is leading you down the path to perdition. You must make a choice now, or you will suffer the same fate that is destined for him." Her voice grew weaker. She was finding it increasingly difficult to catch her breath.

Juan Carlos burst into laughter that echoed through the alley.

After his laughter subsided, he wiped a tear from his eye. "So, not only do you sell tamales. You know the future as well? Perhaps I should talk to you before I bet at the derby de gallos, eh?"

"You may joke if you like. But you are a wicked, arrogant man, and you have profited greatly from your wretched deeds. But very soon you will pay a far greater price than anything that you have gained. God does not turn his head forever, and you have already given your soul to the devil, so he only waits to collect what is his." The pain in her chest would not subside and began to spread out and consume her left shoulder.

"Old woman, I will tell you now. There is no God and the devil is just a ghost story told to frighten small children."

"You just add blasphemy to your list of sins," she gasped.

"That is fine with me. For there will be no one to account for them when I do die, of that, I am certain." He smiled.

"Poor, poor, son of the godless . . . do you deny the existence of the wind, or the sun or the moon as well?" The color from her face drained away, leaving her cheeks an ashen complexion and her lips turned a tone of blue and gray.

"I know there is no God because the very existence of him offends me. The thought that there could be an omnipotent creature that would create man in his own image and then attempt to keep him in ignorance. Trying to keep him from knowing good from evil only to punish him with death for the sin seeking out understanding I find detestable. If anything, the Devil is the hero in this fable. He was one that liberated man from this twisted tyrant that you pray to."

"Say what you will, but your time is up. Payment for your wickedness has now come due. You will not live past the coming Sabbath and your name will no longer be spoken in trembling hushed whispers, it will be forgotten." She shivered slightly.

"I will take three tamales, por favor." He smiled, seemingly disregarding the tamale woman's last statement.

"Come on Juan, this old woman is giving me a bad feeling. Let's just go," Santiago pleaded.

She turned her clouded eyes once again in the direction of Santiago.

"Your brother will die, there is no helping that . . . but unless you choose to depart from this path, you will bear witness to his death and the authorities will claim you and hold you accountable for everything." She waved her hand in a slow, rigid motion.

"Tres tamales por favor," Juan Carlos spoke through gritted teeth.

"I told you, I have nothing I will sell you," she wheezed.

Juan Carlos ran his manicured fingers through the woman's white stiff hair and pulled her face close to his and said, "Hear me old woman. If there is a God or a Devil in this life, I am both of them at once and you should be wary of offending me." He smiled and then pressed his lips against her wrinkled toothless mouth. When he pulled away, she stumbled backwards against the cart and slowly slid down until she sat upon the pavement.

Juan Carlos reached into her cart and served up six tamales, placing them carefully inside individual plastic grocery bags. He reached into his pocket and pulled out a wad of pesos bound together with a money clip. He took out one hundred pesos and tossed the bill at her feet.

"You may keep the change abuelita." He smiled, then placed his hand on his brother's shoulder and steered him back down the alley toward the newly cleaned car.

Angelina sat kneeling on the floor with her head bowed clutching the silver medallion that Garrett had given her. The pendant bore the image of a man carrying a child across the river with the words:
San Cristóbal, nos protege.

She had been crying for some time and her eyelids felt swollen and burned slightly. The light in the room diffused strangely through her tear-laden eyes, creating a shimmering halo of light from the window. She closed her eyes tightly, forcing the last remaining tears from her eyes, sending them racing down her brown cheeks like luminous runners in a race. With eyes closed, she began to pray.

"Blessed Saint Christopher, you have been given such a beautiful name: Christ bearer. It is said that you safely carried the Christ Child across a raging river. It is also said that you watch over travelers on their journeys. I pray that you watch over my love, my unborn child and me. Help us to safety, protect us not only on our exodus from this place, but teach us to be true Christ bearers in this world. Amen."

The knock on the door startled her from her prayer. She carefully placed the medallion on her dresser next to the framed picture of the Virgin, her locket and her sacred tortoise shell hairbrush. Then, with deliberate caution, approached the door.

She placed her hand on the latch and drew a deep breath. She was relieved and at the same time alarmed when she saw the familiar face of the Dueña. She never visited any of the girls unless there was a problem.

"May I come in?" she asked flatly.

"Por supuesto . . . come in." Angelina opened the door wide.

The Dueña entered the room with the elegance of a woman raised in sophistication. She glided around the perimeter of the room before asking if she could take a seat. Angelina told her that she could. The Dueña sat at the edge of her bed and was silent for a long moment.

"I have come to appeal to your better judgment," she said finally.

"I mean no disrespect to you, but I think that you have come to ask me to submit to him," Angelina replied.

"You do not understand. Juan Carlos is not accustomed to being refused . . . by anyone." The Dueña rose to her feet and walked to the dresser and adjusted the hand mirror that rested atop.

"I know. But I can no longer give myself to him. He knows this."

"Why? Because you think that some American boy has fallen in love with you, and will take you away from all of this?" she snapped coldly.

She was quiet for a moment. She closed her eyes and took a deep breath before responding to the Dueña, as though she were trying to recite from memory her lines.

"Ever since I came to this place, I have prayed everyday and every night to God and I asked him to let me feel His love. I prayed that He would not forsake me, and that he would deliver me from this place. He answered my prayers in more ways than I could have expected. He gave to me a man who loves me and for me to love in return."

"Do you believe that this man loves you? You are putting a lot of faith in the words of a boy from the North . . . and you are putting everything on the line."

"I know he loves me. I am sure of it. Just as I am sure that the sun will rise in the morning. Haven't you loved a man? If ever you did, you would understand the certainty that I feel and you would not call into question my judgment." Angelina's throat tightened.

"It is easy to fall in love when you are young mija. You are naively optimistic about the world; everything is beautiful and full of promise because time and experience has not yet cured you of such starry-eyed sentiments. It takes courage to fall in love when you are older." The Dueña picked up the Medallion of Saint Christopher from the top of the drawer.

"The patron saint of travelers . . . are you planning a trip?" The Dueña asked smiling.

"I am going to leave this place," she replied.

"If you continue on as you are doing, I do not doubt that is true, but you might not be leaving in the romantic fashion that you imagine," the Dueña stated.

"What do you mean?" Angelina asked.

"I mean that El Cacique has no intention of letting you go. He has invested too much in you. Do you think that the clothes and the perfume and the makeup and jewelry that you wear come cheap? The satin sheets that you sleep in . . . do you think that they just fall out of the sky?"

"Juan Carlos lied to me. He professed to love me, he presented himself to my grandparents and me as a businessman. He was a lie. Now he tries to imprison me here. I do not care that he gives me fine things. A cage adorned with pretty things is still a cage!" she shouted at the Dueña and surprised herself with the strength in her voice.

"Besides," she continued. "Garret wishes to speak with Juan Carlos. He wants to compensate him for . . ."

"Ah! I see, the American wants to buy his whore! Is that it?" The Dueña shot back.

Angelina lowered her head. The Dueña placed her hand beneath her chin and lifted Angelina's face and her voice softened.

"It is possible that this man loves you, and will do the things that he has promised you, but I am telling you that Juan Carlos is not the kind of man who takes refusals lightly."

"When I told him that I could not give myself to him or to any other man, he said that he understood. He gave me his blessing," Angelina protested.

"You have been here long enough to know Juan Carlos and you know in your heart that he has no intention of letting you go. I can tell you for certain that history indicates that. No woman has ever left Juan Carlos, and lived to go on to better things," the Dueña spoke solemnly.

"What should I do?" Angelina asked.

"I think you know what to do."

"I cannot lay down with him." Tears began to well in her eyes again.

"Then there is nothing more that I can tell you. You will face the consequences . . . and so will your man." The Dueña tossed the Medallion of San Cristóbal on the bed, where it bounced once and came to rest face down on the crushed velvet comforter.

The black Mercedes pulled up to a chain link fence guarded by two large men wearing western hats. One held a shotgun draped across his folded arms while the other approached the car.

Pelón rolled down the tinted window.

"Buenas," Juan Carlos said grinning.

"¡Buenas, El Cacique!" the cowboy hat wearing man replied eagerly. "The Padre just arrived."

"Ah! How nice. I hope you have treated him hospitably."

"Of course, El Cacique. He is comfortable and just waits for you."

"Very well."

The man walked back to the entrance and rolled the gate open allowing the car to drive through. The car came to a stop outside of a warehouse composed of gray sheet metal siding. Outside sat a motorhome that had the flooring panels removed and were leaning against the outside of the gray building while several men busily moved about the vehicle. The driver remained inside the vehicle while Santiago and Juan Carlos left and approached the building.

The inside of the warehouse resembled a strange sort of sweatshop. There were no clothing or shoes or purses being manufactured here. This was an assembly line of another sort. There were two sets of several long tables that filled the first half of the building with about ten men wearing surgical masks and gloves who were carefully placing white powder into tinfoil packets and then placed the full packets onto trays where they were passed down to another group who carefully placed them inside rubber balloons where they carefully squeezed out any air bubbles and tied them tight. These balloons were passed on down to the next row of tables where thirty men and women sat nervously awaiting instructions.

A middle aged, gentle looking man walked up to each individual and asked them their names and wrote them down on a pad and then took a small camera from his pocket and took their picture. When he finished with his inventory, six men carrying trays laden with the oval shaped balloons sat down across from six of the thirty-seated people. After providing them with a brief set of instructions, they began placing the balloons to their lips and swallowed them, one at a time. The tray bearers kept close count of how many balloons each individual consumed. When they were satisfied that they could swallow no more, they moved to the next seated person and began the process again.

Juan Carlos and Santiago walked through the office door with the large plate glass window that overlooked the entire operation. Sitting at one of the chairs was a pale, well dressed man who rose to his feet at the sound of their entrance.

"Ah! Padre!" How good of you to come! I am sorry that we are late." Juan Carlos embraced the man.

"El Cacique, it is good to see you but I have to admit, I was getting nervous!"

"Please, Father, call me Juan Carlos." He smiled.

"Of course, I was just being a respectful business partner . . . Juan Carlos." The reverend smiled.

"Nonsense Father, we are more than business partners, we are friends! Am I right Santiago?" Juan Carlos prompted his brother.

"Of course, Juan Carlos," he replied.

"Now were you able to process the gift I gave you?" Juan Carlos asked.

"Two hundred thousand dollars is hard to hide—but everything has been taken care of. The funds have been transferred into the accounts that hold our charitable contributions and I have made the arrangements with the Grace Christian Academy for your company to start the construction on the new school library. We will pay you for your good works, the money is clean and the children get a much-needed library. Everybody wins!" The reverend smiled.

"Yes indeed! Everybody does win!" Juan Carlos removed a large manila envelope from his coat pocket and handed it to the reverend. "Including you Father. Consider this my tithe."

"Thank you Juan Carlos, and God bless you." The reverend replied as he slipped the package into his coat.

"Now onto business, Father. There has been a slight change in plans. I know that you are used to . . . ah . . . processing smaller groups. But demands require that I send more your way."

The Father looked out the plate glass window. "Is this the next group that you are sending?" he asked.

"Yes. The drivers should be here any moment. An old white couple from San Diego are going to drive the RV across the border with their five year old grandson. You can't get any less suspicious than that!" Juan Carlos laughed.

"I don't mean any disrespect Juan Carlos, I want to be helpful to you . . . but I am used to dealing with . . . um . . . the women you send. I am not comfortable dealing with men. They can cause trouble and such a large group is bound to raise suspicion. What if INS starts poking around?" the Reverend stammered.

"I can assure you that none of them will cause you trouble. You just need to give them a place to stay until the cargo they are carrying passes through and my men can come by and collect."

"That cargo . . . is it what I think it is?" he asked nervously.

"It is best that you do not think about it at all Father. Just accept my generosity and do not offend me," Juan Carlos said through gritted teeth.

The reverend could sense the irritability in Juan Carlos' voice and he knew that such a thing was dangerous.

"Of course, you have always been generous Juan Carlos. I would not dream of offending you." He smiled weakly.

Juan Carlos' posture softened slightly. "Of course not my friend. I realized that handling such a large delivery could be somewhat intimidating. That is why my brother and I are going to pay you double what you normally receive, along with a special bonus, just to show you how much we value this partnership. Santiago, go fetch our little Aztec flower."

Santiago walked to the back of the office and opened the closed door. "It is okay little one, come out."

Slowly, a wide-eyed brown skinned little girl emerged from the dark. Her brown hair was tied back with a blue ribbon in a ponytail that spilled down her back. She wore a yellow blouse and a blue skirt that was slightly too big for her stature causing her narrow almond colored legs to appear more stick-like.

"This is Xotchil. The poor girl is an orphan. No family and no home. She will work for me in the reeds, but I think that she will need some training. I thought that you might help her with that Father." Juan Carlos smiled.

The reverend's eyes widened and he ran his tongue across his dry, bleached white teeth. "Oh I always have time to offer private lessons to eager young students." He smiled.

"Then you do not worry about the INS?" Santiago asked harshly.

"Oh! The INS? Well, I will handle them." He continued without taking his eyes off of the girl. "Besides, worst case scenario, the church will offer them sanctuary." He smiled.

Juan Carlos laughed. "Perfecto! My drivers will deliver the cargo to you in the morning, and I will be by in the afternoon to makes sure things have gone smoothly." He lifted her ponytail and pressed his nose into her warm brown hair. "And to deliver to you our little flower."

She had finished brushing her ebony hair when the knock came to the door. It was not Juan Carlos's distinct knock and it was too heavy to be that of the Dueña's. She opened the door to see the man everyone called Pelón standing before her. She could not see his eyes through the sunglasses he wore.

"Yes?" she said inquisitively.

"The fiesta is about to begin. El Cacique wants you there, on time," he emphasized.

"Ok. Thank you Pelón. I will be there shortly."

"Not shortly, he wants you there now," he barked.

Angelina outgrew her fear of monsters long ago. La Llorona, the ghost of the woman who, in a fit of jealousy, drowned her own children and was cursed to walk the earth searching for their souls had no hold on her. Nor did the mythical *chupacabra* who was said to suck the blood from livestock concern her. As a woman, she had come to realize that the most fearsome monsters were not supernatural, but were made of flesh and blood and born unto men. Sometimes, these monsters had no choice. They were born with a darkness in them that no light could penetrate, others were born children of God, but the cruelty of their surroundings drove kindness and decency from them and they became monsters as a means of survival. Pelón was the worst kind of monster, for he was born into wickedness with a darkness already deep in his heart.

She never had to deal with Pelón directly before, but she was very much aware of his brutality and his lack of regard for women. It was well known that his own mother had been a prostitute who had worked for Felix Cárdenas years ago. It was rumored that his mother gave birth to him while she was serving a prison sentence in Nuevo Laredo's El Penal II. He stayed with her until she died of an overdose and he was placed in an orphanage and his path finally led him to Juan Carlos.

She had witnessed on more than one occasion Pelón discipline the prostitutes that he thought were holding out money and the look of sheer joy on his face while he did so. Juan Carlos permitted it, so long as he never struck any of the women in the face.

"Okay then—I am ready. ¿Listo?" she asked playfully.

"Let's go." He grabbed her by the arm and pulled her into the hallway.

"Ouch!" she cried out. "You are hurting my arm!"

"Then walk faster. It won't hurt as much," he replied.

When they entered the cantina, everyone applauded. She peered into the dimly lit room and saw everyone she worked with—the Dueña, the other girls, the barkeep. Even the janitor with the crippled arm was present. She could smell the carne asada cooking in the kitchen. They continued to applaud and they all seemed to be cheering for her.

Juan Carlos raised his hands and gradually the cheers subsided. He waited until silence fell across the room.

"My friends. Thank you for coming. All of you. Today, I would like to make a toast as we celebrate your dedication to one of the greatest gifts one human being can offer another. Hospitality." Juan Carlos smiled and picked up a salted margarita glass from the bar and lifted it toward the crowd.

"To hospitality!"

"To hospitality!" the residents of the cantina roared back.

He took a drink, and then continued.

"There are those who criticize what we do here as sinful. But I tell you that each of you are doing not only what pleases the Lord, but is in accordance to his commands," he reasoned.

The cantina remained silent.

"Disregard the hypocrites who would tell you that the services we offer are unclean or ungodly. Nothing could be closer to godliness than what we do!"

Two of the prostitutes sitting at the back table applauded.

"The Lord commands us in the Bible that we are to love one another with mutual affection. To contribute to the needs of the saints and to extend our hospitality to strangers. That is precisely what we do, we love and extend our tender hospitalities to all of those who visit Casa de Diana and then we do much good with the proceeds. I just donated money to go toward the construction of a new library for underprivileged school children. I have donated money to houses of God. None of this would have been possible without you. You each conduct your proper role here at Casa de Diana in a manner that is pleasing to God, and he has blessed us."

The cantina exploded in applause.

"Now, I want you to think for a moment. How is it that you came to this place? What brought you here? On this road of life that we all pass through, what was it that guided you here into the comforting arms of Casa de Diana, oh weary travelers?" He continued.

"Some of you came here out of desperation—tired, hungry and without so much as two pesos to rub together. Others may have known someone who told you about this place. It does not matter how you got here. Each of you answered a calling and you did so of your own free will. That is how the Lord has intended it. We all make our own choices and these choices either bring us to, or take us away from our destiny. God has designed each of us with a specific purpose. He knew your purpose even before you were in womb. It was written upon you that He should conduct His will through your bodies, and you should fulfill His command of love and hospitality." He smiled.

"However, there is one of you here today who does not view her role in such a way. In fact, she has come to feel that she is somehow elevated above the rest of us and has decided to disregard the purpose for which she was designed. She would be like the others who would look down on you and call you whores."

The prostitutes began to murmur among themselves and the sounds of discontent began spread throughout the crowd.

"Who is she Juan Carlos? Who is this hypocrite who thinks that she is better than the rest of us?" One prostitute shouted out.

"She knows who she is, and if she had any conviction in her at all, she would show herself to you," he replied.

Her stomach felt tight and she was slightly nauseous from the moment Pelón had drug her into the room. Angelina knew what he was doing and she knew that the Dueña was right, Juan Carlos had no intention of ever letting her leave, no matter how much money Garrett paid him. A strange calmness filled her. The tightness in her stomach relaxed and the nausea had faded away. At that moment, the thoughts in her mind became clear and she spoke.

"God asks us to be loving. God asks us to be hospitable . . . but He does not expect us to suffer because of our hospitality. He does not ask us to surrender our dignity."

The cantina fell silent.

Juan Carlos smiled. "So, the arrogant one has found the courage to speak."

"You try to paint me as arrogant, you try to portray me as one who is proud and thinks myself above God or anyone else, but the truth is Juan Carlos, you are the one who is proud and you are the one who thinks himself above God."

"You have forgotten your purpose. You were nothing but a sad eyed orphan, poor and drifting without a place in the world. You were brought here by Grace, and now you wish to disregard all the kindness and blessings that has been bestowed upon you like an ungrateful child and like an ungrateful child . . . you will be reprimanded," he replied.

Angry murmurs began to emerge from the crowd and drifted throughout the cantina.

"I was not brought here by Grace, Juan Carlos."

"Ah! See! She denies the good works of our Lord!" He shouted to the mob of spectators.

"Turn her over to us, El Cacique! Let us take her to the alley and we will teach her the meaning of Grace!" one of the women shouted as the crowd burst into laughter.

"You know I was not brought here by Grace. I came here because you said you loved me. You swore your undying love of me to my grandparents and promised them that I would have a better life with you. I came here because you are a liar!"

"And you are a stupid whore!" Juan Carlos drew back his fist and struck Angelina in the mouth, knocking her to the floor.

She could taste the blood in her mouth as she ran her tongue across her front teeth where she found an empty socket that gave testimony to where one tooth had resided.

"I am a whore no more. I am reclaiming my freedom from you. You no longer have claim over my dignity." She coughed.

"I am afraid not, mijita. Once a whore, always a whore. You just need to re-learn your purpose," he replied.

She rose from the floor. "You can do to me what you like, Juan Carlos. You can threaten me, you can beat me, you can even kill me . . . but you will not take my dignity from me any more and as long as there is breath in this body, I will not lie down with you."

Juan Carlos pulled out his silver hay hook from the pocket of a trench coat that lay draped across one of the barstools and stormed over to where she stood. He grabbed a fistful of her ebony hair and jerked her toward him and placed the hook at her throat.

"You will not deny me. You were nothing when I found you. I own you," he hissed.

She could feel clumps of her hair tear loose from her scalp and the pain was excruciating. She clutched at his hand in an effort to bring some relief.

"You do not own me Juan Carlos and you cannot break the will of a woman who does not respect you. If you wish to lay down with me, it will be with my cold and lifeless corpse!" She gasped.

"I may just decide to do that. Who knows? You may be more satisfying as a dead whore than a live one." He released her from his grasp and struck her across her face with the curved, outside edge of his hook, dropping her once again to the cantina floor.

Her head was spinning as she lay on ground feeling the coolness of the tile beneath her when she felt a sharp pain at the back of her scalp as she was pulled once again to her feet.

"I will ask you again, mijita. Take me to your bed." He smiled.

"No!" she spat back.

The crowd inside the cantina watched in silence as he drew back as once again the backside of the hook struck her face, reducing her to a crumpled mass on the floor.

He pulled her to her feet and again she denied him and again he struck her down. This episode played out over and again with the outcome never changing, until she finally succumbed to the numbing comfort of unconsciousness.

12

I *guess one of the lessons you learn when you are in combat is that not everybody who goes in with you is coming back out. You can't help but take that little bit of that hard won worldly wisdom with you when you go back home. I have lost people that I have cared about. First my mom and then my dad, but I guess in a way that is expected. On one hand, if you are lucky, your parents have always been there with you and for you . . . and it's hard to imagine life without them being in it. But on the other hand, you know deep inside that they are going leave. They have to, it's the natural order of things. The previous generation has to move on to make room for the next. That is the way it has always been.*

But when it comes down to the young passing on before they even lived. Well, I can think of nothing in the world that is more tragic. Some of the boys that died over there were just that—boys. Some of them was like me and came over without even having a girl back home to write to. They never married, never fathered a child, never had the chance to grow old. Now they're gone, wiped from the earth as though they never walked it.

I was lucky. I went over and I came back. But I sure as Hell ain't the same person that I was before I left. When you come back from combat you are intently aware of how quickly it can all come to an end. Some say that you develop a new appreciation for life; I don't know if that is true, I think I had a pretty healthy appreciation for life before I went. I think that mostly you try to forget what you saw while you was there . . . and for some, what you did.

Another lesson you learn is that evil is real. I ain't talking in a metaphorical or psychological sense, I mean it's authentic. You can see it. You can smell it. It is something that can be measured. But most often, evil presents itself by default. In the absence of good, wickedness is all too willing to fill the vacuum.

My old man talked a lot about evil. He talked about how each of us have to make a stand and take sides and that choosing to not to make a stand was no better than deciding to carry the banner of darkness, cheering all the way.

I read awhile back about how a couple of guys in Texas drove their car through an apartment complex and accidentally run over a four year-old who ran out in front of them chasing after a ball or something. When the driver got out of his car to check on the kid, about six or seven bystanders jumped on top of him and started beating the life out of him. The passenger in the car got out and started pulling the guys off of his buddy and they turned on him. The driver made it back to the car and took off, leaving his buddy to the hands of the mob.

These fellas continued to give this guy a pounding in front of a gathering crowd of about twenty people. The queer thing was is that nobody did a thing to try an put a stop to it, they all just watched it happen as though a half a dozen men beating on one was as natural as breathing.

When the police arrived, the man was found lying in the parking lot. He was taken to a hospital and was pronounced dead. The autopsy listed blunt force trauma to the head as the cause of death. The little girl suffered a mild concussion, but was expected to make a full recovery.

I don't know what I thought was worse—the indifference of the crowd or the cowardice of the dead man's buddy. But I think that my old man was right, choosing to do nothing in the face of a wrong doing don't make you no better than the ones carrying out the deed.

Friday, November 7, 2008

G.H.

It was nearly six o'clock when Garrett Harrison stepped into the cantina at Casa de Diana. The place was deserted of patrons and its only occupants were the barkeep, several whores who sat gossiping at the back of the bar and an old man with crippled arm who was doing his best to push a broom across the floor with his good one.

Garrett stepped up to the bar.

"¿Qué toma?" the barkeep asked.

"Una cerveza y una lima, por favor," Garrett responded.

The barkeep nodded. He returned with a Tecate beer in a bottle, popped off the lid and sat down a small bowl with sliced limes in front of Garrett.

"¿Dónde está Juan Carlos?" Garrett asked.

"¿Quién?" the barkeep asked.

"Juan Carlos . . . El Cacique . . . ¿Dónde está?"

"No sé," the barkeep responded.

"¿No está?" Garrett asked.

"No, no está aquí," the Barkeep replied.

"¿Cuándo volverá?" he asked.

"No sé," the barkeep insisted.

Garrett felt a presence behind him, and turned to find the Dueña. She was an attractive woman who appeared to be in her early sixties, yet her narrow waist and curved physique confided an age much more youthful. Her face bore not the craggy leathery creases of many her age, instead her complexion revealed soft gentle wrinkles of a person of leisure.

"May I be of assistance to you?" she asked in perfect English.

"I hope so. I am looking for Juan Carlos," he said.

"What business do you have with him?"

"I have a business proposition I would like to make him. I told his brother I would be back today to discuss it with him," Garrett responded.

"That is too bad, Juan Carlos is not here," she replied.

"When will he return?"

"He has gone north. He may not be back for many days," the Dueña explained.

"Damn!" he drank deeply from his bottle of beer.

"I know you." She smiled wistfully.

"You don't know me." He swallowed.

"Yes, I do. You and your friends came here about a month ago and created such a commotion that you were asked to leave. But you have been back since, haven't you? Yes, you have. You have been here to see the girl, yes?"

"That's right."

"Well, what matter of business do you have with Juan Carlos today?" she asked.

"Well, you seem to know everything about me, why don't you tell me?" Garrett replied.

"Well, I think that you are here about the girl. I think that you want to make some kind of deal with El Cacique so that you can take her from this place. Yes?"

"That's right."

"How do you intend to do this?" she asked.

"I want to offer him cash payment in exchange for her contract with him."

"You think that she is here because of a contract? You have not considered that she is here because she wants to be?" She raised her eyebrow.

"She don't want to be here. She told me that."

"Whores will say many things, mijo," she said softly. "And she is a whore to the depths of her soul; do not think for a moment that she does this against her will."

"Are you telling me she is a free agent?" he asked.

"A what?" asked the Dueña.

"A free agent, are you telling me that she is here of her own free will? Are you telling me that she is free to come and go as she chooses?"

"We are all free agents in our own minds," The Dueña replied. "Perhaps that is all of the freedom any of us needs."

"She told me how he brought her here. She told me how she is constantly threatened by him. She ain't here because she wants to be," Garrett argued.

"She is a whore," the Dueña answered.

"I have one dead man and two dead girls back in the states that was the result of your boss's handy work. I can have the testimony of Angelina too. If he ain't willing to deal with me, I will give a call to the people at the District Attorney's office, and then he can deal with them instead," Garrett growled.

"Do you think for a moment that the law is not capricious and arbitrary?" she asked. "The law is manmade. It is fallible and it may not work out for you the way that you think it should. You spent the night with the whore two weeks ago, didn't you?" she asked.

"I stayed with Angelina, yes," he replied.

"On her birthday too, how very romantic." She smiled. "Laws are romantic notions too. They are written, as poetry, to capture an idea— to encapsulate justice. But the laws that you seek to invoke are just as fickle as romance," she continued. "Take for example, the Saturday that you spent with her. The laws that said if you fucked her at 11:00 PM you are a pedophile and she is a victim, these are the same laws that say if you fucked her instead at midnight, you are both lawful, consenting adults. So you see, if you put your faith in the law to help you, you are placing your faith in the wind."

"I have a considerable amount of money with me. I want to buy her out of her obligation to Juan Carlos," he reiterated.

"What then? Will you take the whore with you back to your country? Will you marry her, buy a home an have many babies?" She laughed.

"Can you arrange a meeting with Juan Carlos or not?" He gritted his teeth.

"Santiago told you that he was a busy man. Too busy for an American boy with such foolish romantic ideas," she replied.

"Then I want to see Angelina," he demanded.

"She is no longer here," the Dueña answered coldly.

"What? Where is she then?"

"Juan Carlos always keeps his promises," she replied. "He told her that he would take her to the United States one day, and he made good on his word."

"The United States? Where?" he demanded.

"I have said too much already," she scoffed.

"Look. I need to know where she is." He pulled out the two thousand dollars that he withdrew from his savings earlier that day. He counted out three hundred dollars and placed it in her hand.

"All I need is an address," he pleaded.

She nervously eyed the barkeep who was taking inventory of the liquor. She discretely rolled the bills up and placed them in her blouse.

"I cannot give you an address, I do not know it. But I can tell you that when El Cacique takes his girls north, he brings them to a place called Los Carrizales."

"Los Carrizales? The reeds? What is that, like a club or another whorehouse?" he asked.

"No," the Dueña hissed. "It is a riverbed in California in the town of Oceanside."

"A Riverbed?" Garrett asked confused.

"Sí. It runs alongside large fields of strawberries where many Mexicans work to harvest. They are called the 'Fields of Love.' Juan Carlos takes the girls that he thinks are no longer profitable or grateful for their positions here at Casa de Diana to work there," she explained.

"So what? Do I look for a trailer or a farmhouse? Where do I find her in these reeds?" he asked.

"You do not understand," she explained. "The girls there work in the fields to provide services for the granjeros every day, at every hour. Sometimes they serve as many as a hundred men each day. There are no buildings; they are out in the open, without walls, without windows, without beds or sheets. Without any forms of sanitation or dignity. They give themselves to the workers on the ground in caves made from the reeds like animals. For twenty dollars, a man can have any of the women he wants. If he is willing to pay thirty dollars, he can have her without a condom. At the end of the day the only taste left in the mouths of these women is the taste of dirt, alcohol and the sweat of the granjeros."

"Why did he do this? Why did he send her there?" Garrett's eyes watered and his voice began to tremble.

"Because she would no longer lay down with him," the Dueña replied.

"I tried to tell her that it was foolish. She insisted that if she lay down with Juan Carlos, or any other man, it would be a greater sin than she has committed in the past because now God has answered her prayers, he gave to her a man to love her and to be loved by her."

"Juan Carlos became angry and took her out into the middle of the cantina after the patrons had gone home. He called all of us to see what happens when someone disobeys him. He pulled out a hay hook, and proceeded to beat her with the curved end of it until she lost consciousness. He then revived her, and asked her if she still would refuse him. She told him that she would not lay down with him as long as she was alive. So he announced to us that he would send her to work in Los Carrizales, and if she continued to be disobedient, he would not spare the hook." A single tear streaked down the Dueña's face as she recounted the event.

"Listen to what I'm telling you lady," Garrett hissed. "You are gonna tell me where I can find her and you are gonna do it right now."

"I am afraid that we will never see her again. If she is not dead already, she will be soon," the Dueña whispered regretfully.

"I hope you got your fill of this town of yours," Garrett said.

"What?" the Dueña asked.

"Have you seen everything that you wanted to see?" he questioned.

"I do not understand your foolish questions," she hissed.

Garrett leaned in close to the Dueña and placed his lips to her ear.

"I'm not asking your opinion on the subject. I ain't even making a request. I'm telling you that you are gonna tell me how to find these 'Reeds of Love', or you ain't walking out them doors," he whispered harshly.

She laughed.

"If you touch me you will not make it out those doors either." She smiled.

"Look at me and tell me if you think I care," he growled.

She paused and regarded him. The conviction in his voice, the gleam of unshed tears welling in his eye moved her to tell him all she knew. She emphasized that she was not sure where the reeds were exactly. But she understood that lay in the San Luis Rey Riverbed in the city of Oceanside. She knew that a church rested on a hill overlooking the reeds, but the precise location was unknown to her.

Garrett sat silently for a moment staring at the Dueña. He felt something deep inside of him break in two and the canvas bag that he held dropped from his hand onto the floor and all at once he began to shake. When he found his words, Garrett rose from the bar and began shouting.

"None of you even lifted a hand? That greasy son of a bitch beat that girl to near death and none of you lifted a hand to stop him?" he roared.

The whores stopped their gossiping to look at him. The old man ceased pushing his broom and the barkeep turned from his inventory.

He reached down and picked up the bag from the floor.

"You are all just pitiful. Goddamn pitiful. You can all go to Hell! You and your whole damn kind!" He turned and walked out of the Casa de Diana for the last time.

13

I never really talk much about my time in Iraq. I left a decorated Navy Seal; most people who know me don't even know that. It ain't that I'm humble neither, it's just that I don't know what I would say if I ever did decide to talk about it.

Once, I had a reporter from a newspaper ask me what was the saddest moment I had while I was serving in the Navy and as a follow up, she wanted to know what was the happiest moment. I thought about it for a while and I told her. The saddest, most pitiful moment I ever had was looking at the bottom of the Golden Gate Bridge when we shipped out, and the most beautiful, magnificent moment I ever had was looking at the bottom of the Golden Gate Bridge on the way back home. She kinda just sat there looking at me not sure what to say next. And that is just the thing—nobody knows what to say next, so I pretty much shut up about the whole damned thing.

Every now an again, I think about it. One moment, I was a happy go lucky kid graduating from high school, shooting off at the mouth, playing video games, downloading songs that I pirated from the internet. The next moment, I was carrying a German made MP5 submachine gun clearing out Iraqi insurgents from the port city of Umm Qasr. It didn't seem at all strange to me at the time. It never ceases to amaze me what kinds of things that a person's mind can accommodate.

There was one day I was doing a rotation as ground support at a make shift landing strip just outside of Umm Qasr when a horribly shot up CH-53E Super Stallion made an emergency landing. It drooped down at the end of the runway with black smoke pouring out of the engine compartment.

Me and five others were dispatched in an ambulance to assist the survivors. We quickly set about to putting out the smoking engine and then turned our attention to those on board. Of the thirty-one crew, only the pilot was alive. He'd passed out from his own wounds after setting it down onto the runway. The medics sped away in the ambulance with the broken body of the pilot leaving two others and me to clean up the mess.

That chopper was shot all to Hell. There was blood and the smell of death everywhere. After several hours in the sweltering heat, with thirty dead soldiers, the chopper was finally towed back to one of the hangars. I was never the same.

Even now, I shudder when I remember me and those two other boys groping across all of them bodies, examining the red, sticky dog tags. When I recall the stench and wrestling to pull limp bodies out of gun turrets and un-strap them from their seats. When I think about dragging them out and laying them on the ground outside of the aircraft. When I remember them thirty corpses lined up in a row, falling in for their final formation.

I can remember too what happened after they towed the chopper away. There I was . . . Garrett Harrison, Petty Officer, twenty-one years old, Navy Seal. Tough as nails and a member of what is arguably the preeminent defensive force in the world. I was overcome with emotion when I took it all in. I gagged, I vomited, I lit a cigarette and took a long drag and sat down on the runway. In the dry Mediterranean twilight I laid my head down, cradled in my arms crossed over my knees and I cried.

How are you supposed to talk about that?

Saturday, November 8, 2008

G.H.

For the first time in his life, he went to bed resolved to kill a man. When he awoke in the morning, the desire had not left him. He would either kill Juan Carlos or be killed by him.

Garrett informed John Parker that he was going to take his two-week vacation. He apologized for giving such short notice, but he had some personal matters to attend to. John reassured him that he shouldn't worry about it and reminded him that is what vacation time is for. He inquired if everything was okay with him. Garrett reassured him that everything was fine and that he had some personal matters that he had to take care of.

Garrett returned to the confines of his silver Airstream trailer. He pulled out his canvass Navy issue bag from the footlocker that served as his coffee table. He unzipped it and pulled from it a locked silver box. He opened the box and removed a compact gray Kimber .45 Ultra Raptor. It was a handsome piece of weaponry.

He had obtained it in the Navy. One of his fellow sailors had gotten his girlfriend pregnant and wanted to marry her. He offered to sell Garrett his handgun so that he could buy his girl a ring. Garrett paid him five hundred dollars for it. He liked the way the textured feathered panel wooden grips felt in his hand. It weighed roughly twenty-five ounces and sported a 3-inch barrel. It was designed specifically for concealment and stopping power. The .45 caliber slug was nearly a half-inch in diameter, and would knock down anything it hit. The standard magazine clip held five rounds, but Garrett had purchased the modified ten clip magazines simply for convenience. When Garrett had left the Navy and resigned his position with his demolition unit, he figured that he would never again have to wrestle with the dilemma of whether or not to take a human life. From the moment he walked off the naval base until now, he had never thought he would use this handgun for anything beyond target practice. But today, the world changed, and so had he.

He rolled up his pant leg and strapped on his ankle holster, locking his Kimber into place. He slipped on his shoulder holster and slid in his Border Patrol issue Beretta 96D Brigadier pistol. He was intimately familiar with his Berretta. It was specifically designed for the United States Border Patrol in order to meet the requirements of the agency. It contained a max of twelve rounds of ammunition and was designed for high volume shooting. He was not certain what he would encounter in his hunt for Juan Carlos, so he wanted to error on the side of caution.

He placed his two-way radio inside the bag as well. He figured that it would help him keep tabs on emergency radio transmissions, that way, he would know what the police and fire department would know.

He noticed a rectangular shaped bulge peeking out from one of the side pockets of the drab, olive colored bag. He felt the edges of it with his hand to see if the contours would trigger any recollection as to what it might be. He unzipped the pocket and reached inside and his fingers recalled a distant memory of when they last held the familiar soft leather cover. It was the Bible his father gave him.

When he made the decision to join the Navy, his father was furious. When he left for boot camp, his father did not speak a word to him. However, just prior to his arrival aboard the SS New Orleans, the ship that would serve as his home for the four years that followed, he received a package containing a Bible along with two hundred dollars in twenties and a note that read:

So you don't lose your way.—Dad

Garrett recalled leaving home on a Monday. He had thought about attending church service to hear his father conduct the sermon before he departed for training. He didn't go. A year later, his father died. He never dreamed that that Sunday would be his last opportunity to hear his father preach before his parish, or to even hear the sound of his father's voice.

He held the black leather book in his hand and gently thumbed through the thin, gold lined pages when it occurred to him that he had not prayed in a long, long time. His father had always emphasized the idea that you didn't have to be so formal with the Almighty. A person didn't have to recite verbatim, prescribed prayers to be heard by Him. You could approach God as you would a close, dear friend and simply speak to Him and if you listened closely, He would speak back. When Garrett was a boy, he spoke to God often just as his father told him to and he would concentrate and listen for the sound of God's voice often impatient for an answer.

Garrett wasn't sure when was the last time he had attempted

to hold a conversation with God. He was certain that it was when his mother was still alive. After the aneurysm . . . after she died, he no longer felt it in him to even try.

Now, as he was finishing packing his bag in preparation to exact vengeance against El Cacique, it occurred to him that praying was about the only thing left that he hadn't tried. He remembered a scripture that called for exacting an eye for an eye and a tooth for a tooth, but also recalled Jesus advising his followers to forgive those who transgress against us, not once, but seven times seventy times.

He thought about Angelina and how El Cacique had seduced her into falling in love with him, promised her that he would find her work in the North and then forced her into prostitution. He thought about the many other young women that suffered the same fate or even worse at his hands. He thought about the lives that were lost and the innumerable more that were ruined by drugs that he smuggled across the border. He thought about how he beat Angelina when she would not lay down with him and sent her to the reeds to be used and degraded. He thought about the unborn child that she carried. He determined that he had no use for a God who would offer unconditional forgiveness and decided instead that he would appeal to the Old Testament God who demands an eye for an eye.

He hit his knees clutching the black, softbound leather Bible to his chest and spoke.

"Lord, I know that we ain't talked in a long time an I guess you can chalk it up to differences of opinion. I ain't always been too pleased with the way you figured things ought to go down here . . . and if I ever make it up to see you, you're gonna have a hell of a lot of explainin' to do.

"Now, when I prayed to you in the past as much as I can recall, I ain't never asked you for anything. I guess I just always figured that kind of praying was nothing more than begging and I don't accept handouts from nobody . . . not even you.

"So as far as I can tell Lord, I don't owe you nothing and you don't owe nothing to me. So I ain't really sure that I have grounds to even ask what I'm gonna ask you, but I'm gonna ask it anyway.

"You know what's been going on down here. Although, sometimes I wonder if you are even payin' attention. 'Cause if you were, and if you had any sense of justice in you at all, you wouldn't stand for even one tenth of what I've seen. My dad always said that you have some kind of divine plan that we don't understand . . . and maybe that's true, but I have seen some heinous things and right now, I am pretty much in the thick of it all. I know you might not approve of me and you might not approve of Angelina but I ain't coming to you seeking redemption on my account. I ain't even asking you for any kind of miracle. I just hope that you recognize that she didn't have no choice in the matter and if there was anybody on the face of your green creation that ever was deserving of forgiveness, it's her and the child she is carrying. I promise you that if I make it through this, I'll look after and love them both like they was mine to lose.

"El Cacique is as bad a character as they come an as far as I'm concerned, he's a waste of skin. He's responsible for all kinds of wickedness down here. I know in your book, you talk about forgiveness and how vengeance is something reserved for you. But I can't forgive him for what he's done to Angelina, I just can't. And I don't have the patience to wait for you. So, I'm fixing to hunt him down and send him on up your way to let you handle matters from there. I would just appreciate you throwing a little bit of luck my way as I set out to doing it.

"I guess if you decide to disregard this request of mine, that's your call. You are the Almighty. On the other hand, if it ain't too far out of the way for you and your eternal plan . . . and you care to bless my efforts, well, I guess that'd be all right.

Amen."

He rose to his feet and then resumed packing his bag. When finished, he heard a knock on the door. He looked through the portal window and saw Brophy.

He opened the door and Brophy climbed into the trailer.

"What are you doing here?" Garrett asked.

"You didn't think that I would let you do this alone, now did you?"

"Do what alone?" Garrett asked.

Brophy jutted his chin toward the packed canvass bag. "Parker told me that you had some personal business to take care of, and were taking the next two weeks off. Unless that bag is full of yarn and darning needles, my guess is that your personal business has something to do with the girl and the pimp."

"Well, if that is the case, you had better keep on moving bud. The girl is Mexican, and I wouldn't want you wading into the same deep shit that I am wading into," Garrett responded coldly.

"Hey bud, I gave that some thought, and I was out of line. It don't matter what she is or ain't, you are my best friend . . . and if you are in it deep, then I am too," Brophy said. "Besides, you might need the benefit of my wisdom of experience. You may be officially a GS-7 now, but I have been at it longer than you, you wet behind the ears son of a bitch!" Brophy grinned.

"You sure about that bud?" Garrett asked.

"Is a frog's ass water tight? Hell yes I am sure!" Brophy laughed. "Besides, if you don't let me come along, I won't let you use my new toy." He unzipped his backpack to showcase a device that resembled a laptop without the keyboard.

"What in the hell is that?" Garrett inquired.

"I lifted it from one of the new Jeeps back at the station. I am surprised that you ain't seen one before Navy boy!" Brophy said grinning.

"Not before today I haven't."

"This, my friend, is the ICAD Dispatch Receiver," Brophy replied.

"All right. What does that mean to me?" Garrett asked.

"Well, this here is a high tech piece of equipment designed to help us Border Patrol Agents regain control of the regions between the United States and Mexico, compliments of Operation Gatekeeper," Brophy said patting it affectionately.

"Hey! That's great!" remarked Garrett enthusiastically. "Now just what in the hell does it do?"

"Well," Brophy began to explain as he powered up the device. "It is part of the ICAD sensor network that allows field agents like you and me to monitor video feeds, database updates provided by other agents, GPS tracking systems, infrared cameras, and satellite images.

By coordinating all of this data, this baby can give us accurate and high color resolution maps of the area we are patrolling. Hot spots of human activity are represented by a series of dots on the screen here. I tell you cousin, if we are going to track Juan Carlos' movement through the Los Carrizales, this will provide us the means to do it."

The screen flickered on. A digital keyboard appeared on the screen. Brophy grinned. "She is ready! All we need is to feed in the numbers." He began punching in the coordinates.

"Wait a minute, how do you know about Los Carrizales?" Garrett asked.

"Come on bud. Your old dad here doesn't have to explain everything to you now? You have heard of pillow talk, ain't ya?"

"Yeah," Garrett responded.

"Well, let's just say that when the Dueña is satisfied, she really likes to talk! " Brophy grinned.

"She told you about Los Carrizales?" he asked.

"Yep. She told me how Juan Carlos likes to send the women who are problems to work off their infractions in the reeds."

"She told me she didn't know the exact location," Garrett protested.

"She didn't, but she mentioned the name of the church that sits on the edge of the riverbed. The First Congregation Church is what she said, headed by Reverend Robert Caffrey. It turns out the good Reverend has an appetite for underage migrant girls that El Cacique is all too happy to fill. Anyway, I just Googled the name of the church, and not only do I have the address, I have the coordinates as well. Now ain't you glad I ain't Amish?" Brophy grinned.

"Well, I don't know now Brophy, I may need to have a barn raising some day and I think that you would be pretty useless at that!" Garrett smiled.

"Well, I can only be so gifted now bud. It wouldn't be fair to all the other men in the world if I was a world class lover, technological wiz kid and a champion barn raiser now would it? Are you ready to find your woman?" He smiled.

"Yes I am," Garrett replied.

"Then, let's get to it!" Brophy shouted.

"Hey bud . . ." Garrett said resolutely.

"Yeah?" replied Brophy as he carefully placed the ICAD Dispatch Receiver back into his bag.

"It's good to have you back." Garrett looked downward and swallowed hard.

Brophy laid his badge on the counter top and smiled. "I was never gone bud, I was never gone."

It was 3:13 AM when Garrett and Brophy found themselves outside the First Congregation Church in Oceanside. The building resembled two intersecting shoeboxes, sitting on a hilltop overlooking the river valley of San Luis Rey. According to the Dueña, Reverend Caffrey has presided over the church for the last five years. The Reverend oversaw a conservative, primarily white congregation. By the nature of his position, he was a primary candidate for corruption. For who would suspect a man of the cloth to be involved in the flesh trade? The Dueña confided to Brophy that the Reverend had worked closely with El Cacique in acquiring shelter and jobs for the illegal migrants that he smuggled across the border. In exchange, Reverend Caffrey received protection from El Cacique and large cash donations for the church. It has also been known that on many occasions, the Reverend enjoys the company of the young girls brought to work in Los Carrizales. He will often arrange for his favorites to work in the church performing domestic services under his direct supervision.

Garrett and Brophy parked the Chevy Silverado in a vacant lot on North River Road and Stallion Drive. The church sat on the hill above them.

"You think the Dueña was telling you stories out of church Brophy?" Garrett asked.

"What do you mean?" Brophy's forehead wrinkled quizzically.

"Do you think she was telling you the truth about the Reverend?" he clarified.

"Well, I can't be exactly certain . . . but I think we should find out."

Brophy grinned as he reached behind his seat and pulled out a bag containing two black ski masks. He pulled one over his head and tossed Garrett the other.

"Well lookee here! Ain't you a goddamn bone fide outlaw!" Garrett grinned.

"I figure there ain't no sense given away our alias to the bad guys, Batman! You ready?" Brophy replied.

"I am now," he said, pulling the mask over his head.

Garrett placed his hand on the door lever.

"Wait!" Brophy hissed.

"What?" Garrett asked.

"Wait for this . . ." Brophy pulled the light bulb from the truck's interior cargo light. "We can't have this giving off our location." Brophy grinned.

"It seems to me that you have done this before," Garrett observed. "I don't know if I should be happy or nervous about that."

The two crept up the hillside in the dark of night, careful to steer clear of the street. When they reached the top of the hill, they began to scan the perimeter of the church looking for the utility box. Garrett located it on the Northwest facing wall and alerted Brophy.

"Okay, you lovesick son of a bitch," Brophy explained to Garrett, "these are night vision goggles. The military just calls 'em NVG's. You ain't used 'em yet, because . . . well, your duties have been primarily that of kiosk boy. You don't exactly need these to ask drivers if they are US citizens or if they are bringing any plants into the region."

"Okay smart ass, maybe you forgot that I was a Navy SEAL. I practically slept with these things on," Garrett whispered.

"Fine, but I need you to listen to me carefully. Are you hearing me?"

"Yeah, I am hearing you."

"Goddamn it Garrett. I need to know that you are on board."

"I am."

"Good. Because if we are going to pull this off, we have to play this out exactly as I am telling you. ¿Sabes?"

"I got it," Garrett hissed.

"If any of this rubs you the wrong way, or you can't handle it, you tell me right now."

"I'm fine."

"You sure?"

"Yeah."

"All right. I am going to need you to cut the phone line in order to disable the alarm system. When I cut the power, it is going to be pitch black in there, but you will see as plain as day. You better be ready, because if that bastard has a back up generator or even a halogen flashlight, you better be ready to flip the visor up or it is going to be like looking into the face of the sun. You understand?"

Garrett's face furrowed into a frown as he pulled the night vision goggles over his mask and extended his middle finger in Brophy's direction.

"I just don't want you getting lost in the moment. You gotta treat this like business. You following me?" Brophy asked.

"I follow."

"And another thing Garrett . . ." Brophy started.

"Yes?" Garrett asked.

"If your girl is in there, you let me handle the Reverend."

"I can't do that," Garrett replied.

"I will let you have Juan Carlos, that will be easy enough to explain if we get caught. But if you kill a respectable church leader, I won't be able to help you there. I am telling you, let me have him, or we ain't going in!" Brophy hissed.

"All right," Garrett whispered.

Brophy grabbed Garrett by his face and held it in both hands. "I mean it Goddamn it! If you ain't gonna play this out like I say, and I mean to the letter—we ain't going in!"

"All right! I said!" Garrett grunted.

"All right." Brophy released his hold on Garrett's face.

Brophy lifted the panel cover revealing the circuit breakers to the entire church. He rapidly flipped all of the breakers into the off position, while the entire building went dark. Garrett went around to the east side of the building where the phone line ran from the utility post to the building. He climbed onto the fence adjoining the church wall, and climbed onto the roof. He pulled out his utility knife from his pocket and sliced the phone line. When he returned to the utility box, he found that Brophy had already unlocked the door and was ready to go inside.

The two entered through the church's immense main hall. The hall was adorned in a manner that revealed the wealth of the parishioners. Each pew was polished oak, adorned with silver inlays. The high ceilings show cased stain glass windows that each depicted a scene from the book of Revelations. With the electric green halo effect that accompanies most night vision technologies, an eerie glow emanated from the moonlight shining through the stain glass images on the men below. Garrett and Brophy passed by the pews making their way to the residents' quarters, reserved for guests of the church, and the Reverend himself.

They pushed the doors open and entered into the study. Again, opulence ruled the day. Ceiling high bookshelves made up the perimeter of the room. Two high back leather chairs sat before a large mahogany desk with a glass top.

"This must be where the Reverend has his help assist him in orally preparing for his sermons," Brophy whispered.

They passed through the study and entered a hallway. To the left, resided the kitchen and the dining hall. To the right was the Reverend's bedroom.

"You keep your weapon in you holster cowboy!" Brophy warned Garrett as he disengaged the safety on his Beretta and made certain the clip was secure and there was a bullet in the chamber.

"All right!" Garrett hissed.

"Wait a second . . ." Brophy whispered. "Take this." He pulled his backpack off, and pulled from it his digital camera and handed it to Garrett.

"In case we see anything worthwhile. You know, for posterity!" Brophy grinned.

"On the count of three," Brophy whispered. "Ready . . . one . . . two . . . three!"

Both men hit the door hard, bursting into the other side. The room was large and decorated with great canvassed paintings inspired by the gospels. There was a large cherry wood armoire in the corner, near the door leading into the bathroom. Across from that was a matching chest of drawers. A large four-poster bed complimented the rest of the furnishings.

Through the NVG's, both men could clearly see two people in the bed. A scream burst from one of the bed's occupants.

"Shut up!" Brophy shouted. "We are with the INS."

The quivering voice shouted again, "La migra!"

"Cayete!" shouted the man in the bed.

"Reverend, I would follow your own advice if I were you," Garrett shouted back.

"Who are you people? What are you doing here? This is a house of God!" Reverend Caffrey proclaimed defiantly.

"You may want to remove your NVG's bud," Brophy whispered to Garrett.

Both men removed their headgear. Brophy held his Beretta in one hand and his flashlight in the other and shined his light onto the bed.

Reverend Caffrey sat up clutching a pillow to his chest and squinted as Brophy shined his flashlight into his bed.

"Who do you have in there with you Reverend?" Brophy asked.

Beneath the covers, someone stirred.

"It's okay, you are safe here. Come out," Brophy said reassuringly.

"¡No le diga nada!" Reverend Caffrey hissed.

"Hey! Hey! Hey!" Brophy backhanded the Reverend across his face. "No one said you could talk Reverend! Don't go giving me a reason to kick your perverted ass!"

"Todo está bien. Usted es segura," Garrett whispered.

Slowly a tiny hand emerged from the covers. Then the round face and dark eyes of a girl not more than thirteen years of age peaked out from the covers.

"¿Cómo se llama mijita?" Garrett asked the girl.

"Mi nombre es Xotchil," the girl replied.

"¡Qué bonito nombre! ¿Cuántos años tienes?" Garrett tried to smile through the darkness.

"Yo tengo doce años," Xotchil replied.

"¿Dónde vives?" Garrett asked the girl.

"Yo no sé," she whispered.

"¿Dónde viviste antes?" he whispered.

"Yo vivia en Mexico."

"¿Quién te trajo aquí?" He inquired.

"El," she said.

"¿El Padre?" Garrett pressed.

"No . . . El Cacique," she answered.

Garrett offered the girl a bathrobe that he found hanging in the armoire and invited her to climb out of the bed. He reassured her that she was safe. He told her that they were good men and they were going to make sure that she was taken care of. He asked the girl to wait in the bathroom and that he would call her out when it was time to go. He told Brophy that he would not photograph her and the Reverend because of the indignity of it all.

Brophy agreed that it would not be proper. He pulled out some large plastic zip ties from his bag, and had Garrett secure the Reverend's hands and feet. He sat before them on the tile floor of the bedroom, naked, shivering and bleeding from his mouth.

The Reverend's responses ran the range from anger to denial, never quite arriving at acceptance. He threatened the two men, attempted to bribe them and finally tried to bargain, explaining that the entire incident was as innocent as can be. The girl, he clarified was staying with him while her family visited an ailing relative. She had become frightened in the night, and she wanted to sleep with him for comfort.

"Well, what do you think?" Garrett asked.

"I think we should take one of them pillow cases, pull it over his head, and do whatever comes natural," Brophy spat.

"Well, I think we should get some information from him first, don't you think?" Garrett asked.

"Well, okay . . . but we still get to do my pillow case idea, right?" Brophy asked.

"Only if the good Reverend is uncooperative," Garrett replied.

Brophy grabbed Reverend Caffrey by his thinning hair and pulled him up off the ground and sat him down on the bed.

"We are looking for some answers, Reverend," Garrett growled. "And we don't have the time or patience for bullshit. I am going to ask you a question, and if I think you are lying, I am going to let my partner here break one of your fingers. If I think you are lying to me ten times and I run out of fingers . . . well, then I am going to let my partner wrap your head in a pillowcase, and have his way with you. Do we understand each other?"

"Yes," the Reverend responded.

"Okay! We are off to a good start." Garrett grinned through his ski mask.

"We are looking for a man named Juan Carlos. You may know him as El Cacique. Where is he?" Garrett asked.

"I do not know anyone by either of those names," the Reverend answered.

Garrett looked at Brophy.

"That would be a lie, Reverend. The twelve-year-old girl in your bed told me that El Cacique brought her here. Okay bud, break one of his fingers!" Garrett commanded.

"No! Please God, no!" the Reverend begged. "I know him, but I do not know where he is. I swear!"

"Now I am confused. First you don't know him, then you do, but you don't know where he is . . . I think you lied twice. Break two of his fingers bud."

Brophy pushed the Reverend down on the floor, his hands were bound behind his back, and he writhed and cried on the ground like some great pale amphibious thing. Brophy placed his boot on the back of his hand and pressed his weight into it until he heard a series of pops followed by the Reverend's agonizing scream.

"I think I broke three bones by accident bud," Brophy admitted.

"That's all right. The good Reverend knows that forgiveness is divine. Ain't that right, Reverend?" Garrett asked.

The Reverend did not answer, he only continued to sob on the ground.

"Okay. I will ask you two questions Reverend. One will be familiar to you and the other is brand new. Where is Juan Carlos? And when will he be picking up the girl? Now before you rush to answer, keep in mind that my friend is clumsy, he may accidentally break every bone in your hand this time," Garrett cautioned.

"I swear to you. I know him but I have no idea where he is or how to contact him. He dropped the girl by last night. He told me I could have her until this evening. I never contact him. He contacts me when he has some new workers coming through that he has to hide."

"Hmmm . . . how do you contact him then, when you get a taste in your mouth for little girls?" Garrett asked.

Tears streamed down the Reverend's pale sagging jowls.

Garrett sighed. "Okay bud, break some more."

"No! Please! No!" The Reverend desperately pleaded again.

Brophy lifted his right foot and brought the boot down hard on the other hand. The sound of splintering bones merged with agonizing screams and sobs. Brophy pulled the Reverend off of the ground and sat him back on the bed.

"Now Reverend. We know that you take money from this man. We know that you hide his prostitutes. We also know that you are a pedophile. You are going to jail for a long, long time. What can you possibly hope to gain by protecting this man?"

"My life," the Reverend sobbed.

"What?" Garrett questioned. "Your life ain't worth shit now."

"My life will be worth even less if I give him up. Juan Carlos has connections all over the country, inside and outside of prison. If I tell you anything, my life will be worth less than nothing."

"I see. Did you know that we know all about Los Carrizales?" Garrett asked.

Reverend Caffrey stopped sobbing for a moment and looked at him. "How do you know about Los Carrizales?" he asked.

"Oh, that is not important really. What is important is that we know that the 'Reeds of Love' are right here below the church, and tomorrow, we will have a hundred FBI and Border Patrol Agents descend on those fields. When we find El Cacique, and we will find him, we are going to tell him that you told us all about it," Brophy said smiling."

"You can't do that to me!" the Reverend shouted.

"Oh, but we are doing this to you. How does it feel to get fucked, Bob?" Garrett asked as he slapped him across the top of his balding head.

The Reverend collapsed into a naked, translucent sobbing mass on the tile floor.

"I don't think we're gonna get much more out of him bud. His days are numbered and he knows it," Brophy observed.

"I think you are right. But we can't just leave him here," Garrett replied.

"Au contraire mon frère! I think that we can." Brophy reached into his bag and pulled out a roll of duct tape.

"Well ain't you a goddamn Boy Scout!" Garrett smiled.

Garrett and Brophy pulled the Reverend up off of the ground and laid him on the bed. Brophy wrapped several layers of duct tape around his mouth taking care to not cover his nostrils. Then laid him diagonally across the bed securing his zip tied hands to one bedpost with several passes of the gray adhesive, doing the same to his feet hitching them to the other bedpost.

"I think that'll hold 'em for a while," Brophy said approvingly.

"Let's get the girl out of here," Garrett suggested.

The men opened the bathroom door and found Xotchil crouched in the corner. Garrett spoke to her again and asked her to come out. She hesitated. Garrett pulled his mask off of his head so that she could see his face. Once again, he spoke reassurance to her and asked her to come out. Slowly the girl rose and approached him. Garrett explained once again to her that they were good men who had come to help her.

Garrett and Brophy took the secluded path down the side of the hill in order to benefit from the cover of night. When they approached the truck, he told her that he wanted her to sit in the cab and lay low on the floorboard. He told her that he did not want her to get up no matter what. He asked her if she understood. She said that she did. He asked her to promise him. She gave her word.

14

*I*t has been over a year since I dreamt about the city of Umm Qasr or the dark horseman, but last night my dreams returned me once again to that place. The images were the same . . . the cratered landscape, the burned out buildings, the lifeless bodies littering the streets. Only this time, I was not on horseback, I found myself on foot and I was wearing my U.S. Border Patrol uniform. I walked through the streets, my ears straining intently in the silence for some evidence of life. Then, behind me, I heard the unmistakable sound of an equine grunt. My mind immediately raced to my memories of the dark horseman. I spun on my heels and I saw the familiar hunched figure of the ancient white haired tamale woman riding a gold colored stallion. As she rode by, she looked down at me and her eyes were a deep chocolate brown, completely clear of the milky white cataracts that clouded them when I had visited her before.

I thought to speak to her but I could not think of anything to say. She carried in her right hand a long brass chain from which swung a large Byzantine censer with burning incense. As she passed, she turned her eyes from me and returned them to the road. I could hear her voice, soft and low reciting the Lord's Prayer. I stood listening as she rode slowly past the cratered earth and the rising plumes of black smoke until she was so far down the road that her voice could no longer be carried to me.

I watched her proceed down the road for what seemed like a long time and when I could no longer see her; I felt this sense of urgency wash over me, like I should follow the path that she made for me. I also felt at peace, somehow knowing that we shared a common destination and that she would prepare a place for me and would be waiting for me when I got there.

Sunday, November 9, 2008

G.H.

Before the sun began to break above the horizon, Brophy and Garrett descended into the reeds. Each knew what was at stake. The reeds were a maze and chances were good that the pimps, prostitutes and patrons knew the area much better than they did. If they were not careful, they could lose their target, or worse yet, get ambushed. Either proposition did not sit well with the two men.

They walked into the reeds about a quarter of a mile in from the road. The reeds got thicker as they moved farther away from the road. They found a small clearing near a towering eucalyptus tree and sat down. Brophy pulled the ICAD Dispatch Receiver from his bag and turned it on. He had pre-programmed the coordinates of the church before they left. Within moments, they had a lock on their location.

"This will give us an aerial view of the reeds. The screen displayed a GPS style map of the region," Brophy explained.

"The black triangle in the middle is our location. In a minute, we should be able to download a satellite image of the area for a map overlay, then we can see where we are in relation to the trails."

"Can we see where they are?" Garrett asked.

"Only if they happen to be in place when the satellite snaps a picture, which the odds are against us on that one. But the image should be clear enough that we can navigate our way through these reeds and find where the girls are doing business."

The sun was higher in the sky now and the valley was lit up and coming to life. As the air warmed, the sounds of the early morning commute began to fill the air.

"You don't think he'll show? Do you bud?" Brophy asked him.

"I don't know if he will or not. He is slick," Garrett replied. "I think that if we don't find this bastard soon, we had better wait for him back at the church. He will be looking to collect the girl and if he finds out we are on to him . . . he will disappear just like a ghost." Garrett suggested.

"Hey Bud?" Brophy asked.

"Yeah?"

"You know, all of this don't mean that there ain't a God."

"Sure it don't."

"I mean, Caffrey is a son of a bitch, there's no denying that . . . but he don't represent the Almighty."

"I know it."

"It's just we see a lot of shit in this line of work, and it is sometimes easy to lose sight of the good stuff."

"Yeah, there's a silver lining around every goddamn storm cloud."

"You have got a gift, Bud. You see the world differently than anyone else I know. Maybe it is because your old man was a preacher or maybe you are a just a plain old optimist, I am just tellin' you, don't lose faith."

"I ain't lost faith. I believe in the Almighty but the way I figure it, you can never tell which Almighty you are gonna get on a given day."

"I don't follow you," Brophy replied.

"Damn it Brophy, I don't have time to give you a sermon here, you just got to look in the book to figure it out for yourself. God loves you, except for when he's smiting you with floods or fire. He loves the children, except when he is taking every first born or commanding you to offer them up as a sacrifice. He forgives you except when he is casting you into a lake of fire. He tells you to turn the other cheek except for when he calls an eye for an eye. I am telling you, the Almighty ain't all knowing and he sure as Hell ain't benevolent, he's just older. The way I see it, God is either suffering from a bi-polar disorder or he has got one queer sense of humor. Either way, I don't have much faith that he's gonna do much of anything in the way of helping me out. If we're gonna save her, it's because we took the initiative . . . not because we got assistance from some celestial hand."

"Hey Bud," Brophy added.

"Yeah?" Garrett responded.

"For what it's worth, I think you are doing the right thing."

"I know I am."

Oceanside, California is one of the more desirable residential areas in Southern California. It shares San Diego's pleasant climate without the price tag and has everything a prospective, upwardly mobile homeowner would look for in a community—beaches and lush green farmland. If one drives along North River Avenue, at first glance, one only sees the enormous residential California-style homes with the red tile roofs, painted from cream to orange, adorned with vibrant gardens. Just behind these half million dollar houses are the strawberry fields of Japanese farmer Rodney Shimizu. Depending on the time of year, he employs from fifty to four hundred migrant workers to plant, harvest and maintain his crops.

To get to Los Carrizales, one has to pass by Maria's Family Kitchen and the 7-Eleven gas station on the corner of North River Avenue and College Boulevard. Just a few feet from the 7-Eleven gas station, sitting in the shadow of The First Congregation Church, a sign marks the location of an oil pipeline which is wrapped in a gray towel and duct tape, beyond that is a scenic bike trail.

Just off the bike trail is a narrow footpath that leads to a field of bamboo and reeds so thick that it is almost impossible to see who is standing next to you. About a half a mile from the street, the vegetation is even thicker and it becomes necessary to bend low to the ground in order to press forward. In this dense jungle of reeds and bamboo, there are eight or nine "caves" made within the thickets, each one right next to the other. Plastic grocery bags are tied to the bamboo shoots and are used by the prostitutes to dispose of the condoms and the toilet paper that they use to clean up with after each encounter with a client. Once the bags are filled, the prostitutes discard them in the brush so that they leave no evidence of the nature of activities that occur there. In the heat of the afternoon, a human stench fills the air, choking out the natural aroma of manzanita, oak and strawberry blossoms, making one realize that they are in Hell . . . literal fields of fire and brimstone.

If one arrives in the early morning, before business begins, within the caves on the ground can be found empty beer bottles and boxes of empty liquor bottles, shreds of cloth, pieces of blankets, empty cigarette packages, shoes, hats, tee-shirts, underwear and a single, large five gallon paint bucket serves as the community toilet. All of this debris is amalgamated with open condom packets and myriads of used condoms leaking semen onto the ground, each bearing silent witnesses to hours of subjugation and humiliation suffered by the women forced to work in Los Carrizales.

It was 8:30 AM when the van pulled up and stopped along the roadside above the riverbed. It parked on a turn out on North River Road where the neatly groomed strawberry fields end and the wild reeds and bamboo of the San Luis Rey river bottom begin. The morning commute had slowed. The workers were toiling in the fields and none of the occupants of the houses with manicured lawns were present to witness the delivery of human cargo.

Juan Carlos and his brother Santiago stepped out in front of the van and walked along back to open the door. Santiago stepped inside and withdrew carrying the limp, lifeless body of a girl.

He smiled at Santiago. "Look around you and tell me, what do you see?"

Santiago squinted as his eyes scanned the landscape. "I see what we always see here."

"He placed his hand on the back of Santiago's neck. No my brother, look closely."

"No sé. I see the strawberry fields . . . houses . . . the riverbed."

Juan Carlos laughed. "You only see the obvious."

"What do you see then?" Santiago asked.

"I see a classroom."

"A classroom?"

"Sí. Today, this is our classroom, we are the teachers and this whore is going to learn an important lesson."

Santiago looked to his brother. "I do not understand why teaching this whore a lesson has to cost us revenue," Santiago complained.

"Ah! My little brother. There is so much that you do not understand. Let me see if I can explain it to you. This little whore has forgotten what she is for, so I tried to help her understand her place. When that did not work, I tried to discipline her. I tried to make an example of her but she was stubborn. So, I bring her here to Los Carrizales to help her to remember her purpose, and perhaps teach her a little humility."

"We have over a dozen whores to work this field. You gave them the day off, you gave the youngest to that priest and you only brought this one to work. We could be making ten times the revenue!" Santiago argued.

"Oh no, my little brother. That is where you are wrong. First, the little girl was a gift to a friend, a business partner if you will. That kind gesture will bring us much in return. As for this little whore here—she will do the work of our entire moving brothel. If a dozen whores would serve one hundred men—so will this whore, if we have to stay here all day and night to make sure she does. So, you see? We get the revenue, our little whore learns her place, the other whores are happy and rested on account of having a little holiday, and we have the gratitude of a valued business partner—everybody wins!" Juan Carlos smiled broadly.

Angelina lay on the ground where Santiago placed her. She still bore the fresh wounds inflicted on her from the beating Juan Carlos gave to her at Casa de Diana. She feverishly murmured the prayers of the incoherent as she lay there in the dust.

"Come now. Our clients will be arriving soon!" Juan Carlos suggested. He nodded at Pelón who sat solemnly behind the wheel and proceeded to honk the horn several times. The *granjeros* in the strawberry fields heard the horn and looked up from their work. Like children heeding the melodious chime of an ice cream truck with their coins clutched in their hands, many of the *granjeros* sat down their tools and quickly headed in the direction of the sound of the horn.

Santiago lifted Angelina up across his shoulder and carried her into the reeds with Juan Carlos following behind.

Santiago laid her down in the shade of one of the many caves hidden within the network of trails in the reeds. She was feverish and barely conscious as she lay there among the empty condom wrappers and cigarette cartons.

"I think she might need medical attention Juan. Let's take her to a doctor," Santiago pleaded.

"Our doctor is dead. She must attend her lesson," Juan Carlos snapped.

"I don't know. She might die," Santiago reasoned.

"If the whore dies, she dies. If the whore lives, she lives. It is of no consequence."

"If she is of no consequence, why are we spending so much energy trying to teach her a lesson?" Santiago asked.

"You wonder about too many things, mi hermano. That will only get you into trouble," Juan Carlos growled.

The first of the *granjeros* arrived for business. Each knew what was expected of them. They would form a line of sorts along the trail, and wait for the one in the front to be summoned forward by Pelón. They would pay their $20.00 and were given a condom and directed to wait for instructions. Those who wished for a more intimate encounter paid thirty dollars, received a stamp on their wrist and were spared the condom. When Pelón felt the area was safe to proceed, he directed the men to the path that would lead them to the reeds.

Some of the *granjeros* were confused by the new format. Today, instead of a dozen whores, there was only one—a badly beaten, unconscious woman. The news of this spread rapidly down the line in hushed whispers and many chose to leave, stating that it was improper to take advantage of a sick girl in that way. Others had consciences that bothered them less and they chose to remain in line and wait their turn.

The first patron to visit was a large man who stood over six feet tall. His dirty, sweat soaked tank top revealed to the world his hairy back and clung tightly to his body, making him appear like a contestant in some freakish wet t-shirt contest.

He paid his twenty dollars and approached the unconscious woman. He began to unbuckle his belt and unzip his pants when a gunshot rang across the riverbed. A man's voice shouted,

"United States Border Patrol! Everybody down!"

The *granjeros* scattered through the bamboo and reeds shouting, "la Migra! la Migra!"

The large patron had his pants tangled around his ankles, causing him to fall several times before he simply tore off his pants and ran through the overgrowth in his underwear.

Brophy and Garrett had heard the horn and witnessed the vast migration of farm workers leaving the fields and entering into the reeds. They followed the *granjeros* straight to the brothers.

Brophy hollered to Garrett that Santiago had taken off toward the van.

Garrett told him to go after him.

Brophy sprinted after Santiago in the direction of the street.

Garrett saw her laying on the ground, beneath the shade of the curved bamboo stalks. He kneeled beside her and brushed her cheek. Her breathing was labored and raspy. She was bruised, swollen and hot. Numerous deep abrasions on her face crisscrossed like lines on a roadmap. He touched her trembling hands and found them cold and clammy. He saw that she was clutching a silver chain in one hand. He gently peeled back her fingers and saw that she held the silver medallion of San Cristóbal that he had given to her. He swallowed hard and placed his hand gently on her abdomen just below her navel and gently kissed her face, holding her hand against his cheek. He spoke to her but she did not respond to the sound of his voice.

"Now, isn't this a sad ending galán?" Juan Carlos stood behind him clutching a silver hay hook in his hand.

"It's about to get a lot more pleasant in a minute, Salazar," Garrett growled.

"Why do you say that, galán?" Juan Carlos smiled.

"Because, I'm going to kill you," Garrett spat back.

"You are going to kill me, galán? Over what? A whore?" Juan Carlos chided as he paced in front of one of the bamboo caves.

"I'm going to kill you because the world has no use for flesh pedaling psychopaths like you," Garrett growled.

"Ah! First you try to take something that is not yours to have, then you threaten me and now you call me names. That is sad. I think you are wasting your time, galán. Time that I think would be precious to you. I do not believe your whore will be alive much longer—ah, yes, you know that it is true. I will tell you what I will do. You pay me twenty dollars and I will let you have her for the next twenty minutes to do with as you will." Juan Carlos laughed.

Garrett began to rise and before he could straighten to his full height, Juan Carlos lunged at him striking his face with the hook. Garrett felt the flesh on his face tear as he fell backwards into the reeds.

"I think it is poetic, don't you galán? For two lovers to be killed by the same man, with the same weapon?" Juan Carlos hissed.

He reached for his Beretta, but found the holster was empty. It had fallen out when he and Brophy had pursued the workers through the brush.

"Please galán, let us keep this fair. You don't want to bring a gun to a duel such as this. Where would be the sport in that? Now please, stand up so that I may kill you like a man and not like some whimpering whore laying on the ground." He jutted his chin towards Angelina's quiet form.

Garrett stood up. His face was throbbing and he could feel his shirt soaking up his blood.

"It seems I have injured your face, galán. Perhaps your whore would find it to be an attractive scar?" Juan Carlos laughed.

"It is a shame that she will not live to see it! Do you know why I beat her like that, galán? Do you understand the lesson I was trying to teach her?"

"I don't care your reasons, you had no right to touch her," Garrett growled.

"I beat her because she was arrogant," Juan Carlos explained. "She thought that she was too good to be a whore. So I beat her. She forgot her station and I had to remind her what it was."

"You beat her because she wouldn't submit to you, you sick son of a bitch!" Garrett could feel his hands begin to tremble. El Cacique was getting to him and he knew it. He had to keep a clear head if he was going to be the one to walk away.

"Ah, yes. She refused me then, but now she refuses no one. Just look at her galán, now she is obedient. I think she would make even a better whore now. It is a shame the she will not recover. "

Juan Carlos stepped in to strike Garrett again with the hook and recoiled in pain. The hook connected with Garrett's arm, tearing his shirt, but not before Garrett pushed the open blade of his knife through Juan Carlos' right forearm.

Juan Carlos began to move the silver hook in his left hand, waving in front of Garrett as he moved about.

"So now we are kindred. We have spilled each other's blood. We are connected. Even after I kill you, we will have a rapport, for you see, blood is sacred."

Garrett spat on the ground. "You are gonna bleed a lot more than that Salizar. I am going to shred you so badly, not even your mama is gonna recognize you."

"You make jokes even in your last breath." Juan Carlos laughed. "I have always loved you Americans with your cowboy optimism. It is sad that your abundance and greed has made you soft. You walk the earth living like gods, taking what does not belong to you and arrogantly think that you will never have to pay your debt."

He lunged forward and Garrett saw a flash of sunlight reflecting against the steel hook and felt metal bite into the flesh below his right eye.

Garrett recoiled in pain and felt blood run down the contours of his face. He eyed Juan Carlos cautiously, glancing occasionally at Angelina's lifeless form lying silently on the ground.

"Your whore is dying galán, there is no stopping that. I cannot imagine a pain so great as watching the one that you love most in life take their last breath. I can ease your pain, galán. I can kill you first . . . or I can simply pluck your eyes from their sockets to spare you the sight of your whore's last moments. Which would you ask of me, galán? Shall I take your eyes? Or shall I tear out your heart?"

His face throbbed and the blood stung Garrett's eyes, blurring his vision. His shirt was soaked crimson and clung tightly to his body. He raised his hand to wipe his face when Juan Carlos once again slashed the hook at Garrett, where he sidestepped the attack too late. The hook tore into his shoulder. Garrett stumbled and dropped to his knees, clutching the fresh wound with one hand while at the same time unfastening the strap on his ankle holster with the other.

"Come on, galán, must I give you yet another chance? Stand up, and die like a man."

Garrett slowly rose to his feet taking with him the Kimber from his concealed holster.

As he rose, Juan Carlos charged Garrett thrusting the hay hook upward piercing his flesh, puncturing his diaphragm and cutting into the outer arterial wall of his heart. While at the same moment, Garrett fired off a shot from his Kimber placing a half-inch diameter slug into Juan Carlos' face, right below his left eye. The bullet made its exit leaving a gaping and bloody grapefruit sized hole in the back of his head.

Both men collapsed to the ground. Juan Carlos was dead before he hit the dust.

Garrett could not seem to fill his lungs with air. Each breath he took, he could hear the sucking wind whistle through the hole in his chest. He attempted to rise to his feet and could feel the world spin around him. A heaviness began to fill his lungs and he began to cough in uncontrollable spasms. He could taste the bitterness of blood and bile in his mouth while pink foam began to bubble out of the hole in his chest, darkening to crimson. His legs buckled beneath him, sending him once again into the warm embrace of the dusty earth.

He raised his head and saw Angelina laying just a few feet away from him but it could have been a whole world. He tried to ignore the searing pain that possessed his body as he crawled to her and laid his bloodied head upon her chest. He could not hear her heart beat. He reached for her hands and clasped them in his and found that they had stopped trembling. Everything around him seemed to grow farther and farther away. He thought he heard Brophy call his name. There were voices of other men too, but he could not see them.

"Oh damn bud, what in the hell did you do?" Brophy asked.

"I shot the son of a bitch," Garrett gasped.

"I heard." Brophy kneeled down, placing his index and ring finger on Angelina's neck.

"She's gone, ain't she bud?" Garrett asked weakly.

"She ain't suffering." Brophy swallowed hard.

"Did I get him?" Garrett wheezed into Angelina's bloodied blouse.

"Yeah, bud, you got him." Brophy placed his hand beneath Garrett's head and gently rolled him onto his back.

"Don't . . . don't move me!" Garrett coughed.

"I got to bud." He unfolded his knife and cut open Garrett's shirt exposing his chest.

"Is it bad? Cause it feels bad . . ."

"You've had worse paper-cuts working in the kiosk than this bud." Brophy smiled feebly.

Garrett lifted his head slightly and glanced at the dark red foam bubbling out of his chest and running down his abdomen.

"I appreciate your attempt at optimism, but you are a shitty liar." Garrett smiled back.

"Do all of you Navy boys cry like this, bud? I told you, you're fine." Brophy could tell by the darkening froth coming from the opening in his chest that Garrett was hurt bad. He was bleeding internally, but his breathing is what mattered now. The hole left by el Cacique's hay hook left Garrett with a sucking chest wound and his lungs were deflating. He knew that there was nothing he could do for the bleeding at the moment. Right now, keeping him breathing was all that mattered.

"Damn . . . it hurts bud." Garrett coughed up red foam.

Brophy knew that time was running out. He had to close the opening in Garrett's chest and give his lungs a chance to fill with air. He scanned the landscape desperately searching for something that he could use. He rose and tore a plastic grocery bag that was tied to the entrance of a nearby bamboo cave and emptied the used condoms, their wrappers and the wadded tissues onto the ground. He spat in disgust and folded the bag so the cleanest side faced out. Sterility was a luxury he did not have at the moment. He knelt down and waited for Garrett to exhale, pressing the plastic bag against the opening in his chest. When he inhaled, Brophy immediately felt a suction pull at the bag, creating a seal. Brophy kept his hand on Garrett's chest and with each breath, he could feel his lungs inflate slightly.

"She was beautiful, bud."

"Yes, she was something," Brophy replied.

"He had no right to do what he did. No right at all."

"I know it." Brophy placed his fingers lightly against Garrett's carotid artery and could feel his pulse weakening.

"I'm sorry for a lot of things I've done bud . . . but I ain't sorry that I killed him. He got what was coming."

"Just take it easy . . . save your strength. I called for backup. They'll be here any minute, " Brophy said.

"I won't be, bud . . . I'm done."

"You ain't done," Brophy whispered.

"Back in the trailer, in the cabinet above the fridge is the cash I got for sellin' the Indian. I want you to keep it . . . do something good with it."

"Quiet now. You're gonna need that money when you get back because your sorry ass is probably gonna get fired when they get wind of this . . . we both will." Brophy smiled.

"She didn't choose this. He forced her. She wanted to do right. She wanted out. You think that counts for anything?" Garrett wheezed.

"It counts with me," Brophy said.

"It counted with me too." Garrett closed his eyes.

"No! No! No! Stay with me! Keep your eyes open . . . look at me, bud!" Brophy shouted.

Garrett quickly opened his eyes like a man startled from a dream and attempted to bring them into focus on Brophy's face, but the landscape darkened into shadows against a wide, circling blue sky. He knew that Brophy was speaking to him and he struggled to concentrate on his words but Garrett could derive no meaning from them. He knew that his head lay against the breasts of his beloved but he had become numb and could no longer feel her. He desperately wanted one more time to sense her warmth, to feel the thickness of her lips against his, to taste her skin, but all he could feel was a cold weightlessness enveloping him.

The numbness, the urgency in Brophy's voice and the immense blue sky rising above him told only a part of the story. Just beyond Brophy's frantically working silhouette, Garrett could see the tiny, shimmering forms of green and red fluttering above him. Two humming birds were darting in and out among the interweaving colors of brown, green and blue. Pausing, then rising and falling together in a sort of dance, each coming close, but never touching the other. A light breeze pushed in from the west, causing the bamboo and the tall grass along the riverbed to sway in a slow and gentle rhythm.

Garrett's eyelids fluttered then closed as he drifted into the darkness knowing desire.

Epilogue

Friday, November 13, 2009

The morning sky burned a deep crimson like the color of grapes pressed into wine, with streaks of orange, purple and hues of blue emerging from a horizon made bright from the rising sun. Brophy stood at the edge of North River Road and Stallion Drive, pointing out toward the broad swath of freshly torn earth below, where only weeks before a thick tangled growth of reeds and bamboo demarcated the edge of the riverbed. In stark contradiction to the newly emaciated wasteland were the strawberry fields. Neat, vibrant green rows, contrasted sharply against the warm brown earth. The fragrant smell of strawberries rose and drifted with the sweet subtlety of a first kiss over a countryside painted in the colors of a Spanish love story.

The reporter stood next to Brophy while a man wearing a Padres baseball cap adjusted the wireless microphone on his collar. She smiled at him and turned to face the two cameramen.

"Thank you, Mister Brophy, for consenting to this interview. I realize this last year has been a difficult one for you: the death of your partner, your indefinite suspension from the Border Patrol, and the recent jury verdict acquitting Reverend Caffrey. Any of these taken alone would have left anyone in your position reeling. How are you holding up?" her teeth as bright as tombstones flashed in a feigned consolatory smile.

"I'm above ground," he replied.

"We are overlooking what some in the community called the 'Reeds of Love'. An outdoor brothel hidden within the thick bamboo reeds growing along the San Luis Rey Riverbed." She pointed out toward the freshly plowed wetlands along the banks below.

"Yes. This is where Xotchil, Angelina and dozens of other

young girls were brought and exploited. All of them minors," he spoke solemnly, facing the news cameras.

"The city acted quickly and cleared the riverbed to discourage further activity. Do you believe their efforts will be successful?" she asked quizzically.

"Well, I wouldn't go as far as saying that the city acted quickly. The girls were rescued last year. The city officials decided just a few weeks ago to level the wetlands," Brophy replied.

"Well, do you think that the actions of you and Officer Harrison were successful in shutting this particular prostitution ring down for good?" she asked.

"Santiago Salazar and his accomplice are in jail awaiting extradition to Mexico, and his brother Juan Carlos was killed while resisting arrest, which will definitely slow things down a bit . . . but I suspect this network has just been shut down temporarily, after all, it is damn near impossible to legislate morality and we are talking about the world's oldest profession. I think that clearing the reeds is just a way for city officials to give the appearance that they are doing something," Brophy said.

"If it's true that these women were victims, why couldn't the authorities get any of them to testify against the Salazar brothers, Reverend Caffrey, or any of the men involved in this operation?" she asked.

"Think about it. These are young girls who have been threatened, brutalized, raped, sodomized and had all sorts of cruelty thrown at 'em by these bastards as a means of keeping them in line. Made to walk in their shoes, I'd think you'd be reluctant to speak up too." His face began to redden.

"How long do you think this particular brothel was in operation?" she asked.

"It is hard to say for sure. Six months? A year? We located the church that laundered money for the Salazar brothers and served as their main operation center where they housed the girls. Where they slept, ate and where the ones who served as *mulas* delivered their cargo."

"Mulas?" the reporter blinked.

"Yes. Many of the undocumented migrants traveled here carrying several bags of cocaine that they swallowed. It's one of the ways that El Cacique smuggled drugs across the border and it is one of the conditions he set for those who wanted to cross over. He would make arrangements to get them across but it would come at a price. It's not a new technique. Drug smugglers have been using mulas for years; however, it's the age of some of the girls used in this operation that makes this case unique and very disturbing."

"How old were the women that you and Agent Harrison discovered working here, Mister Brophy?" the reporter asked with a level of enthusiasm that made him uncomfortable.

Brophy glared. "That's the thing, most weren't women at all. The ages of the girls that were brought here were surprisingly young. Xotchil was only twelve."

"I understand that most of the . . . er . . . clients were undocumented workers employed at the local farms. Do you think that illegal immigration is the root cause of the flesh trade and drug trafficking in this area?" the reporter asked, as her blonde hair cascaded down the middle of her back and fluttered slightly in the morning breeze.

"Well, in my experience, you can't have drug dealers without drug users and you can't have prostitutes without Johns. You would be surprised who the clients are. Hell, you might've even ate dinner with a druggie or a John this week and not even known it," he replied flatly.

"But the mulas and the prostitutes were here illegally, weren't they Mister Brophy?" she pressed.

"Christ! We are talking about defenseless people here . . . most of them babies, who by a stroke of shitty luck led tragic lives. They got swept up in this because of the actions of two evil sons a' bitches, not because they were undocumented."

"I am sorry to hear the loss of your partner, Garrett Harrison," the reporter said shifting to a more sympathetic tone.

Brophy took a breath. "Thank you. It has been a terrible loss for the whole agency. Everybody is still reeling from it."

"Isn't it true that your partner, Officer Harrison, was romantically involved with one of these undocumented prostitutes? What is the Border Patrol's position on that?" The reporter's blue eyes widened slightly and her mouth turned upward in a faint smile.

"I can't speak for the agency, I don't work for them any more but I will tell you Garrett Harrison was the finest man I ever knew and a damn good officer," Brophy replied harshly.

"I am just following up all ends. It isn't personal, but it is news," the woman pressed.

"Well, there are worse people in the world than Garrett and I resent you trying to smear his name and the name of the woman he loved for the sake of some goddamn news story!" Brophy growled.

"Well, wasn't it Officer Harrison and his relationship with Angelina that resulted in the two of you breaking protocol and you getting suspended?" she asked.

"I'd think that the story you would want to tell isn't about Garrett, Angelina or me. The story should be about how these people are being bought, sold and abused right under our noses and nobody seems to give a shit." Brophy gritted his teeth.

"Is it true that you and Agent Harrison as well as other Border Patrol Agents frequently visited Casa de Diana, a popular brothel in Tecate?" One of the cameramen adjusted the zoom lens on his camera to focus in on Brophy's face.

A large man clad in a Border Patrol uniform stepped in front of the camera and spat a thick, brown stream from his lips, saturating the camera lens and splattering the man behind it.

"Hey!" the man behind the camera shouted.

"I am sorry about that. I should really be more careful," the man said as he stepped in front of the second cameraman and pulled a wad of nearly black, saliva soaked tobacco from his lower lip and smeared it over the second camera lens.

"We all should." He spat on the ground.

The cameramen looked up at the man's towering form and lowered their cameras.

"This interview is over. Let's go Brophy," the man hissed.

Brophy pulled the wireless microphone off his belt, tossed it on the ground and followed the man across the street to the parked Chevy Silverado. The reporter motioned to the two cameramen and followed them in eager pursuit.

"Is it true that Angelina and Agent Harrison were both murdered by the pimp known as El Cacique? " she hollered after him as both men climbed into the cab of the truck.

"I said it's over!" The man shot back.

"Was El Cacique's death an act of revenge? Officer . . ." the reporter squinted to read the name on the agent's badge.

"Officer Parker! What about Angelina's age? Is it true that Garrett Harrison became involved with her while she was still a minor?" she shouted.

"We are done here!" Parker shouted back.

"Do you support the agency's decision to indefinitely suspend Officer Brophy from the Border Patrol? How do you feel about Reverend Caffrey's acquittal? Do you think that the actions of Officer Harrison and Officer Brophy jeopardized the verdict?"

Parker glared at the reporter silently and pulled his mirrored sunglasses from his pocket, placing them squarely on his face.

Mister Brophy, what do you have to say to Reverend Caffrey regarding the civil law suit he has filed personally against you?" she shouted into the cab.

Parker glanced at Brophy sitting in the passenger seat and then looked ahead, barely giving the glow plug enough time to heat up when he disengaged the clutch and pressed the gas pedal to the floor. The diesel engine belched out black smoke and the tires kicked up a cloud of dirt and gravel as the truck pulled away. The reporter and the two cameramen coughed and tried to shield their eyes from the dust and smoke as the truck rattled east down North River Road, beyond the green manicured lawns and past the rolling strawberry fields dotted with the *granjeros* who marched solemnly beneath a golden sun like weary soldiers, pushing forward with slow deliberation to some far off place, dust covered, brown and anonymous.

Reflections from the Author
Acknowledgements
Reading Group Discussion Questions

Reflections from the Author on *Without Sin*

I have heard it said that writers do not choose their subjects; it is in fact, the other way around. Looking back, I cannot argue with that assertion. The muse speaks to us in a variety of ways. For some writers, they hear a song, read a poem or perhaps see a photograph and begin to contemplate the real-life story behind it. For me, I was inspired by the tragic events that occurred along a stretch of the San Luis Rey River in Oceanside, California. My effort here in many ways, is a testimony to what Jules Renard asserted when he said that "The story I am writing exists, written in absolutely perfect fashion, some place, in the air. All I must do is find it, and copy it." I suppose in many ways, there is nothing magical about writing; it essentially comes down to your psyche being open and your light being on, like a neon vacancy sign in a hotel awaiting a weary traveler.

At its heart, *Without Sin* is tale of two ill-starred lovers. Garrett and Angelina are two broken souls who have endured crippling difficulties in their young lives, but have tried to press on with courage and hope. Their love affair, perhaps like most, was made here on earth, rather than in heaven and was not without hardship. I became increasingly fond of them both as they grew; their relationship with one another developed and as they attempted to assert their will on the world around them. However, in the background of this tale, there are the hundreds of thousands of immigrants from the south who every day, leave behind the comfort of their family and the familiar to endure unimaginable hardships inflicted upon them by both man and nature in a far too often tragic attempt to seek out a better life in el Norte. There are numerous talented journalists, sociologists and ethnographers who have dedicated their efforts to recording these stories in an effort to give a voice to those who might otherwise remain voiceless. I praise each of them deeply, but it is my belief that, documentary alone is not sufficient. It is my hope, that the stories of each of these men and women have echoes and that the sound of these echoes resonate within us as a nation of immigrants and awaken us from our deep, collective nap. But, enough of the author's intentions, for those can quickly fade and in the end, it is the reader who puts together shape and meaning, the author merely provides the clay.

After reading numerous articles on the plight of the young, undocumented girls in Los Carrizales, I had in my mind's eye, the image of a young woman, forced into a hopelessly dark place, on her knees praying to Saint Christopher for deliverance. Where did she come from? How did she arrive here? Where was her family? What circumstances led her to the reeds of love? These were the questions for which I sought answers, and if a storyteller has any worth at all, it is to the extent that he or she can give testimony and dignity to the human narratives around us. When the poet and activist Murial Rukeyser asserted that "the universe is made of stories, not atoms," she reminded us, that it is critical for us to recognize that every person, every place, every object has a story, bears witness to stories and, in fact, is a story. It is essential, to the human narrative, that we realize that all of these stories interconnect, and that each of us are, in fact, surrounded by stories, embedded in stories and composed of stories. As a grown man, I know that there are people in the world who are cold and indifferent. There are butchers, there are racists and there are opportunists. I know too, that the world also has its share of Angelina Marguerite's and Garrett Harrison's who, in spite of their own personal hardships and the numerous violent horrors they encounter, are full of hope that their love will persevere and that their lot will improve. It was difficult to say goodbye to them and I miss them both, but their optimism remains with me.

—David S. McCabe, August 2011

Acknowledgements

The writing of this book has been a large undertaking and I have many people to thank in helping me bring it to life. If I have omitted anyone, please know that it is an oversight. First, I want to thank my publisher James Clois Smith Jr. for acquiring it, understanding its potential, and being willing to take a risk. My dear friends Teresa and Sean Clark, Glafira Tinoco-Carr, Nick Fliter, Christine Oh, David Schrodetzki, Jennifer McAdams, Sheila Rahnama, Silvia Villanueva, Angela Dancev and Joanne DeCaro Afornalli for your many reads, re-reads and encouragement.

I would like to express my deep appreciation to all of my friends, colleagues and mentors at Pasadena City College who strive every day to make our world a better place-one student at a time. Special thanks goes to Adelaide Hixon for her generous and passionate support of Education and the Arts, and heartfelt gratitude goes to my Dean, Michael Finkenbinder for his leadership and support of all students. I would also like to thank Carlo Gébler, Deanne Stillman and Mary Otis— your guidance and mentoring have made me a better writer.

A tip of the hat goes to journalist and author Charles Bowden for his illuminating prose that gives voice to the thousands silenced by the violence along the U.S. Mexico Border. Thanks go also to Marisa Ugarte for her work as the Executive Director of the Bilateral Safety Corridor Coalition and her lifetime commitment to ending the exploitation of women and children throughout the United States and Latin America. I thank Kathryn Rodriguez for her work with Coalición de Derechos Humanos and her dedication to ending deaths in the desert along the border between the U.S. and Mexico. I learned much from you on our seventy-mile hike along the migrant trail. Much appreciation and respect goes out to the men and women of the U.S. Border Patrol who in the execution of their duties, save lives. A debt is owed to Agent Dennis Michelini who provides to the world a vibrant and truthful testimony to life on the U.S. Mexico border through his many interviews and editorials. Your work and your words played no small part in inspiring my writing.

The completion of my book would not have been possible without the love and support of my family. I would like to thank my parents Vivian and James Wright and David and Louella McCabe for their encouragement, specifically James for his help in gathering research for this novel. I would like to recognize my grandmothers Dixie Carter and Susan Wright for believing in me as well as my grandfathers Raymond Carter and Keith Wright; even though you are no longer with us, you both continue to guide and inspire me. I would also like to acknowledge my brother, Jonathan McCabe for his support, and to my niece Haylee who I encourage to continue to seek out books that will make you think.

Deepest thanks to my wife Lisa, who exemplifies Faith, Hope and Love every day, and to my beloved son Carter for tolerating my absence during the writing of this novel. To you both I say: "*Níl aon tintéan mar do thintéan féin.*"

Reading Group Discussion Questions for *Without Sin*

1. Each chapter of the novel begins with journal entries written by the protagonist, Garrett Harrison, in an effort to cope with his Post Traumatic Stress Disorder. The entries are Garrett's reflections on current events or some past experience that has marked him. How did these reflections enhance the overall story? Were there any entries that confused you? Give an example of a particular phrase or entry that challenged you. What other writers use this or similar techniques in their work?

2. What determines the path that led Garrett and Angelina to Casa de Diana's? Were they victims of circumstance or are they each responsible for their own plight?

3. How does the role of the tamale woman move the novel forward? Describe the tamale woman's relationship with Garrett and Juan Carlos.

4. What advice did the tamale woman give to Garrett that he did not heed, leading to his tragic end? Could the outcome have been different?

5. Garrett lost both of his parents—his mother when he was a young boy and his father as a young man. He makes many references to his father throughout the novel but his mother is mentioned rarely. Why do you suppose his father dominates his memory?

6. How is the rendezvous at the mango orchard similar to Garrett and Angelina's first night together at Casa de Diana's? Discuss what factors (including their age, individual circumstances and cultural background) contribute to their decision to commit to each other and attempt to negotiate with Juan Carlos (el Cacique)?

7. "Do you love me? Will you love me all of your life?" Angelina asks Garrett, to which he replies, "Angelina, I have no life if you ain't in it." Why are Angelina and Garrett so drawn to each other? What qualities do they share?

8. "In the America that my father grew up in, a man knew his own mind. The icons of manhood back then, from Gene Autry to John Wayne to my own red-blooded father weren't ever confused. Right and wrong was clearly demarcated and it was easy to tell the good guys from the bad guys." How are contemporary constructions of masculinity challenged or reinforced in the novel?

9. What does *Without Sin* have to say about America's current immigration policies? Has your view on immigration changed since reading the novel? How so?

10. What does *Without Sin* have to say about the wars in Iraq and Afghanistan and the treatment of the veterans of those wars?

11. What does *Without Sin* have to say about the obligations that society and individuals have towards children?

12. How does this novel address the theme of good and evil?

13. Which character best personifies good? Evil? Does anyone character stand out as being "without sin"?

14. Is Garrett a tragic hero? Is the world a better place for having Garrett in it? Did his actions lead to change?

15. How are religious themes (faith, hope, love, forgiveness, etc) explored in this novel?

16. What is the significance of the title? Explain how the title relates to the characters presented in the novel.

17. Fun Question! If Garrett Harrison, Taylor Brophy and John Parker were to vote in the next presidential election, which political party or candidates would they vote for and why?

18. Fun Question! Many reviewers have commented that this novel would make a compelling and powerful movie. Which actors could you imagine playing the main characters? What challenges would a screenwriter have in the process of adapting it?

CPSIA information can be obtained at www.ICGtesting.com
Printed in the USA
LVOW090606010512

279778LV00002B/2/P